Land of Marvels

Land of Marvels

A Novel

Barry Unsworth

NAN A. TALESE

Doubleday

New York   London   Toronto   Sydney   Auckland

This book is a work of fiction. Names, characters, businesses, organizations, places, events, and incidents either are the product of the author's imagination or are used fictitiously. Any resemblance to actual persons, living or dead, events, or locales is entirely coincidental.

Published in the United States by Nan A. Talese, an imprint of The Doubleday Publishing Group, a division of Random House, Inc., New York.
www.nanatalese.com

DOUBLEDAY is a registered trademark of Random House, Inc.

Book design by Donna Sinisgalli

Library of Congress Cataloging-in-Publication Data
Unsworth, Barry, 1930–
Land of marvels : a novel / Barry Unsworth. — 1st ed.
p. cm.
1. Archaeologists—Great Britain—Fiction.   2. British—
Iraq—Fiction.   3. Geologists—United States—Fiction.
4. Americans—Iraq—Fiction.   5. Excavations (Archaeology)—
Iraq—Fiction.   6. Petroleum—Prospecting—Iraq—Fiction.
7. Petroleum industry and trade—Middle East—History—
Fiction.   8. Great Britain—Foreign relations—1910–1936—
Fiction.   9. Iraq—History—20th century—Fiction.   I. Title.
PR6071.N8L36 2009
823'.914—dc22
2008009201

ISBN 978-0-385-52007-2

PRINTED IN THE UNITED STATES OF AMERICA

1 2 3 4 5 6 7 8 9 10

First Edition

For Aira, with love

Far-call'd our navies melt away—
    On dune and headland sinks the fire—
Lo, all our pomp of yesterday
    Is one with Nineveh and Tyre!
Judge of the Nations, spare us yet,
Lest we forget, lest we forget!
            —*Rudyard Kipling*

. . . Certainly the American people have no more interest in talking up the Chester concessions diplomatically than they would have if the Admiral were proposing to open a candy store in Piccadilly, a dressmaking establishment in the Rue de la Paix, or a beauty parlor on the Riviera. If the Admiral and his friends wish to invest money in Turkey, they no doubt know what they are doing. They will expect profits commensurate with the risks, and they should not expect the United States Government, which will enjoy none of the profits, to insure them against the risks.

            —From an editorial in the New York World *of*
            April 23, 1923, in reference to the efforts of
            the Chester Group to obtain oil prospecting rights

Land of Marvels

1.

He knew they would come that day or the next. Jehar had sent word. But it was only by chance that he saw them approach. He had risen soon after dawn, tense with the fears that came to him in these early hours of the morning, and fumbled his clothes on, taking care to make no noise that might disturb his wife, who slept in the adjacent bedroom, only separated from him by a thin wall. Crossing the courtyard, he saw that Hassan, the boy who kept the gate, was asleep under his blanket, and he took the same care to avoid arousing him.

By habit—it was the only route he ever took whether on foot or on horseback, though rarely so early—he followed the track that led for a half mile or so through low outcrops of limestone toward the hump of Tell Erdek, the mound they were excavating. This seemed to fill the sky as he drew nearer to it, black still, like an outpost of night. Then he saw a sparkle of silver from the floodlands in the distance and knew that the sun was showing behind him.

It was above the horizon by the time he reached the tell and bright enough to dazzle the eyes, though there was no warmth in it yet. He stood for a while in the shadow of the mound, strangely at a loss now that he was here, uneasy, almost, at the silence of the place, at the sense it gave of violation, this ancient heap of earth and rock and rubble, gashed and trenched for no purpose immediately apparent, as if some beast of inconceivable size had raked it savagely along the flanks. Before long it would resound to the thudding of the pick and the scraping of the shovel, the shouted orders of the foremen, the cries of the two hundred and more Bedouin tribesmen, who would come with their baskets and harness—valuable property, often fought over—to resume their antlike task of carrying away the loose earth and stones from the digging.

But it was now, as he felt the silence of violation in this place where so much of his hope and his money were invested, that he saw the men approach. News of the railway came to him in a variety of ways, but the reports he paid for were announced in the same way always: the dust of the riders, lit this morning to a glinting ash color by the early rays of the sun, seen far off across the flatland to the west. He knew in every detail the route they had taken: the rail yards of Aleppo, then Jerablus on the Euphrates, passing within sight of Carchemish, where Woolley and Lawrence had made the Hittite finds barely a year ago, then the desert steppeland rising and falling, dusted with green in this early-spring weather, scattered with mounds like this one, the tombs of long-dead cities. And so to this little swarm of dust in the middle distance.

It was the way the line would take, straight toward him,

straight toward his hill, between the village where his workforce came from and the floodlands of the Khabur River. Sometimes he imagined he could catch the shine of the rails as they reached toward him. Mica, salt, asphalt, quartz, any glinting thing in the landscape might work this effect on him, even the fields of pitch where the oil seeped up, which were too far away to be seen at all, except in occasional, shifting gleams. It kept his worry alive, though he knew it for illusion; the journey on horseback from Jerablus, where the line had reached, where the Germans were building the bridge, took four days.

Sometimes it took longer, and Jehar would enumerate the reasons: desert storms, problems with the horses, attacks by raiding parties. He was grave-faced in recounting these things; his tone was charged with sincerity; further details were ready if required. But it was never possible to know whether he was merely inventing these episodes; such things happened on occasion to any traveler in these lands; why not, on this occasion, to them? The motive was clear enough—no secret was made of it—and it was this that made the accounts less than fully reliable: Jehar was seeking to extract a few more piastres for their hardships and their loyalty. He took care not to do it too often. He was a man of the Harb people; but he had traveled widely outside the tribal lands, and his travels had taught him that moderation, whether in truth or in falsehood, was likely to be more profitable than excess.

When the figures were near enough to be distinguished, Somerville stepped out into the open so that they should see him as they followed the track toward the expedition house. They dismounted at a distance of a hundred paces or so and left the horses in the care of one of their number. The others, headed by Jehar, walked toward him, inclining their heads in greeting as they drew near. None would have dreamed of approaching mounted when the *khwaja* was on foot. Jehar, as always, would be the spokesman. The others drew around him in a half circle. The hoods of their cloaks were thrown back, but they wore the folds of the headcloths still drawn over the mouth against the cold they had ridden through. They would say nothing, but they would keep a close eye on the sum handed over to Jehar; he was their employer, as the archaeologist was his, four being deemed a sufficient escort to ensure safe passage through lands in the main unfriendly, guard against ambush by day and depredation by night. Often enough, of course, they were themselves the raiders and despoilers; in their saddle slings they carried Mauser repeating rifles of recent make, weapons that had been issued to the Sultan's irregular cavalry units in Syria. But none of these men belonged to any unit at all, however irregular . . .

Jehar uncovered his face, which was handsome, narrow-boned, and level-browed, fierce in its serenity. "Oh noble one," he said in Arabic, the only language they had in common.

"Well," Somerville said, "speak out, why do you wait?" The delay, he knew, was more due to Jehar's relish for drama than to any diffidence about delivering unwelcome news.

Jehar raised his arms on either side. "Lord, the bridge is made, its claws have come to rest on our side of the Great River." He continued to gesture, lifting his arms higher, then lowering them to make the sweeping shape of an arc. "A great marvel, this bridge of the Germans," he said. "It is all made of steel, the span is greater than any floods can reach."

He looked keenly as he spoke at the face of the man before him, who had sustained the infliction of this news without change of expression. "Farther than ten throws of a stone," he said in a tone of wonder. "High in the sky, the sparrows cannot fly over it." He was disappointed by the other's failure to show feeling but not deceived by it; he was sensitive in certain ways and had understood very early in their acquaintance that the Englishman was one of those—he had met others in his time—whom Allah for reasons inscrutable to mortals had predisposed to feel singled out for harm. He was himself an optimist, blessed with a belief in his destiny. Only one such as he could set out to raise one hundred gold pounds, starting from nothing. This was the bride-price of the Circassian girl who filled his thoughts. He knew that this man was searching for treasure and was possessed by fear that the people of the railway would bring the line too close and take the treasure for themselves. It must be an enormous treasure, for one to spend so much on the finding of it. They had not found it yet; this was the third year they had come; they had dug down and down, but they had not found it yet . . .

"We were approached by a *ghazwa* of the Shammar people," he said. "A dozen men. They followed us for some miles and fired at us. We killed one and they fled, the cowards."

There was nothing in the attentive faces around him that could be taken to confirm or deny this story. Next time he spoke of it the Shammar raiding party would be fifty strong at least, the deaths five or six, and the encounter would already belong to the realm of legend.

"Now we will be pestered by his relatives with demands for blood money," Somerville said.

"No, no, they did not know us." For the first time Jehar glanced around at his companions, who all shook their heads.

"Well, we shall see. Now that the bridge is completed, have they started immediately to lay the rails on this side of the river?"

"No, lord, there will be some delay. New rails have come from the steelworks in Germany, they have come by sea to Beirut. Now they wait for the unloading of the rails and the transporting of them to Aleppo and so to Jerablus. They will bring the rails and the coal into the yards in Jerablus. All this will take time, perhaps ten days. Also, they lack timber. It must be brought from the north, from Urfa. This I was told by one whose word can be trusted. For this very precious information I gave him money from my own purse."

"But they had already laid some miles of track on this side of the river, even before they started work on the bridge. They were already engaged on it in my first season here, three years ago. Then the work was abandoned, the rails were left to rust. Now there are German surveyors and engineers here, they have rented houses in the village, they have taken some of our workpeople to build their storage sheds."

He paused, aware of having spoken too rapidly, with too much emphasis, aware of Jehar's eyes on him. There was always something unsettling in the man's gaze, something too intent. "Under our noses," he said. "They brought the stuff downriver." In fact the warehouses had been there already when he arrived in mid-February. The sight of them, the presence of the Germans, had been a grievous blow to him; before that it had been possible to hope that they intended to take the line farther north, toward Mardin. He said, "The sheds are stacked to the roof. Strange they should be waiting for supplies at Jerablus when they have the timbers and the rails stacked up here."

"But they are intended for this part of the line," Jehar said with extreme simplicity. "A railway is made in stretches, like a garden. When you grow palms, you plant here because the ground is easy. In another place you wait until you can make the ground better. Twenty piastres I gave him."

"I am not carrying any money," Somerville said. "I did not expect to meet you here. But I will remember what is owed. Four Turkish pounds as usual. We agreed at the beginning that I would not be responsible for your expenses."

He did not believe that Jehar had disbursed any of his own money, but in any case it would have been a great mistake to undertake to meet costs of this kind; he knew Jehar well enough to know that the costs would multiply. It was little enough he gave them anyway; how much Jehar would keep he did not know, but thought it probable that the others might get half the money to share among them, a meager amount but they found it sufficient; this job of escorting Jehar was much coveted, he had been told. "Well," he said, "in view of the delay at Jerablus you can take some days for your own business before setting out again. But I must be informed when they start again with the laying of the track."

On this, with low bows, the men retired to where their horses waited and turned toward the village. But Somerville was not given time to ponder the news. His two foremen were approaching, and behind them came the first of the workpeople, talking and laughing together. He moved forward to greet the two men, deriving comfort, as always, from the air of competence they carried with them, like an aura; they were united in it in spite of the physical dissimilarity between them. Elias, who was from Konia and Greek by birth, he had known for some years now. They had been together on a dig at Hamman Ali, south of Mosul, in the days when Somerville had been still an assistant. He had been delighted—and flattered—when Elias offered his services here. He was stout of build and corpulent, though quick and sure-footed on the ground of the site, with a round, good-humored face that could turn to fury with fearsome speed when he found something amiss, some slackness in the work. The other, Halil, was a Syrian, tall for an Arab and sinewy, with a stentorian voice and an expression of severity and melancholy.

Somerville had complete confidence in both and knew that they could be safely left to organize the groups and set the people on to work; there would in any case be little change from previous days in the distribution of the labor and the areas of excavation: Most of the people would be employed at different levels of the pit, which in three seasons of excavation they had dug down to a depth of sixty feet; others would be extending the lateral trenches in the hope of finding some remains of connecting walls. Walls were of utmost importance, even if no more than a few inches of them were left. They could lead to rooms, to gates and portals, to temples and palaces. So far, however, they had found nothing but the foundation lines of humbler and more recent habitations, Roman and Byzantine, not greatly interesting.

He was about to start making his way back to the expedition house when his assistant, Palmer, arrived, a sturdy figure in his white cotton suit and soft-brimmed white hat.

"I thought I'd come and see the work started," he said. "I didn't know you were here. Lovely morning, isn't it?"

Somerville assented to this but without much conviction. He liked Palmer and knew he was lucky to have an assistant who, in addition to knowing something of field archaeology, was an acknowledged expert on Assyrian and Sumerian inscriptions. But there were occasions when he wished—irrationally—that Palmer's looks might sometimes betray some faltering, even some hint of dismay, something to correspond to the extremely disappointing nature of their excavation so far. But no, he was always equable, his eyes gentle and shrewd behind the glasses, ready for the momentous discovery just around the corner. Of course Palmer was young, only twenty-seven, eight years younger than himself. And it wasn't Palmer's money that was draining away . . .

Together they watched as the villagers were assembled into their work parties of six. This was a more noisy and complicated procedure than any not accustomed to the ways of the Bedouin and the group dynamics of large-scale excavations might have expected, and it called for firmness and tact in equal measure on the part of the foremen. Quarrels would flare up, a dispute over nothing, and words lead to blows sometimes and blows to knives and knives to feuds. Previous trouble of this sort would have to be remembered, and the men set in different groups at the next assembly. Then the pickman, the most important member of the group since it was he who cut into the ground, or sometimes the spademan, his second-in-command, whose pay was slightly less, would object to the inclusion of a particular basketman in his group on the grounds of laziness or stupidity or because of some former fault or simply out of dislike, and this could lead to heated dispute. And as all the men, in addition to a daily wage, were paid baksheesh for anything of interest or value they found, there was always keen competition for the areas of the mound rumored to be more productive.

"Amazing, isn't it?" Palmer said. "A microcosm of our divided world. No wonder Europe is on the edge of war."

Somerville nodded. This same morning scene was being enacted, with the same disputes, all over Mesopotamia, where French and German and British and American archaeologists were digging and tunneling into mounds pretty much like this one. Some were making important finds—and the recurrent awareness that he was not among these fortunate ones was like the intermittent throb of a sore tooth—but all were in haste, no matter what the place, Tell Halaf, Tell Chagar, Khorsabad, Nineveh, Babylon. Haste, in this spring of 1914, to get out of the earth as much as possible, before it was barred to them. Fear in this haste too, he thought: fear of the cataclysm, the abyss . . .

"They have no slightest reason for thinking one spot better than another," Palmer said. "Not as things are at present. It's a toss-up. But they go on making a fuss about it. It's a form of superstition, I suppose."

He had spoken with the cheerful skepticism that belonged to him, and he paused now, smiling at Somerville. "Or perhaps a form of gambling," he said, noting the lines of strain and fatigue in the other's face.

"Quite a few of them are eager to be sent over to the trench on the eastern side, which is scarcely begun yet, where that piece of ivory was found yesterday," Somerville said. "But the thing was out of context. I don't think there'll be anything more. All the same, we will have to keep our eyes open for any fragments of the part missing."

"It's hard to know what it was doing there."

They discussed it as they walked back to the house together. It had been one of the few interesting finds of the season so far, slightly more than half of a circular ivory plaque, broken across diagonally, showing the head and right foreleg of a lion, carved in relief against the background of what looked like papyrus flowers, the head lowered in a fashion almost dainty, fastidious, the teeth gripping into the throat of a man not supine but resting back on his arms, straddled by the beast, head raised, near death, the upturned face African in looks, the hair bunched in tight curls. It had been found in the vertical pit that went down from the summit, a little way along a trench on the eastern side.

"It can't date from the level where it was found," Palmer said. "It's a thousand years too early. There was no ivory in circulation then, none that we know of."

It was something of a mystery to both of them how carved ivory of sophisticated workmanship could have found its way to such a deep level; it had been lying amid mud-brick rubble and fragments of painted pottery dating back to the third millennium before Christ.

"It seems that there were elephants in Syria then," Somerville said. "There might have been some local carving in ivory, though none has come to light. But I don't think it is Syrian work in any case. It's too refined, too ceremonious somehow."

He enjoyed speculations of this kind, and his spirits had lifted by the time they were drawing near the house. "There will be a reason," he said. "There is always a reason, if you can find it. Someone made it who was once alive in the world. And someone else brought it here."

"The level needn't be such a problem," Palmer said as Hassan ran to open the gate for them. "It's probably the doing of our little friend, the jumping mouse."

This was an accustomed joke between them, the jumping mouse, or jerboa, being a creature that had reached legendary status, having bedeviled generations of archaeologists in the lands between the two tributaries of the Euphrates, the Belikh and Khabur rivers, by its habit of building its nest in very deep burrows—sometimes deep enough to reach the living rock—and in the process throwing up shards and flints from the deepest layers onto the surface. Palmer was convinced—or affected to be—that this little animal seized upon various more recent objects, anything that took its fancy, and bore them down into the depths of the earth, even things bigger and heavier than itself. In this two-way traffic the layers were jumbled up and the dawn of history confused with the day before yesterday.

The houseboys had laid the table on the shaded side of the courtyard, and the other members of the expedition had already started breakfast. Edith Somerville, sitting at the head of the table, saw Hassan, who had been squatting against the wall, scramble up to open the gate, saw her husband and his assistant enter side by side. They had been laughing together, but this laughter tailed off as they passed through the gate and came into the courtyard. She watched her husband come toward them though without seeming to look in their direction. And it was this, the habit of aloofness, something that belonged to him but was also assumed, especially when there was a group to be faced, greetings to be exchanged, that struck her anew as he approached, belied as it always was by something incongruously jaunty in his gait, a slight jerking upward motion of the feet, involuntary and almost pathetic when combined with his abstracted expression, as if he had suffered some blow and was exerting himself not to show the damage.

The impression was not new to her, nor was the dislike for it that followed immediately; she hated any flicker of pity in herself, felt it demeaning. But the mixture of feelings was strong on this occasion, seeming to sum up, in these few moments, all that was contradictory and unresolved in the relations between them. So much was this so that she glanced quickly at the other faces around the table, as if she might see a similar feeling registered there, at that of Gregory, her husband's Armenian secretary, his sallowness in contrast with the dark red complexion of Major Manning beside him, who had arrived among them the day before, and of Patricia, sitting opposite her, fresh from Girton College, who was there for no particular reason except that she was the daughter of a London friend and had liked the idea of joining the expedition. None of these faces seemed any different, except that of Patricia, whose looks had brightened at Palmer's appearance.

Then the two were at the table, apologizing for their lateness. She met her husband's glance and smile, with its usual
combination of irony and resignation, and returned to the enjoyment of her breakfast.

It was easily her favorite meal. The bread here, east of the
Euphrates, had been new to her, quite a revelation in its way,
cooked on an upturned cauldron with a fire inside, beaten thin
so it came in large, crisp wafers. Accompanied by wild honey,
dried dates, and goat milk cheese, it made a delicious breakfast.
She enjoyed her food and unlike most of her women friends at
home had never needed to take care of her weight. She was a
tall, full-bodied woman, but at thirty-five she was as light and
graceful as she had been at twenty.

Conversation during the meal mainly concerned the recent
speech from the throne, news of which had been brought them
by the major, who had been in Mosul the week before, staying as
a guest at the consulate. A message of hope and more than
hope, even confidence, that an accord with Germany and Turkey
would be reached, was on the verge of being reached.

"Approaching a satisfactory issue," Manning said. "Those
were His Majesty's words. He was speaking with particular reference to our commercial interests in Mesopotamia."

He had a mannerism, fairly frequent, in the pauses between his words, an involuntary tightening of his lips, marked by
a slight bristling movement of his fair, carefully clipped mustache, as if he were controlling an impulse to more violent
speech.

"Approaching, well, yes," Somerville said. "We are not

standing still, so much is true. But approaches can be long or short, can't they? No disrespect to King George, his speeches are designed to reassure the nation, but 'satisfactory issue' is a bit on the vague side, don't you think?"

He caught his wife's eye and saw something in her expression, something of admonition or reproof. He had spoken to their guest with a lightness that was sardonic, almost gibing, a tone that he knew had become more common with him of late, as his worries accumulated. It made him disliked; Manning didn't like him, he knew that, though without much caring.

The very fact of the major's presence among them was proof that a language less vague was being spoken elsewhere. Manning spoke Arabic, he had an escort of armed Shammar tribesmen, he had traveled on camelback through the regions west of the Tigris and southward across al-Jazirah. After some days of ranging about among the headwaters of the Khabur he was leaving for Damascus next morning, a journey that would involve crossing the northern part of the Syrian Desert. The reason given out for these extensive travels was the need for reliable survey maps, and in fact Manning did occupy himself with these. But his main employment—Somerville knew this from Jehar, who sometimes, in the hope of baksheesh, included such items of information in his news of the railway line—was speaking to tribal leaders, offering rewards in the name of King George for promises of allegiance in the event of war, seeking to determine the number of friendly rifles. It was an enterprise that had caused a good deal of mirth to Palmer when he had heard of it. To take the trouble to record this information and transmit it to military intelligence in London for future reference in the event of war, when it was known on every hand that the promises of the sheikhs shifted with the desert breezes . . .

"Rapidly approaching," the major said now, pointedly looking away from Somerville. "Those were the words used."

A silence followed this, broken by Patricia, not out of tact so much as out of impatience with people who got so huffy over what was after all only a form of words. "Too many prophecies flying around, royal and otherwise," she said briskly. "It's dead easy to make prophecies, you can always adapt them to events and pretend you meant something different."

It was a presumptuous thing to say, in Edith's view, improper too, unwomanly, trying to tell the men their business. Seeing the way Palmer smiled and nodded in full approval, she felt an increase of contempt for him. She noted the steady, unabashed regard of the girl's gray eyes, the delicate flush of the complexion, the mouth still childlike in its softness. To have studied modern history at Cambridge was all very well, but women should behave as women, not try to talk about politics on equal terms with the men. The girl was so heedless, so inviolable in her self-absorption . . . Edith drank some coffee, thought it needed more sugar, reached for the bowl.

"The only important commercial interest that is approaching rapidly is a German one." Somerville at once regretted this remark. He had not mentioned the news of the bridge, held back by an instinct of secrecy betrayed by his words now, he felt, and absurd in any case since everyone at the table must know he was referring to the Baghdad Railway. This great project, financed by the Deutsche Bank, was designed to link Constantinople to the Persian Gulf. It was not the fact of it he had wanted to disguise, but his own private belief, gaining on him daily in spite of his efforts to resist it, that it was aiming at him.

He had risen as he spoke as if to forestall any further talk of the line, and he now smiled around the table in farewell. "I'd better walk over and see how things are going," he said. And then, to Palmer: "Shall we have another look at that piece of ivory first?"

Palmer got to his feet, though it seemed with a certain unwillingness to leave Patricia's side. Together the two men made their way to the large stone-flagged room opening onto the courtyard, where most of the work of restoration was carried out.

The ivory lay flat on one of the small tables, resting on a thick bed of black felt. Patricia had been eager to be given the task of preliminary cleaning, and Palmer had wanted to please her, so Somerville, after some hesitation, had agreed. It had meant no more than removing the marks of clay on the surface by means of a soft brush with wetted bristles, but he was obliged to admit that she had done it well. It was possible to see now that the background consisted of a pattern of lilies and papyrus flowers and that the tight curls of the victim's head were not carved in the block but made up of a number of very small pegs with rounded heads that had been fashioned separately and inserted with astonishing skill. There were still some traces of the gold that had been used to highlight these curls, traces too on the victim's skirt.

Somerville took from his pocket a small magnifying glass he always carried with him. "There is quite a bit of clay still in the eyes," he said, after some moments of scrutiny. "But the eyes themselves are made of pitch. The lion's, I mean. It has run a little as if the lion were weeping. And there is what looks like compacted ash in some of the incisions." He passed the glass to Palmer. "What would make the bitumen run like that?"

"It must have melted," Palmer said. "Must have been in a fire, or pretty close to one. Hard to know what else but heat would do it, the stuff sets like a rock and lasts forever. And then these traces of ash, if that is what they are."

"If so, the fire must have been here. No one would have brought a fire-damaged ivory plaque to this place with him. There was probably an inlay once, here in the arches formed by the lily petals."

There was nothing left of the stones they had used for this, cornelian or lapis lazuli, whatever it had been, but there were traces of some vitreous powder here and there that could have been part of the original cement. Once again it came to Somerville, as he continued to look closely down, that the victim was somehow collaborating in his fate, supporting himself on his arms, holding his face upward, offering his throat. This was no ravening spring of the beast on its prey. There was something stately and ceremonious in the inclined head of the lion, the enclosing grip of the paws as it held the man in its embrace and took the last of his ebbing life. It was power that was being celebrated here, power absolute and unquestioned. But whose?

"It has something in common with a few of the ivories found at Nimrud in the 1850s," he said. "Those they found in the fortified palace built by Shalmaneser. No one has yet established where they came from." In the interest of the object before him, as the dim notion came to him that with luck he might add something to this debate, even finally settle it, he felt the rush of an emotion like relief; the specter of defeat, so close to him lately, shrank away, receded. "That would put it somewhere in the middle of the ninth century," he said. "Getting on for three thousand years ago."

"If it was made for him," Palmer said. "But it could be quite a bit earlier. The Assyrian kings of the period brought back booty from all over. A lot of it was someone else's booty first."

"Or else tribute from subject peoples, more or less the same thing. A luxury product in any case." Somerville straightened up from his examination and smiled suddenly. Smiles were rare with him, but they were attractive when they came, narrowing his eyes and bringing something youthful and almost reckless to his face. "No telling, not for the moment anyway," he said. "But you can be sure this bit of ivory has seen a thing or two in its time."

"Starting with the beast they took it from. Can't have been much fun for the elephant with the weapons they disposed of then."

On this note they parted, Palmer to resume the study of some cuneiform inscriptions that had been found on fragmented clay tablets at a depth of twenty feet, Somerville to return to the tell and see how the work was going. Before setting off, however, he looked in on his wife, who, together with Patricia, was busy in the smaller, adjoining workroom. They were occupied with assembling and trying to fit together some sizable fragments of pottery that had been found lying close together not far below the surface. It was Islamic ware, dating to the period of domination by the Seljuk Turks and beautiful in its color-

ing, with an opaque bluish and green glaze that had stayed fresh
through the eight hundred years or so of its life. For Somerville
it was too recent to be of great interest, medieval, in fact. Such
pieces were common throughout the area; you sometimes
kicked against them as you walked, the pots having been made
in considerable quantities not far away, at ar-Raqqah, a prosperous trading center until it was destroyed in the Mongol invasions
of the thirteenth century.

For Edith, he knew, the age of the pieces had no slightest
importance. The main thing was the promise of beauty, the
achievement of a finished form that would crown the work, restore the original vessel complete in every part. The odds against
this were tremendous, but Edith was not interested in the odds;
people who thought about odds were unheroic and would never
achieve anything. She continued her efforts in spite of all disappointments. In broken pots as such, those at the deepest and
most ancient levels, fragmented and dispersed beyond all possibility of restoration, she took no smallest interest; they were
meaningless to her. Life had to glow with promise; there had to
be a fire of purpose. She had been disappointed in this too, without losing belief in it. And Somerville, as he stood watching her,
knew himself to be part of that disappointment.

She had looked up and smiled at his entrance but returned
almost at once to the work. Her fingers were deft as she handled
the pieces. Some hair had escaped from her headband and hung
in tendrils over her brow. Patricia's movements were slower;
her lips were parted a little in the effort of concentration, and
she held her head low as if it were burdensome. Not long, he
thought, since she had sat thus on a bench in a lecture room.

They did not get on very well, these two; he had no sense that he was interrupting anything like a conversation between them. But he had been too preoccupied with his own troubles to give much thought to what might divide them. It came to him now that Edith might simply be resentful of the girl's presence there, that she would have wished to be the only woman in the company. The thought was strangely displeasing to him. Suddenly he felt like an intruder in the silence here, and he turned away and left without speaking.

2.

§

The mound presented a very different picture now from that desolate one of earlier. The men were working in their groups; voices resounded; there was the regular sharp impact of metal on stone and the softer sound, all-pervasive, as if the whole mound were afflicted by a scraping thickness of breathing, of the earth and rubble being shoveled into the baskets to be borne away. Two files of people were in constant movement, one mounting with baskets already emptied, the other descending, stooped to take the weight of the loaded baskets on their shoulders.

Only now, as he felt within him the resumption of a steadier breathing and a greater sense of the open sky, did Somerville become properly aware of the tension he had felt, disguised from others, not fully acknowledged to himself, since early morning and the receiving of Jehar's report. He began to mount the slope on the southern side, that facing toward the expedition house, making his way among low crags of granite and the rubble of ancient habitations.

The summit on this side was his preferred viewing place. He stood still here and looked toward the horizon across the long sweep of the steppelands, dressed now in their spring green. It was the third time, standing here in the same place, that he had witnessed this brief tide of green. At the beginning it had accompanied his hopes, augured well for the momentous discoveries he had hoped to make here. Now it seemed a cheat to him, as did everything he looked at, the huddled mud-brick houses of the village, the dark tents of nomad herdsmen in the far distance, the scattered heaps where communities of people had once lived. He could see the glint of the streams that marked the upper reaches of the Khabur River and, at the farthest limits of vision, brief enough to seem illusionary, the occasional gleam elicited by the sun from the swamps of pitch. Sets like rock, Palmer had said. Only strong heat could have put those tears in the lion's eyes. Might the pitch for the eyes have come from somewhere here?

Beyond this, far beyond, still to westward, lay the imagined banks of the Great River, as Jehar had called it. Suddenly, disagreeably, he remembered the way the man had watched him, that predatory intentness. How far away was the left bank of the Euphrates, where the piles of the bridge now rested? A hundred miles, perhaps a little more. When they started work again, how long would they take to reach him? Fifteen days, twenty? In certain lights, on the verge of the horizon, he could persuade himself that he saw, luminous and fleeting, the steel of the girders, the green of the palms that lined the banks. It appealed to his imagination as strongly now as ever to think of the powers that had marched and countermarched across this land of the

Two Rivers: Sumerians, Babylonians, Hittites, Assyrians, Medes, Chaldeans, all bent on conquest, all convinced they would last forever, building their cities and proclaiming their power, empires following one upon another, their only memorial now the scraps that lay belowground, which he and his like competed in digging for.

Now, to replace these invading hosts, there was the railway. With this thought, perhaps the cause of it, he became aware of shouting voices, a sudden clangor, as if sheets of metal were being thrown down. The sounds were familiar; they came from below, from beyond the eastern slope of the mound, ground invisible to him here, where he had never set foot, where the railway people had built their storage sheds and stacked the timbers for the line. Like a garden, Jehar had said. A railway line is built in patches, like a garden. He was clever with comparisons as liars often were. Not a liar exactly, he didn't know the difference; truth, falsehood, it was all the same ground to him, he could step where he liked.

A series of muffled hammer strokes reached him, and the run of wheels on the light track the Germans had built for transporting the rails. Once again the question came to him, sickening in its quality of irresolution: Was he not a much worse liar, a real liar, one who told lies to himself? Deep within him did he not really want this railway track to come crashing through his mound, or close enough at least to put paid to any hope of further excavation? Convenient, a salve to his pride, if he could lay the blame for his failure on the incursion of the line. If the failure were seen to be his, it would reduce his chances—already not great—of finding a sponsor, raising money for other digs.

His own money was running out; there would not be enough for another season . . .

The mound had seemed so promising. Higher than most, more than a hundred feet from ground level to summit, surmounted by a long ridge running east to west, the western end bumped up higher by a dozen feet, as if to indicate some more important edifice lying beneath, citadel or palace or the tower of a temple, stone perhaps, leaving a debris more substantial than the sun-dried mud brick generally used in this land of abundant alluvial deposit. Close to the base, exposed by the thousands of years of wind and water, they had come upon fragments of painted pottery of the late Ubaid period, which Somerville had thought might have been imported here, perhaps from as far away as Uruk, a great city in its day, whose ruins lay on the Tigris between Baghdad and Basra. This, if it were so, would argue a considerable degree of commercial importance as early as the sixth millennium before Christ.

But perhaps most important of all there had been the remembered advice of the man, much revered, whom Somerville had worked under as an assistant field archaeologist at Tell Harmal on the lower Tigris, his first work of excavation in Mesopotamia. *If you want to make your mark, find somewhere to dig between the Belikh and the Khabur. Tell Erdek, say, or Tell Mahdin. Never been touched. You are on the borderlands of empire there. Find the right place and you will go down through half a dozen cultures, all the way to Neolithic.*

Tell Erdek was the one he had chosen. It had the advantage of water not far away that could be drunk after filtering and boiling, and the village was close by, giving access to a labor force.

They had leased the land from the local sheikh, had a house built, kept relations good by promising him the house—palatial by local standards—as a gift when the work there was finished.

They had proceeded in regular fashion, cutting the trench from the top of the mound to a point well beyond its foot; at exact intervals, in descending order, the work gangs were positioned, each with a measured square to work in. Quite soon, in their first season there, they had come to the remains of walls running across the line of the trench. But this had led to nothing much except an immense labor of clearance. So far only the ground plans of two small houses had come to light. They had found no substantial remains below the raised area on the west side; the rampart, so promising at first sight, had proved a purely accidental configuration. It was true that their pit had descended through empires: Layers of Parthian, Byzantine, Roman occupation had been found, then a thousand years or so of apparent nonhabitation, then Aramaean potsherds, then evidence of devastation by fire. Below the ash of this conflagration were the chipped flint ax heads of Neolithic man, a time before recorded history began.

The sequence was impeccable. But in all this time of digging nothing of major interest had been found, nothing that did more than reinforce what was known already. There was this piece of ivory, which had no context—so far at least—and therefore no meaning; in the previous season they had unearthed a stone-built Sumerian shrine with the small, badly damaged statue of a worshiper, further proof that the influence of Sumer had extended into this northern region, a fact amply demonstrated by others before him.

It was not much to show for all the work and all the money. He had pinned his hopes on Tell Erdek. It was the first time he had been in charge of an expedition, after the years as assistant at different sites in Anatolia and Mesopotamia. He had not come to archaeology in the usual way, through the usual stages, as Palmer had: distinguished university career, postgraduate studies in ancient history and Semitic languages, an assistant curatorship. After his years at Rugby he had joined the family firm and worked with his father, who had made a modest fortune in the Manchester cotton trade; there had not been much choice in this, he was the only child. He had not been happy, but he had gone on with it while his parents lived, spending what leisure time he had on studies begun in early boyhood relating to the history and archaeology of the Near East.

It had been his consuming passion. In an age of explorers and empire builders his hero had been an archaeologist, Henry Layard, whose excavations had revealed to the world the glories of ancient Assyria. In 1830, at the age of twenty-two, Layard had given up his position in a London law office and traveled on horseback through Anatolia and Syria. He had excavated Nimrud, with its colossal human-headed, five-legged bulls, uncovered the palace of Sennacherib at Nineveh and the many hundreds of cuneiform tablets from the archives of the Assyrian kings, an immense addition to human knowledge. And he was still not yet thirty! Somerville too, in conscious emulation, had given up everything for the sake of archaeology. His mother had died when he was still young. On his father's death he had sold the business and the family home, invested the money, and offered himself as unpaid assistant to Sir William Forben, who was about to leave for Mesopotamia. He had always held to the similarity of circumstance between Layard and himself; their lives were connected by a bright and glittering thread; he too would become famous for his discoveries; he too would reveal to the world a splendor from underground, long unsuspected.

He was farther away from this now than ever. By the end of this third season, with the wages of two hundred workers to pay and the cost of transport to meet, he would be left with funds insufficient for another year. And now there was this sudden threat of the railway—for both sudden and insidious it had been. In 1912 and most of 1913, during the course of his first two seasons at Tell Erdek, the railway company had run into money problems; the line had been to all appearance abandoned. A branch line to Alexandretta had been completed and opened to traffic, but work on the Euphrates bridge had been suspended; the track had been halted just east of the river and might well have stuck there some years more. But in the previous December, while preparing to set out, he had learned from the *Times* that the Deutsche Bank had disposed of its holdings in the Macedonian Railways to an Austro-Hungarian syndicate and reinvested the funds thus obtained in the main line, confirming the company's intention of taking it across Mesopotamia to Baghdad and Basra. He had had the proof of it this morning from the mouth of Jehar, who always looked at him so closely and intently, as if something more were expected, awaited, some inevitable end. Once again, with the same feeling of sickness, he was swept by the same question: Was it not he who was waiting for the end, for the line to come and pierce this bump of ancient ground and smash his hopes—hopes smashed already?

Jehar had watched the *khwaja* ascend to the summit of the mound and stand there looking toward the horizon, a motionless figure in his invariable dress of broad-brimmed hat and long-sleeved shirt and khaki shorts that came to his knees. It was important to keep the Englishman under observation as far as possible so as to know what progress was being made in the search for the treasure. There was of course no possibility of knowing what was passing through the other's mind as he stood there, and Jehar did not speculate: better the vacant mind than the mind occupied fruitlessly. But he would not have been in the least surprised to learn that he himself was featuring in the Englishman's thoughts; he was convinced that their two lives were closely intertwined; it was this man who had singled him out, sent him to Aleppo first and then Jerablus to report on the progress of the railway; and it was in the railyards of Jerablus that he had seen the girl who had changed the whole course of his life, made him a different man.

She was called Ninanna, a beautiful name, unusual for a Circassian girl, and she was fifteen years old. This he had discovered from the man who called himself her uncle and perhaps was. They were Muhammadan people from the Caucasus Mountains who had fled south from the Russian Cossacks and taken refuge in parts of northern Syria. The uncle ran a bar with a few tables in the yards of Jerablus. Customers were not lacking; work on the bridge had been going on for two years, and in that time a township of hovels and shacks had sprung up to house the men who came to work on the construction or in the sawmills and coal sheds and to entertain them and skim off their wages: brothels and bars and gambling houses and pits for dogfights and makeshift stalls.

But it was not there, amid the fumes and clamor of the shunting yards, that he had seen her first. She had been getting water from the pump near the offices of the German engineers, laughing and talking with two older women, and their eyes had met while the laughter was still in her face. He had known at that moment that she was for him. He had watched her walk away, with the tall jar held in place on its pad with one raised arm. And he had felt the deep disturbance of love at the sway of her walk, her beauty and strength and stateliness. Her head was covered by a scarf worn well forward, by which Jehar knew she was a respectable girl and unmarried, a fact confirmed when he spoke to the uncle, who was asking a hundred gold pounds for her.

From that moment the course of his life had changed. It was not a life that had been marked up till then by any great virtue or distinction. He was a Bedouin of the Harb people, a tribe not very numerous, pastoral and nomadic in their way of life. He had quitted the tribal lands before reaching the age of twenty, driven by a restlessness that had taken him far afield. He had worked in the kitchens of a Damascus hotel, in the fish market below the Galata Bridge in Constantinople, as a boatman on the Euphrates, transporting bitumen downriver from Hit to Baghdad. Sometimes, when he had no work and no money, he had stolen articles left unguarded. And sometimes, in lonely places, he had attacked and robbed some passerby. Then, in Mosul, in a dispute over cards, he had stabbed a man and wounded him badly. The man did not die; but he did not walk upright again, and Jehar was sent to prison for a term of seven years. Halfway through this he was offered an amnesty on condition he joined one of the forced labor gangs that were working under armed guard on the Baghdad Railway, blasting a way through the difficult terrain of the Amanus Mountains in Anatolia. He spent six years working on the railway, first as a laborer, then, when his quickness of mind was noted, as a courier along the line. It was during these years that he had learned some German, his great asset as a news bearer in Somerville's eyes.

Was I that man? he thought, with continuing wonder, watching the figure above him, which remained motionless among the toiling people. This care, this deliberate waiting, was new to him. Through all the vicissitudes of his life the needs of the moment had been all that counted with him, the one constant element. He had taken what work he could find, leaving on a whim, an impulse, an urge for new horizons. Like many who live from day to day, he had always had a passion for gambling; a week's pay would go on the turn of a card. Now, at thirty-four, cunning and care had descended on him; he had become a person who postponed his pleasures, planned ahead.

He knew where he would take the girl when they were married. He would take her to Deir ez-Zor on the right bank of the Great River. He had seen this town when he worked on the rafts that carried pitch to ar-Raqqah and the upper reaches of the river. It had a green islet in midstream and a permanent bridge that led over to the other bank. Six white minarets rose above the flat roofs, and to the east of the houses there were gardens and sown fields, a mass of green . . .

He was saving money, putting coin to coin. His savings were

in a goatskin bag, resting against his stomach, below the robe, below the cloth belt and the knife. But he was far away from the sum he needed, the hundred gold pounds the uncle was asking for her. And he was ridden by fears: Some other man would look at her and want her, someone richer than he; the uncle, whom he didn't like and didn't trust, would lose patience and seek to use the girl for the pleasure of his customers.

He saw the man above him turn, begin to descend. Their destinies were linked; he knew it. Through this man he would make money more quickly. There were treasures of great price in the bowels of this hill, and now the railway line was threatening to come before these could be found. Profit could be made out of this by a man who kept watch and bided his time—a man such as he.

3.

◈

In late afternoon the foremen's whistles sounded, and Somerville, accompanied by Palmer and by his secretary, Gregory, began the checking of the finds, moving from one gang to the next. Gregory had his own secretary in attendance, a proudly smiling boy named Yusuf, whose special duty it was to bear the pen and the large red account book. Bringing up the rear were two men, one with a wicker basket, the other with a number of small boxes, not regular jobs these, but assigned from day to day and much coveted—the standard rate was three piastres per man.

At his approach the groups stopped work and squatted in a line. He began always with the senior member, the pickman, first inquiring the name.

"*Qasmagi?*"

"Daud Muhammad."

"What have you got?"

Daud Muhammad had the handle and lower part of a large

terra-cotta pot with a crude design of crosses incised around the base, some very small pieces of copper beaten out flat, fragments of painted pottery, and the bone haft of a knife much chipped away.

The smaller things Somerville scrutinized briefly then cast aside, without regard for any hopes the pickman might have set on them. The bone implement went into one of the boxes; the pieces of pottery were placed in the basket. This done, he considered for some moments. It was general practice to pay baksheesh for objects found, in addition to the daily wage. It was an insurance against theft and encouraged the workpeople to keep their eyes open. And the possibility of some large reward appealed to the gambling instinct, strong in most Arabs. Baksheesh accounted for about 20 percent of the total wage bill. But it was always necessary to lend weight by a pause for consideration.

"Four piastres," he said, in clear and distinct tones.

This was immediately repeated in a loud voice by the pickman, both as public acknowledgment and as an aid to memory. The pen and the account book were handed to Gregory; Yusuf crouched and presented his back so that the name and the amount could be entered. There were four Daud Muhammads working on the site, and some further name or distinguishing feature had to be added so as to avoid confusion. This one was Daud Muhammad the Pockmarked. At the end of the week Gregory would add up the amounts, a difficult and complicated feat of arithmetic, sometimes disputed by the men themselves if the total did not correspond to their memory of it.

Somerville repeated the procedure with the remaining members of the group before moving on. The basket people sometimes made small finds, beads, rings, seals—objects that had escaped the notice of the spademan when the baskets were being filled.

Moving from group to group, he worked his way up the side of the mound. There were more fragments of pottery, some lapis lazuli beads, an almost intact cylinder seal with a design of foliage on it. A better than usual day, nothing outstanding. The seal looked interesting, though it would need careful cleaning with a solution of alcohol before much could be known for sure about it.

"Where was this found?" he asked the spademan who had found it. The man pointed some yards to his right, on the eastern side of the mound, where a short lateral trench had been dug. It was in this area that the piece of ivory had been found.

Another group was working at the limit of this trench, and Somerville approached them now.

"*Qasmagi?*"

"Hassan Muhammad Ibrahim."

"What have you got?"

But Hassan Muhammad did not answer at once, giving instead a broad and triumphant smile. There was a cloth at his feet as he squatted there, and he glanced down at this now, still delaying.

"What is it?" Palmer said. "What have you got?"

With the air of a conjurer the pickman drew the cloth away and lifted out with both hands a piece of stone, the shape of a narrow rectangle, broken at the edges, about a foot in length.

Somerville took it from him and looked down at it. It weighed less than he had expected, being no more than a couple of inches in thickness. Impacted clay obscured much of the detail, but he was looking at a fragment, part of some larger design, carved in low relief. He made out a descending curve, broken off at a point where it was growing steeper. A slight lump or protuberance, also broken off short, rested on the upper part of the curve. At a slightly lower level there was what looked like part of a two-stranded ring.

"Twenty-five piastres," he said, and heard the sum repeated loudly by the jubilant pickman.

The rest of his rounds revealed nothing much, but he hardly noticed in any case, so taken up was he with thoughts of the stone. Could it have been quarried locally? It looked like gypsum, though the clay adhering to the surface made it difficult to be sure. Carved in relief, with that thickness, it could only have been part of a wall decoration . . .

He was still occupied with these speculations and the growing excitement that attended them when the workpeople began to disperse. The carving would have to be examined carefully before any conclusions could be reached, however tentative. He would have liked to set about this at once, but as always at the close of the day's work there were various claims on his attention, small disputes to be settled, the finds to be taken to the house and laid out there. When these things had been seen to and he had washed and changed, it was time for dinner, which at this season took place in the dining room of the house, the evenings being still too cold after sundown to sit outside.

As almost always he was slightly late. A place had been left for him at the head of the table, facing the major, who sat at the foot, the same place he had occupied at breakfast. Somerville glanced around the table, saw that his wife was halfway down on the right, that his assistant and Patricia were side by side, as was now their usual practice.

This evening, however, he was not the last to arrive. He had barely taken his place when Fahir Bey, the commissioner appointed to report on the progress of the excavation, entered the room quickly and began shaking hands, bowing to the ladies, uttering apologies in his fluent and only slightly accented English for disturbing them at their meal. He had ridden over from Ras el-Ain, where his quarters were. He had intended to arrive earlier but had been delayed by official business at the last minute. He was introduced to the major, who responded stiffly and with what seemed to Somerville some increased bristling of the neatly trimmed mustache.

"Alas, our acquaintance will be short," Fahir said. "You are leaving tomorrow, I understand."

"How did you know that?"

Fahir had very dark eyes, and his eyebrows were jet black and arched in shapes so rounded and precise that they seemed artificial, as if painted on, giving him a theatrical look, strangely enhanced by the small, diagonal dueling scar on his left cheek. There was nothing theatrical now, however, in the way his smile faded and his eyes rested on the major's face. "I was informed of it," he said. "These are Ottoman lands, sir. A British officer, traveling here and there, seeking out the sheikhs, asking questions. Strange if we did not know when he arrived, when he is proposing to leave."

"I am traveling with a pass issued by the Turkish authorities in Constantinople, sir. I am an officer of the Royal Engineers, engaged in the compiling of survey maps on behalf of the Royal Geographical Society."

"Ah, yes, of course," Fahir said. "A very august body. For Damascus, is it not, by way of Palmyra and Homs? The Royal Geographical Society wishes to have survey maps of the desert?"

The major failed to reply to this, but the strain of his silence was relieved by Edith's hospitable urging of the visitor to join them at table and the bustle of Ali, the houseboy, laying a place for him. The dinner was better than average this evening: a mutton broth, quite passable if somewhat too greasy; a salad of radishes and broccoli—plentiful at this season, though not for very long, in the riverbank gardens—followed by a brace of wild duck, shot that day by the cook himself, a man of uncertain temper named Subri. And they still, at this early stage, had a stock of Cypriot wine that had been brought down from Harran with other provisions at the beginning of the season.

Somerville thought it unlikely that Fahir would have done any better at home. He himself hardly noticed what he was served these days, distracted as he was by anxieties of one sort or another. But when there were guests or occasional visitors he felt in some measure responsible for the quality of the food, which quite often came out of tins. Fahir was to be regarded as a guest though he came at regular intervals, once every ten days or so. He had no need to come more often: He had abundant sources of information; any of the workpeople would be ready enough, for the sake of a few gurush, to tell him of significant finds. The site was leased in regular legal form, and the Ottoman state had given consent to the transport of antiquities out of imperial lands. But if objects of material value were found, it was uncertain how far this could be relied on; it was, after all, this same Ottoman state that had appointed Fahir to keep a careful eye on him. And then, of course, his lease counted for nothing, it was a useless scrap of paper, when set against the rights granted to the Germans in the railway concession, prospecting rights of twenty kilometers on either side of the line.

In an effort to drive away these thoughts, so painfully familiar, he glanced around the table. His wife was giving some instructions to Ali; Fahir was exchanging some smiling remarks with Patricia on his right; Palmer seemed to be saying something to the major, something about empires. The major himself had hardly spoken at all since Fahir's arrival and their exchange of words. He had probably taken umbrage. Ridiculous if so, and extraordinarily arrogant. If a major in the Turkish Army, heavily escorted, were traveling about, questioning local chiefs and making maps in some part of the British Empire, some region of India, for example, he would have been at once arrested and locked up. Yet Manning assumed the right to do the same thing in Mesopotamia and seemed ready to take offense if the right was questioned. But of course he had a pass; that was the difference; anything could be bought in Constantinople these days, including licenses for spies.

There was a sudden lull in the conversation, and he could hear more clearly now what Palmer was saying: "A few centuries, yes, but that is not very long in the scale of things."

It seemed he was referring to something Fahir had said earlier about the long subjection of Mesopotamia to Ottoman rule.

Somerville saw Fahir look with sudden interest down the table. "But your British Empire is hardly more than a century old," he said. "Too young to feel the touch of mortality."

"Empires never do feel the touch of mortality, it seems to me," Patricia said. "You might have individuals who see the writing on the wall, but the imperial power as such doesn't seem able to read the signs, it hangs on for dear life and always ends in a bloody mess. I mean, look at the Romans."

These remarks and the decided tone in which they were uttered and the way in which not only Palmer but her husband too gave them—and Patricia—their attention were all deeply provoking to Edith, further evidence of the girl's presumption, her habit of intruding on the talk of men, not just with an expression of interest but with opinions of her own—and expressed with such definiteness, with such an absence of self-deprecation. It was so graceless. She had been too much indulged as a child, that was it, too much encouraged to show off; Edith had never liked to see little girls being trotted out to recite things and show how clever they were. She made up her mind to see less of Patricia's mother when she got back to London.

Palmer raised his hands, made a gap between them, widened it slightly. "When it comes to empires," he said, "a few centuries one way or another makes precious little difference. Anyone who excavates in this part of the world is likely to dig down through half a dozen, going back five thousand years at least."

"And they all thought they'd last forever," Patricia said, with an air of stoutly making her point.

"Only the most optimistic of my fellow countrymen would

nurse such a belief at present." Fahir smiled as he spoke but there was no intention of humor in his words. "We have too many friends, and they all want a piece of us," he said. "Britain, France, Russia. The sick man of Europe, you call us. A term of contempt. But it also brings contempt on those who use it. What do you do with a man who is sick? Do you help him to get well or do you merely prop him up for long enough to go through his pockets, meanwhile uttering hypocritical expressions of good-will? Only Germany is a true friend to us, and she has shown this in various ways, one of them the building of this railway."

"Another is the training of your army," the major said.

"So it is." Fahir had been a cavalry officer, and he made no secret of the fact that he had completed his training in Germany, where he had also acquired the scar. "Now there is no need for our junior officers to go to Berlin," he said. "The German instructors are here among us."

The major tightened his mouth in a way more protracted than usual. "Britain is a friend to Turkey," he said. "We are doing everything in our power to safeguard Turkey's territorial integrity. You only have to look at the settlement signed by our governments last October, scarcely five months ago, when agreement was reached on a whole range of matters, the Baghdad Railway among them."

"This whole range of matters were mainly concessions Turkey was obliged to make. As for the railway, you got what you wanted, the right to control the construction from Baghdad to Basra and the right of veto for any extension of the line to the Persian Gulf."

"A triumph of diplomacy," the major said.

"Some might find other terms for it. Diplomacy works best for those who have the strong cards. You British speak often of the sacrifices you are making for the sake of Turkey. What sacrifice have you made in order to obtain these rights in the railway? You have declared yourselves willing to increase by four percent the duties on goods entering the Ottoman possessions. Such staggering generosity. What other imperial power is obliged to permit foreign nations to determine her customs dues? Major Manning, we Turks do not deceive ourselves. We know we need foreign capital and foreign technical assistance. We know that we have to pay a price for these, that we risk losing control of our possessions in the Near East. We see that the British have designs on Mesopotamia as far as Basra, the French have their eyes on Syria, the Russians are seeking to absorb Armenia. He would be a great fool who did not know these things."

A sudden anger had come into his voice with these last words, and Palmer, perhaps feeling himself to blame for having started this dispute, now made an attempt to shift the focus of the conversation. "Of course," he said, "for an archaeologist only dead empires are interesting, and the longer dead the better."

It was not the most tactful of interventions, and it came too late in any case. Somerville was beginning to say something when Manning cut across him. He was looking at Fahir with unconcealed hostility. "That is a gross misrepresentation of my government's policies," he said.

Fahir's hostility was no less evident, but it came with a slight smile and a pretense of ironic detachment. "Your government's policies are the same as those of any other government, to protect your interests and extend them where possible by any means available."

Edith Somerville now—and rather belatedly—remembered the words of her mother. *If there is disagreement at a dinner table and if this is tending to be expressed other than politely and urbanely, it is always the fault of the hostess.* But she had been stimulated and in a way roused by this quarreling, which had something noble in it to her mind, being due not merely to personal antipathy but to patriotic feeling. There was passion in both men and it warmed her like a fire. In another age they might have fought a duel. She preferred the major's repressed rage to Fahir's irony, but that was a question of taste. And she was on the side of Britain anyway, and proud of the British Empire, which everyone knew was the greatest the world had ever seen. All the same, the two could not be allowed to go on looking at each other like this. She cast around in her mind for a way of smoothing things over.

"But this railway," she said, "surely it only benefits those who have put their money in it and then hope to make a profit from the price of the tickets."

It worked, as it generally did. Both Fahir and the major were immediately eager to enlighten her, as were the other men at the table, so much so that several spoke together. Fahir's was the voice that prevailed, perhaps through a tacit recognition that he was the one most entitled to speak of the benefits to Turkey of a line that was designed to pass exclusively over Turkish imperial possessions.

He spoke eloquently of these benefits. With improved communications the huge resources of minerals and metals in eastern Anatolia could be fully exploited, the copper mines of Diabekir, the meerschaum quarries near Eskishehir—practically a world monopoly—the coalfields already producing half a million tons a year. Then there was the increased prosperity that would come from exploiting the agricultural resources of Mesopotamia, the foreign investment that would follow upon the large-scale irrigation projects. In remote antiquity the Land of the Two Rivers had been an important center of cotton production, and there was no reason why this industry should not be revived. The climate was ideal. Mesopotamia could be one of the world's great cotton-growing regions. Grain too. Once the effects of irrigation and the railway were realized, Anatolia, northern Syria, and Mesopotamia, taken together, would export more grain than Russia . . .

"All this will come from the railway," Fahir said. "It will be of the greatest benefit to everyone. The foreign powers will obtain concessions to prospect and develop, the Turkish state will have direct trade routes from the Persian Gulf to Constantinople and so to the Black Sea. The local populations will see their standard of living tripled within three years of the completion of the line."

Fahir's eyes glowed as he looked around the table. "A truly international enterprise," he said. "Foreign investment, local industry, a process of mutual enrichment practically unlimited. The railway will usher in a golden age of prosperity to these lands."

There was nothing forced or consciously exaggerated in these words, or so at least it seemed to Somerville, who had not seen this fervor in Fahir before and would not have believed it could exist in him. All his habitual irony had dissolved in this vision of paradise, this process of mutual enrichment, continuous, without end; it was as if his own words had transformed him even as he spoke them. A sense of marvelous possibility or a genuine belief that these things, in a Europe so divided, would come to pass? It was impossible to know; Fahir himself would not know. Perhaps no more than a dream of water to a man with a thirst. He was a servant of the Ottoman state, devoted in his way. Now, after the centuries of domination, the empire of the Osmanli Turks was slipping away. When our grip on power is loosening, we will fall back on what is second best, visions of cooperation and mutual benefit . . .

Somerville felt himself convicted of meanness and smallness. He could not share this hope in the future. The wealth was there and the lure of it was real enough. But those who financed and controlled the line were unlikely to have the well-being of local populations or the integrity of the Ottoman Empire high among their priorities. In any case, whatever the intricate pattern of desires and hopes that accompanied the railway, whatever wealth it might bring, his own view of it was starkly simple: It was threatening to put an end to his excavation and with that deal a mortal blow to his whole career.

"Quite a speech," Palmer said a little later, after Fahir had retired for the night. "He forgot to mention a few things, though." His face wore its usual expression of cheerful skepticism. "He forgot to mention one of the chief Turkish interests in the railway, which is to be able to move troops and munitions speedily to the head of the Persian Gulf and threaten British communications with India in the event of war. Quite a few things he forgot to mention, actually. There are substantial deposits of chrome ore in Cilicia, and the line passes close by them. If you have it in mind to manufacture armor-piercing shells, you need chrome."

"Well, it's the Germans who are building the line," Patricia said. "I suppose they would like to get their hands on the chrome too. I mean, if Turkey needs foreign capital to help with her cotton industry, she needs it just as much to help her make jolly good hand grenades and stuff like that."

Palmer and she were very much alike, Somerville thought, very well matched. They talked the same language. Both took a sort of glee in deflating high-flown sentiments. A glee not shared by Edith, who would find it mean-spirited and cynical, she would probably be striving to shut the girl's words out. There were just the four of them now, after dinner; they had moved into the sitting room, where a wood fire was burning. Somerville and the younger people sat close to the hearth, and Edith was a little farther off, in her favorite armchair, reading by the light of an oil lamp on the table beside her.

"How did you know about this chrome business?" Somerville asked.

"Financial pages of the *Times*," Palmer said. "If you want to know how things are going, keep an eye on the market for metals. Better than a hundred so-called authoritative editorials. The prices of certain metals have been increasing steadily for months now. All the international accords and treaties and high-sounding assurances haven't made a scrap of difference. Lead, chrome, zinc, antimony in particular."

He paused for a moment for effect, then straightened his back and adopted an oracular manner. "My friends, I put it to you, what have these metals in common? Bear with me, and I will tell you. They are all found in substantial quantities in Turkish Asia, and they are all very important for the manufacture of field guns and armor plate."

Somerville glanced across at his wife, who had not looked up from her book during this conversation. She was rereading one of her favorite novels, Scott's *Rob Roy*, one of a stock she had brought with her, all of which she had read before, not once but several times. The slightly flickering light cast by the lamp gleamed on her lowered head, the fair tresses at her temples. She was sitting with her legs drawn up beneath the long skirt of her dress. She never sprawled or slumped or adopted ungainly postures, unlike Patricia in this; some principle or instinct of grace informed all her movements. Grace and decorum together—the combination had moved him from the beginning, from the days of their courtship, with something dutiful in it, almost childlike, as if some silent appeal for approval were being made. He had the same feeling, though aware of a lack in logical connection, about her habit of reading novels that were already deeply familiar to her, a habit that she must have had already in adolescence.

The fire flared suddenly, distracting his attention. Fuel was brought to the house by an old man, slightly lame, who had somehow secured a monopoly. He brought dried camel dung, dead sticks from the undergrowth of the riverbanks, wood brought down in the winter floods, which he gathered and dried for them. Some of these pieces had lain in the swamps of pitch before being borne away, and this long ooze of pitch had penetrated to the heart of the wood. These pieces would flare up when the flame had devoured the outer part, and for some moments jets of pale blue and orange and gold would lick eagerly around them, as if in some fierce joy of release, a voracity short-lived but somehow startling.

"You promised to explain to me how the picture signs developed into writing," Patricia said to Palmer, in the tone of one who is sure that a promise will be kept.

"So I did. We'll need some paper and a pencil. Let's sit over here."

Edith Somerville raised her head to watch the pair seat themselves at the small square table that was sometimes used for bridge when there were people who cared to play. Then she looked at her husband and smiled, but it did not seem to Somerville there was much amusement in this smile or any warmth for him. More like resignation, he thought. He said, rather awkwardly, "I'd better get along, before I fall asleep by the fire. I've got one or two things to see to."

The quality of his wife's smile did not change with these words. She made no reply but nodded a little and after a moment returned to her book, leaving him with a vague sense of discomfiture at his own awkwardness, at the constraint that had settled between them, making him feel obliged to announce his purposes, as if he couldn't get out of the room without doing so. He wondered if she had noticed it, his explaining of presences and absences, a sort of politeness that belonged to strangers rather than to man and wife. If so, she gave no sign. She was not herself more explanatory than before, and this too troubled him, like a lack of sympathy.

But as the door closed behind him, all thoughts of Edith, all sense of the scene he was leaving, were immediately erased from his mind, replaced by the image of the carved stone they had found that day, which he was on his way now to look at.

"I'll try to give you an idea of the signs in a minute," Palmer said. "But just to go into the background a bit, the key to it all is the cuneiform script."

"I know that means wedge-shaped." Patricia smiled and shrugged her shoulders a bit. "It's just about all I do know."

"The shape was accidental in a way. It's all down to the humble reed, which is what they used for writing. It was cut on a slant, so the marks it made were wedge-shaped. Trace the development of cuneiform, and you follow the whole course of Mesopotamian civilization. The earliest examples we know of are in Sumerian and date to about three thousand years before Christ. We can read Sumerian now, but no one knows for sure where the language came from. Anyway, this way of writing spread very quickly and was taken over by people with languages entirely different from Sumerian, by the Hittites, for example, whose language was Indo-European, and by the Semitic invaders of Mesopotamia, the Akkadians, who passed it on to the Syrians and Babylonians. It was still being used at the beginning of the Christian Era. Three thousand years, not bad for a system of writing, is it? Empires die young by comparison. I should have pointed that out to Fahir. Are we disturbing your reading? If so, we can push off somewhere else."

"No, not at all," Edith said. "I wasn't trying to read actually. I was listening to what you were saying." They would be glad to be alone together, she knew that. "My eyes are getting tired in any case," she said. "I am going to bed soon."

"John must have told you all about cuneiform writing long ago."

"Yes, but his main interest doesn't lie there, as you know. That's why he is so glad to have you with him. By nature he is a digger and searcher, a man of action really."

She paused for a moment, aware of having spoken more in belittlement of Palmer than in any spirit of praise for her husband. "He can't read the original inscriptions," she said, "so he doesn't get so excited about them as you do."

In fact it had been Palmer's lack of excitement that had struck her in listening. She had not taken much to him from the start, disliking his jocularity, which she thought rather common, his way of questioning and undermining things, the lack of fire in him. He saw everything from below, from ground level, toad's level; there was no splendidness in him. His present behavior confirmed her in this opinion. The girl was hanging on his words; you only needed to look at her face to see that. He was the authority; he was in control; he had an intimate knowledge of what he was talking about. Yet he had not tried in the least to be fascinating, to exercise what Edith thought of as the male pre-rogative, the communication of power and strength and passionate certainty. Instead he had spoken with a sort of casual, confiding friendliness, as if he were telling her about a book he had read or a place he had been to and she hadn't.

The man had devoted practically the whole of his adult life, all the years since leaving Oxford, to these studies that he spoke of now so flatly! She simply could not understand it. How different from John in the days of their courtship, when he had outlined his plans and ambitions to her. How inspiring he had been with his passion for Mesopotamia, carrying her along with him on a tide of great designs and bold projects, and how she had admired him for giving up that pettifogging business and devoting himself to his heart's desire. She had responded to his ardor with all the ardor of her nature. *Follow the dream,* that was it. *In the destructive element immerse.* How true that was. *Lord Jim* was one of the novels she had brought with her. Palmer was too pedestrian, too lacking in impulse, to have even the merest notion of such a thing.

"Well, good night," she said. "I'll toddle off to bed."

Palmer waited till the door had closed behind her, then took up the pencil and drew the sheet of paper toward him with an air of relief. "Well," he said, "in the very earliest tablets, let's say around 3000 B.C., the sign for a star was like this, sort of an asterisk made with six lines of equal thickness and length, scratched in the clay with some sharp instrument, no wedge shape at all. Come round the table a bit so you can see better. It's what they call a pictograph, the picture represents the object. Now look at this, a few hundred years later, in what they call the Third Dynasty of Ur, the period of Akkadian domination. It still has the same form, still six lines, but the three upper ones end in wedge shapes. Now if we come to more recent times, say about 700 B.C., the great age of Assyria, it looks like this."

The two were sitting shoulder to shoulder now, and Palmer's pencil was busy.

"But it's totally different," Patricia said. "It's nothing like a star now. Just a simple cross with the wedge shape on the side instead of at the top."

"Yes, that's right, it has turned through ninety degrees. All the cuneiform signs went through this change, for reasons that are not altogether clear to us. And at the same time they got more and more abstract, less and less like the original object. And they started to take on additional meanings. A bowl was still a bowl, but it could also mean food or bread, depending on the context. Two lateral lines meant a stream, but when they became vertical they could also mean a seed or a father or a son."

"And what does this one mean now?"

"Well, it still means star, but it can also be read as sky or God."

"I think the whole thing is absolutely fascinating," Patricia said.

"Do you really?"

"Yes, I do."

"Some people find it boring. Edith, for instance."

"Well, I don't. Edith doesn't go into things very much, does she? She hasn't got much concentration, have you noticed? The whole course of human thought is there in those signs, the whole process of learning. From object to symbol, it's an essential step; we can't emerge from childhood without making it. No child at school today could learn to read or add up without it."

They were still sitting shoulder to shoulder, their upper arms touching. Palmer put the pencil down without shifting his position. For some moments he maintained a deliberate silence. Patricia did not look at him, but she did not move away. He felt love and desire gather within him, furthered by silence, indistinguishable one from another. Object and symbol, he thought. *Yes*. He had known this girl only three weeks. "I am glad you feel like that about it," he said in a voice that was slightly husky. "It matters a lot to me. To tell you the truth, it has been my whole life up to now. Will you marry me?"

The piece of carved stone lay flat on the table where he had left it. He carried the lamp over and stood looking down. The carving was in shallow relief, and the incisions were impacted with clay, making the detail difficult to distinguish clearly. He noticed now that the clay was speckled with a grayish powder; in some places it was more than a speckling, it was a thick admixture, very hard to the touch. He took the eyeglass from his pocket and looked closely at this filling, which brought the cuts in the stone to the same plane as the surface. Something that had been compounded with the clay from the beginning perhaps . . . Then it came to him: It was the dust of wood ash, the same stuff he had found in the roots of the Nubian's hair, in the eyes and the ears of the lion; that had been more bluish in color, but it was the same stuff.

It would not brush out, it was too hard packed. He went to the long table where various instruments and cleaning materials were laid out, returned with tweezers, a thin scalpel, a dentist's pick. Slowly, very carefully, he began to scrape out the filling of clay. Some he put in a jar for laboratory analysis when they returned to London; they had no facilities for it where they were. The traces remaining in the incisions and in the texture of the surface he removed with a weak solution of hydrochloric acid and a soft cloth, working patiently and with great care.

It was well after midnight by the time he finished. He could see the line of the curve clearly now, and the forward-slanting protuberance at the top, where the stone was broken, not a boss, as he had thought at first, but the stump of something that had been longer. The double band of the ring was some nine inches to the left of this, slightly lower down. But it would be on a level, he thought, with the lower part of the curve if this were continued downward. The curve and the stump and the ring, taken together, reminded him of something . . .

Without much sense of decision, as if moving under some gently exercised propulsion, he got up and made his way across the near corner of the silent courtyard to the drawing office. Here he provided himself with a pencil, some sheets of plain paper, and a square of tracing paper. As he returned with these, the silence that hung over the courtyard and the unaccustomed lateness of the hour brought about a feeling of excitement in him, as if this were an escapade of some kind, something so far out of the common as to seem reckless, even illicit.

Seated again in the workroom, he laid the tracing paper over the stone and lightly traced out the lines of the carving, taking care to keep the spaces and proportions exact. This done, pressing down hard with his pencil, he made an impression on the first piece of paper, then drew in the lines. There before him were the curve, the stump, the ring. The curve descended gently, but at the point where the stone was broken off it seemed, for no more than half an inch, to become steeper, almost vertical. Still as if his movements were being directed, he took up the pencil again and continued the line down from this point, ending it with a hook. The stump he extended, following the line of the slant. He found himself looking, quite unmistakably, at the hooked beak and stiff heraldic crest of a hawk. What he had thought was a ring could not be so; the line below it swelled out a little; it was the beginning of an arm. The ring was a bracelet, and it was enclosing a human wrist.

Head of a hawk, arms and hands of a man. Into Somerville's mind there came the memory of the picture that he had bought at the age of eighteen, which had hung first in his bedroom when he still lived with his father, then on the wall of his study in London, a copy of F. C. Cooper's watercolor of the excavation at Nimrud in 1850, carried out by Henry Layard, depicting the entrance to the shrine of Ninurta built by Ashurnasirpal II in the ninth century before Christ. Later he had seen the originals brought to the Louvre from Khorsabad by Paul Émile Botta and to the British Museum, some years later, by Layard. But it was the painting that had fired his imagination. On either side of the portals and flanking the colossal human-headed bulls, three panels, one above the other, depicted the guardian spirits of the Assyrian kings, the middle one with the head and wings of an eagle and the body of a man, right arm raised in blessing, wrist braceleted. The bracelet too was proof: Only gods and demigods and kings were empowered to wear bracelets.

What was it doing here, so far from the Tigris and the Assyrian heartlands, from Ashur and Nineveh, the great cities of Assyrian power? Somerville peered around him into the dim corners of the room, as if to interrogate all points of the compass, all quarters of the world.

Dawn was not far off when he finally succeeded in sleeping. He had lain awake through the hours of the night, possessed by the excitement of his discovery. The same tension of questioning fastened on him the moment he opened his eyes. The figure of the hawk-headed guardian came to him complete in every detail, as he had seen it first in Cooper's painting, then among the sculptures brought back from the Northwest Palace at Nimrud, slabs of gypsum carved in low relief, which had decorated the portals and walls of the palaces of Assyrian kings, scenes of hunting and warfare and ritual procession. Among them, recurring again and again, the beak, the crest, the human form, always in profile, always with its magical accoutrements, the right hand with its braceleted wrist raising a cone-shaped object toward the branches of a tree, the left lowered, holding a small bucket. Perhaps a sacred tree, the Tree of Life—no agreement had been reached on this, the time was too remote, the evidence lacking. The cone resembled a date spathe, the male flower used for fertilizing palms, but in the sculptures it was not always applied to trees, but sometimes to the king himself to give magical protection to his person, as it was in those portals of the shrine at Nim-

rud, built at a time when Assyria, under Ashurnasirpal, one of
the cruelest and most magnificent of her kings, was about to em-
bark on those wars of conquest that would see her, within two
centuries, mistress of an empire greater in extent than any that
the world had ever seen, stretching from the Taurus Mountains
to the Persian Gulf and westward to Syria and Palestine and
Egypt.

Nimrud—he kept coming back to that. Scene of those early
spectacular discoveries of Henry Layard that had first fired him
with the ambition to be an excavator in the Land of the Two
Rivers and bring fresh marvels to light . . .

Somerville knew he should get up. He could hear his wife
moving about in the adjacent bedroom. The major would be
leaving early; it would be unmannerly not to be there to bid him
farewell. But he lay for a while longer, in the toils of the story
that had begun to knit together in his mind from the moment of
recognizing the shapes in the stone. Kalhu, the ancient name,
mentioned in the Bible as Calah, on the left bank of the Tigris
south of Mosul, a city of great antiquity but not particularly important until Ashurnasirpal chose it for his new capital, setting
thousands of men to work there and lavishing great wealth on
the building of his palace. Why would he want to move away
from Ashur, the old capital city, named after their father god?
Pride? Fear of attacks from the desert tribes of the west? Impossible to know . . . Snatches from his royal inscriptions, read and
reread in translation, came to Somerville's mind as he began to
make the first moves toward getting out of bed. *I built a pillar over
against his city gate and I flayed all the chiefs who had revolted and I
covered the pillar with their skins . . . A palace of cedar, cypress, juniper*

*and tamarisk for my royal dwelling and for my lordly pleasure for all time
I founded therein . . . The spoil of my hand from the lands which I had
brought under my sway, in great quantities I took and placed there . . .*
For all time—he had thought his palace would last forever. All
those precious woods, so boastfully enumerated, burned to ash
by the Medes and Chaldeans allied together when the cities of
Assyria were put to the fire and their empire collapsed.

Clapping his hands, calling across the courtyard from his
window for Hassan to bring him hot water, he thought: No, not
stone, stone might suffer charring but would not be reduced to
ash. Perhaps at the very heart of a conflagration, even stone.
Ivory, yes; fire would melt ivory . . .

He was only just in time to bid farewell to the major, who
departed with his maps and his lists of friendly rifles and his escort of Shammar tribesmen. After breakfast he felt a certain re-
luctance to leave for the tell and see the work started—his usual
practice. The foremen were well able to take care of this, he
knew; it was merely a question of assembling the groups, allot-
ting the work—the area of excavation would be the same. And
perhaps it was this, the sameness, that unsettled him, a nagging
sense that these recent, unusual finds required a breaking of
new ground, a shift in tactics that he felt for the moment unable
to direct.

With the idea of looking once again at the carving and at
the lines he had traced and placing them side by side so as to
examine them in the sober light of morning, he made his way
to the workroom. There was no link between the stone and the
ivory as far as he could see; at least there was nothing that could
associate them through points of similarity; the ivory was not Syr-

ian work, it came from the cities of the coast or from Egypt, it was a statement of power, not a plea for magical protection.

He found Palmer, who had not been at breakfast, there before him, seated at the table, microscope in hand, a lamp at his elbow in spite of the daylight. Before him, laid down on the table, loosely fitted together, were the pieces of a clay tablet found some days before among the thick debris of mud brick. He looked up as Somerville entered. "I was hoping to see you," he said. "It took ages to clean these up and assemble them. This is the first time I've looked at them properly. I didn't feel like going over to the dig this morning, not just yet."

"Nor did I."

There had been something disjointed in these opening remarks of Palmer's, a lack of consequence unusual in him. His eyes looked wider open than usual and had a slightly staring look. "Yes, quite a job," he said. "There are some gaps, of course."

He was silent for several moments, still looking in a curiously detached way at Somerville. Then he said, "I didn't think much of it when they turned up. I thought it would be the usual thing, you know, some scraps from a list, an inventory, some record of an exchange of goods, perhaps Hittite or Mitannian—they both traded in this region. I didn't believe I'd be able to make it out. In any case, the surface looked too much damaged, it was impregnated with a mixture of wood ash and mud dust, devilishly hard to move." He paused again, looked quickly down at the fragments as if to make sure they were still there. "But I was wrong," he said. "Some of the cuneiform is as clear as when the marks were first made. The clay has been baked hard. Thank

God for fire—there's nothing like a good blaze for preserving inscriptions. This is in Akkadian, the dialect of it spoken by the Assyrians."

There was silence between them for some moments. Their eyes met, fell away, met again. "Akkadian caused a lot of trouble at one time," Palmer said. "But once they realized that it is a Semitic language akin to Babylonian, it was deciphered quite soon. What we are looking at here is part of an Assyrian royal inscription. Oh, by the way, Patricia and I are sort of engaged."

Somerville found that his mouth had gone completely dry. "Congratulations," he said. "You couldn't do better. Is there any mention of Ashurnasirpal?"

"No, why? The name of the ruler is missing—we only have some pieces of the lower half. It seems to be a record of the capture of Memphis by an Assyrian force. There's part of a name, but it is not Assyrian. Taha or Tark, it looks like."

"Might be Taharqa—he was king of Egypt when Memphis was taken and sacked by the Assyrians. But that was much later, it was Esarhaddon who was the Assyrian king at that time." He felt an obscure sense of disappointment. "Nothing to do with Ashurnasirpal," he said.

"Why did you think it might be him?"

In as few words as possible Somerville explained what he knew he should have explained already as being due to a colleague but had been held back from doing so by a secrecy that had somehow grown with his disappointments. He told Palmer about the form he had traced out, the ash he had found in both the stone and the ivory.

"They used pitch for the lion's eyes," he said, "and on the

points of the man's hair. Pegs of ivory capped with pitch. This must have been partly melted in some fire before hardening again; it has formed what look like tears in the lion's eyes, and it has run down into the roots of the victim's hair. It is Egyptian work, or work influenced by Egypt. But they had no bitumen industry that we know of. So I thought, you know, that it might have come from somewhere not far from here, perhaps Hit on the Euphrates. There was a trade in bitumen there long before the Assyrians became a power in the region."

"That's right. At Tell Halaf the Germans have found pots that had been broken and repaired with pitch in the Ubaid period, a thousand years before Assyria was on the map at all."

"So it seems likely that the Egyptians, or whoever it was, used imported bitumen when they fashioned the ivory plaque, which I think might have been part of a chair back. But in that case, how did it get here? Then I remembered that Ashurnasirpal took an Assyrian army on an expedition to the shores of the Mediterranean not long after he came to the throne—round about 875. He was the first in a long line of Assyrian empire builders."

"The Great Sea, as they called it. He boasts about it in the annals. *I washed the blood from my weapons in the Great Sea and made sheep offerings to the gods.* Charming chaps, weren't they? There would be rich pickings on that coast. The ivory could have come from there, somewhere like Byblos or Sidon—they had a lively trade with Egypt. I wouldn't call him an empire builder myself, more a sort of large-scale raider."

"Not easy to draw the line. It is more or less how we acquired our African colonies, isn't it? I mean, what else would you call Cecil Rhodes? Anyway, it seems reasonable to think the plaque might be part of the booty they brought back."

"He boasts about that too. The details of the loot are always very important in the annals. He came back with gold, silver, copper, linen garments, large and small monkeys, ebony boxes, things fashioned from the tusks of the walrus . . . Yes, I see what you mean, ivory, in other words."

"And it was Ashurnasirpal who made his capital at Kalhu, on the other side of the Tigris, about the same time. And I think he was the first Assyrian king to use gypsum for sculptures not exposed to the weather. I'm not absolutely sure, but I think they used limestone before that."

Palmer shook his head. "No idea," he said. "Out of my line."

"Gypsum is softer, you can get more detail. And the carved stone we found, that is gypsum, and so I thought, you know, there must be some connection, perhaps he is the link, perhaps there is some clue in the closeness of the dates that will help us to understand how these things got here. But now there is this business of Esarhaddon and the invasion of Egypt, and that was in the early seventh century, about two hundred years later."

"Well, it's still Assyria, isn't it? This is the third year of excavation here, there has been no sign of an Assyrian presence before. These things have all been found recently and all in the same area, on the east side of the mound, where we have opened the new trench."

Somerville felt a tightening of the chest. It was from the eastern side that you could look down on the railway buildings.

This was where the German voices came from, the clatter of metal, the thumping sound of the open trucks as they passed along the rails. "We will go farther on that side," he said. "We'll keep some people on the trench where the things were found, and we'll start a new one in sections, at right angles to it."

4.

⟐

Jehar found himself spending more time in the rail yards at Jerablus than he had ever intended. He had returned there in the company of a trading party, eager to gaze at Ninanna again and to pick up something further about the progress of the railroad that he could sell to the Englishman. But after that great leap of the bridge there had been what seemed like a pause for breath; work on the left bank had not begun; they were still waiting for the rails to come from Aleppo. It had occurred to him that he might invent some story of the line to take back with him, a strike among the workforce, a large-scale ambush by the desert Arabs with great loss of life. Storytelling came naturally to him, he had a gift for it, and the stories became true to him as he told them, as he embroidered them with detail. However, an elementary caution remained: He was held back by the fear that his employer might find the stories contradicted by others and so would cease to trust him and therefore cease to pay him for the information he took back.

Meanwhile, instead of adding to his stock of money, he was experiencing difficulty in holding on to what he had. He kept his eyes open, watching the movements of goods about the yards, the guard that was kept on the warehouses and storage sheds, the hours of opening and closing in the offices of the German surveyors and engineers, the quality of the locks, the fastening of the windows. There were moments of inattention, and one had to be ready for them. He succeeded on different occasions in stealing some pick handles, a tool kit in a leather holster, a three-gallon drum of kerosene. These things he sold for what he could get in the shanties that had sprung up in the area of the docks and by the riverside. The town had swollen greatly with the coming of the railroad and held now a good many people who did not ask where things came from. Sometimes he took serious risks for Ninanna's sake. The police were not much in evidence here, but there was always the justice of the gang to be reckoned with. Once, in a dockside tavern, pretending to pause while he watched a game of dice, he stole a purse from a coat belonging to one of the players, which was hanging over the back of the man's chair. He was seen, and only flight and the refuge of darkness saved him from serious injury. He went in some fear now of being recognized.

His consolation, which was also his torment, was that he could see Ninanna every day, for hours on end, from midmorning till nightfall, while she was there at the café. All that was needed was the price of a glass of tea. The café stayed open until midnight and later, but he had no hope of seeing her after dark; the uncle, aware of having a valuable asset, kept her carefully sequestered from view and from the temptations of darkness.

The sight of her filled him with hope. But all the men there could watch her too, as she moved about with her tray, serving tea and coffee and raki, gathering the empty glasses. Not only were they feasting their eyes on her, but also—in his imagination—nursing schemes similar to his own. He was not capable of distinguishing his own desires from those of others; anyone who set eyes on Ninanna, saw the candidness and beauty of her face, her grace of movement and her shapeliness, would be stricken by love for her just as he had been and would start getting together the gold pounds. He knew that the uncle would not hesitate for a moment if another came to him with the money.

This uncle, in Jehar's eyes, had no fidelity in his nature, no sense of right or wrong whatever. He had complained that Jehar sat all day over one glass of tea and how was he to make a profit if everyone behaved like that? Such a shameless and avaricious person was no use to anyone; he simply cluttered up the earth. It had sometimes come to Jehar's mind that he might put an end to this miserable man if a good chance presented itself, but he was uncertain how the girl would take it, whether she would trust herself to him, whether there were others with whom she might seek refuge . . .

Meanwhile he found ways of talking to her, though never for long. She came for water to the pump that was near the office of the German engineers, where he had first seen her; sometimes on these occasions she was alone and would have some little while for talking, or listening rather—she said very little. The small kitchen where the coffee and the tea were made had a door that gave onto the outside yard, which had always a dark smell of soot and hot metal and spent steam from the shunting of the engines, but which nevertheless was kept open because of the heat from the stove in that narrow place. Keeping a wary eye out for the uncle, who was generally behind the counter inside, taking the money, Jehar would cross the tracks and come to stand at the open doorway, and by these means he sometimes succeeded in talking to her for a few minutes, with the clangor and hissing of the shunting bays on one side and the voices from the café on the other.

Such scattered moments did not make for conversation as this is generally understood, and Jehar had seen from the beginning that he must find one single topic, one that could be resumed at every opportunity, which would in effect, in spite of all interruptions, make an unending story. He found it in a vision of their future together. This, with all that it contained of happiness and fulfillment, was situated in the town of Deir ez-Zor, on the right bank of the Great River, which he had seen when working on the rafts that carried the pitch upstream and downstream from the black fields of Hit.

He described the town to Ninanna, the green islet in the midst of the stream, the permanent bridge that went from one bank to the other, the six white minarets that rose above the roofs of the houses, the great mass of gardens and palm groves and cultivated fields that extended along the river for many miles to the east. Memory and invention combined with love to make him eloquent. Their future at Deir ez-Zor was an amazing story, and no one had ever told her such a story before. She listened at first with her face turned from him; but gradually, as the story took on more and more wondrous detail, she would look directly at him, beguiled alike by the repetition of what was already familiar and the constant addition of what was new. She would sometimes ask questions, and when he answered Jehar would add something more to the story, some novelty that had not been there before. No less than twelve pillars supported the bridge, and these pillars were of stone. The town was lawful and orderly; no one went in fear of his property or his life. Not only was there a garrison of Turkish soldiers, but peace was also ensured by the Bejt Ftejjeh, a very powerful and numerous family long settled in this region, who had prospered under Ottoman rule.

Many members of this family worked in the government offices, he told her, and they gave a sympathetic hearing to Arabs. The Government House was situated on the river, and it was tall and white with many windows, and it had a wide courtyard. There were always two guards at the gate, in uniforms of blue and red. Deir ez-Zor had several primary schools and a high school and a polytechnic school—their sons would have good instruction. And there was land. To the north of the town were the gardens of as-Salhijjeh, the property of the Pasha, the Turkish overlord, but much of it neglected because the Pasha lived in Baghdad and came rarely.

This Pasha entered increasingly into the story, becoming always more corpulent. He sat there in Baghdad, eating halvah and pastries filled with honey and cream and kebabs of every description, getting fatter and fatter and making Jehar, who did not get enough to eat in these days, feel hungrier and hungrier as he invented the dishes. He puffed out his cheeks to make her laugh; he had no idea what the Pasha looked like, or whether he truly existed, but it was obvious that soon he would cease visiting his lands altogether. He would become totally immobile, and Jehar acted out with staring eyes and rigid head this stricken immobility of the overstuffed Pasha. Laughter came easily to Ninanna, widening her eyes, replacing the look of wonder that the story had brought to them.

A piece of land could be rented for the price of the tax on it; the flush wheels that brought the water from the river could be repaired, the irrigation channels dug out again . . . In these snatched moments, amid the dirt and din of the rail yards, these two, who had not once touched each other, who owned nothing, created together a land full of promise, an earthly paradise.

Jehar knew he was gaining ground with the girl; he could see it in her eyes. But the knowledge brought him no peace, rather the contrary, increasing his sense of what he stood to lose. It was a pattern familiar to his experience and his general sense of the nature of life, the crushing of human prospects, just when they seem auspicious, by some stroke of fate, something not envisaged, unpredictable. He had known it often enough in his gambling days, this dark game of fate. It troubled his sleep now; he dreamed of unmaskings, disguised enemies, trusted faces turning ugly.

Driven thus, he visited the uncle in the small shed he called his office, where, in addition to a table made of planks scavenged from the yards and a single chair, there was a low pallet against the wall, because this shed served also as the uncle's sleeping place.

Standing before the seated man, taking care to speak respectfully and show no sign of the contempt and hatred in his heart, glancing around cautiously in the hope of seeing something in the nature of a strongbox where the takings from the café might be kept, Jehar offered his services in any capacity the uncle might choose, as watchman, caretaker, sweeper, handyman. He would ask for no payment, only board and lodging. However, they would agree on a nominal wage, and this would be regularly deducted from the hundred gold pounds, and so, week by week, the debt would be paid and in the end Ninanna would be his.

It had seemed, as he sketched it out in his mind beforehand, a reasonable proposal. It would require patience and self-control, but he would be able to see the girl every day; he would be able to watch out for possible rivals; he might succeed, before the debt was paid, in persuading her to run away with him to Deir ez-Zor. In any event, he would be well placed to kill the uncle if he went back on the agreement or tried to make a whore of the girl or sell her to someone else. Yes, it had seemed eminently reasonable. But the fabulist is not always the best judge of his own fables, and the more hope he has in them, the more he is likely to deceive himself. Well before the uncle's ugly smiling, Jehar had realized that the story would fail to convince.

The uncle chuckled in a way that seemed evil to Jehar. He was a heavy man and would remain quite still for long periods with his small eyes almost closed below the fringe of his headcloth. In fact it was he who had served as Jehar's model for the palsied Pasha of Baghdad. He opened his eyes now, however, to look at the man before him. "Do you take me for a fool?" he said. "I am to give you free board and lodging for months on end and as a result of this generosity lose the bride-price? What work is there here for a watchman or a sweeper except to watch for coins that he can sweep into his pockets?"

He said nothing more, and indeed there was nothing more to be said. Jehar turned and left, confirmed in his antipathy, nursing murder in his heart. The uncle had as good as called him a thief, a gross insult, not to be borne. And what kind of man was it who would sell his own niece to someone whose honesty he doubted?

He thought of crossing the yard and looking in at the doorway of the kitchen in the hope of seeing Ninanna. But as he passed the company drawing office he saw one of the Germans emerge bareheaded and go around the side of the building. He did not lock the door; it was obvious that he was not intending to be away long. Gone around to the privy at the back, Jehar thought. He drew nearer. There was no one else in the office and no one nearby. The work of a moment to mount the wooden steps, enter, sweep together the several papers on the desk, clutch them in one quick handful, and leave as he had come.

For the work on the eastern side of the mound Somerville had decided on a method first used by Flinders Petrie at Lachish in Palestine twenty-five years before. Petrie's mound had been steeper sided than this one of his, but that made no difference as far as he could see. A line was marked from the summit, and a shallow trench was begun, following this line of descent. Groups of six, each consisting of a pickman, a spademan, and four basketmen, were set one below the other three yards apart and, working from within the trench, told to cut a horizontal step. The objects found by each gang were to be kept separate and recorded separately. In this way, working in narrow shafts, he hoped to establish an exact chronological sequence.

On the seventh day, working at about twenty-three feet from the summit, one of the pickmen came upon the traces of a wall six or seven inches high. Somerville was called for and crouched for two hours, first with a small trowel and then with a narrow-bladed pocketknife, carefully scraping at the accretion of clay that obscured the base. At the end of this time he sat back on his heels. The habit of restraint in the presence of the work-people, assumed for the sake of authority, kept his face impassive, gave no hint of the elation that filled him. The base was of stone, cut and shaped; the layer of bricks that surmounted it had kept their form, even under the weight of masonry piled upon them to make new foundations for building. They were not like the disintegrated remains they had found so far, made of compacted mud and dried in the sun: These bricks had been fired in a kiln. Only the rich and powerful had such walls built for their dwellings—and for those of their gods.

The import of this flooded his mind. He felt the need to be alone, apart from others, so as to be able to think calmly. He told the group they would all be remembered when the time for baksheesh came, instructed the pickman to follow the line of the wall with due care, and called for Elias to come and keep an eye on things. Then he made his way a little higher up, beyond the line of the new trench. From here he could look down at the railway buildings and beyond them at a vast and barren expanse marked by long rises of rock and gravel and the ridges of ancient canal embankments and silted irrigation ditches. In the days when that wall was built this land had been well watered, fertile, and prosperous. Always precarious, of course, for the people who worked on the land, because the season of floods was unpredictable and capricious. But for the rulers a green and pleasant land. He knew it as he stood there; this had been more than a stop on a trade route, more than a frontier post on borders contested by warring imperial powers. Higher than the delta lands to the south, cooler in summer, probably well timbered once, freshened by the streams between the two tributaries of the Euphrates. In their great days of empire the Assyrians held undisputed sway over all this ground. Could Tell Erdek once have been a summer resort for their kings, a place of rest and repose after the campaigning, after the washing away of the blood? If so, what more natural than they should have brought here things that they treasured or that held some particular meaning? That would explain the ivory plaque, perhaps even the guardian spirit . . .

"Noble lord, I have a paper for you to see."

Engrossed in his thoughts, with the sound of voices and of metal striking on stone not far away, Somerville had heard no steps approach behind him. Turning, he saw Jehar standing at a respectful distance, holding a square sheet of grayish paper in his hand. "What is it?" he said. "What have you got there?"

Taking the question for encouragement, Jehar advanced and handed him the sheet. After a moment he saw that it was a map, carefully drawn by hand on graph paper. There was a dotted red line that crossed diagonally to the northwest, dipping slightly as it crossed the Khabur River, then rising again north-ward. There were contour lines indicating the steepness of the gradients, and at certain points a small black triangle had been drawn, with the altitude in meters beside it. He saw Zeharat al-Bada, 423, el-Muelehat, 411. These were the rises he had just been looking at. Following the red line to the edge of the paper, he saw that before reaching this edge it passed through the town of Ras el-Ain, a three-hour ride away. It was here that Fahir had his quarters. It took him a moment or two longer to realize that if the red line touched this town, approaching as it would be-tween the hills and the eastern branch of the river, it must come very close indeed to the mound on which they were standing.

"It is the railway," Jehar said softly, choosing the moment to speak when he saw comprehension come to the other's face. "I did not want to show Your Excellency this very important docu-ment at a time when others were close by. I have traveled danger-ously, without the men who should have accompanied me. The cowards deserted me, left me alone. Now, if they saw us, they would try to claim some credit for the obtaining of this map. They are liars from infancy. They would even ask Your Excel-lency for a reward, whereas it was I alone and unaided that ob-tained it."

Even in the stress of the moment Somerville found himself struck once again by the ornately phrased, unfaltering speech. Jehar had probably never attended any sort of school in his life and almost certainly could not read or write and would not be capable of fabricating such a map, though Somerville had been briefly prey to this suspicion. It was as if some angel of eloquence had befriended him. Or demon, he thought suddenly—Jehar was the perpetual bearer of bad news. He felt a sudden throb of pain at his temples. Between the hills and the marshes, through his mound, through his prospects, through five thousand years of human life and death . . .

He was aware of Jehar's gaze upon him with its usual blend, which he had always found unsettling, of intensity and simplicity. The gaze of a savage. He strove to let nothing show on his face; from obduracy, from the long habit of restraint; the other would know he had dealt a blow, but he would see no evidence of it, gain no advantage. "This is a survey map, drawn to scale," he said. "Where did you get it?"

Jehar had been expecting this question and had prepared an answer that he thought would produce the best result. At first he had been inclined to tell the truth and describe how he had stolen it from the survey office. It was an exploit of which he felt proud and would have made a gripping and dramatic story, the adroitness and boldness of it, a miracle of timing. But in the end, not being sure the *khwaja* would appreciate how brilliant he had been, the risk of detection and punishment that the theft had involved, he had decided on a different answer.

"It cost me much time and money," he said. "It was far from easy. There is always someone who can be approached, but it takes time and patience to find him. There is one there, one of those that make the maps, but he is too fond of the liquor they call eau-de-vie that they make from grain, he is often drunk and always in need of money, the more so now as he has lost his post, yes, he has been discharged. His name is Herr Franke. He was one of those that make the drawings, but then he is shaky, his hands he cannot keep still, his eyes are blurred, he cannot see to do the maps, he makes mistakes, so they dismiss him from the work and so he loses the stipend, but he does not lose the desire for schnapps, in fact it is increased by his misfortune. It was he who sold me the map. He has no hair on his head, and he has a way of opening and closing his mouth. Like this, like a fish."

"I see." Somerville did not for one moment believe in this drunken, fishlike German draftsman; the account had been too circumstantial: the name, the appearance, the details of the dismissal; he had noticed before that Jehar was one who fell under the spell of his own stories. But it would not do to show doubt, as then the story would be embroidered and elaborated; Herr Franke would figure increasingly in it until, bald and gasping, he became a permanent element in the saga of Jehar's existence from day to day. He himself, the benefactor who had to be coaxed and deceived, he too was part of the tale.

"Have they resumed work on the line?" he said.

"Not yet, noble one, but it cannot be long now, they say the rails have come from Alexandretta to Aleppo. They can soon be brought to Jerablus from there. The cost of obtaining the map was twelve Turkish pounds. Herr Franke would not accept less."

"We agreed from the beginning there would be no refunding of expenses. I am tired of telling you this. However, I will mark you down for eight pounds. You showed enterprise in obtaining the map, and this should be rewarded. You will have it in a few days when the money is drawn for the payment of the wages."

Jehar rocked his head from side to side in the manner of one dubious, then compressed his lips and nodded slowly as if making the best of things. In fact he was delighted with this promise, which almost doubled his stock. He still had a long way to go; but he was optimistic by nature and a stroke of fortune like this renewed his faith. He rejoiced inwardly as he walked away from the slope. Deir ez-Zor with its white minarets and green gardens, Ninanna's face, her smile, the wonder in her eyes, which was the wonder of their future together, all came close before him.

Somerville stayed where he was awhile longer, holding the square of paper loosely in his hand. Within a few days work would begin again on the line. He had no very precise idea of how much track could be laid in a day. Five miles? It would depend on the nature of the terrain. The map, with its apocalyptic red line and exact topographical detail, had been a shock to him, but it added nothing essential: He had known, since arriving in February and seeing the German storage sheds already half constructed, lying so close below the eastern side of the mound, that the line was making straight toward him. It would pass west of Tell Halaf, where the Germans were excavating under the direction of von Oppenheim. But von Oppenheim was wealthy and had powerful friends; it was said that he had been one of the advisers on the route the line should take; he would take care that there was no danger to his operation. He himself had one solitary possibility of bringing some pressure to bear: He had mentioned it to no one, but the present British Ambassador to Constantinople, recently appointed, while not a friend exactly, would be likely to remember him because they had been at school together.

All doubts were resolved now. It was as he had dreaded— dreaded and hoped in almost equal measure. He felt a gathering of resolution. Things had changed enormously in the few days since he had last stood alone here. It filled him with wonder now to think how a few apparently ill-assorted objects could so transform his prospects. A piece of ivory, a piece of carved stone, some few marks on a clay tablet, a wall with kiln-fired bricks and a stone base . . .

A heavy clatter of metal came from somewhere close below him. He took some steps to the eastern side of the summit. Arab workmen, supervised by a man in blue overalls and a white sun hat, had hoisted a sheet of corrugated iron onto a framework of timber; two others were preparing to rivet the corners of the metal to the support poles. There was no room for doubt now; that anguish had been lifted from him. The line would not come to save him from failure and defeat but to blast these new hopes of success. Finally, unequivocally, he knew it for an enemy.

When Somerville left the site in the evening, the base of the wall had been exposed for a length of two yards. It followed the line of the hillside and showed no sign of coming to an end.

The map Jehar had brought him he spoke of to no one. He was preoccupied at dinner and ate hastily and mainly in silence. Edith was not at the table; he was told by Hassan, who always knew the movements of people about the house, that she had eaten earlier and retired to her room. Rising from the table, he felt a sudden weariness descend on him, a heaviness that made every movement of his limbs seem like a huge effort. The exhilarating discovery of the wall, Jehar's map with its remorseless red line, his lonely travail of spirit that had followed, the long hours of anxious supervision while they worked to uncover the wall, all this had taken a toll on him only recognized now. He had intended to spend some time in the workroom after dinner but decided against this and went almost at once to bed.

He was asleep within seconds of his head touching the pillow and slept profoundly without stirring, for several hours. He had not been conscious of dreaming or of any questioning that might have continued below the surface of his sleep, but when he woke, in the deepest silence of the night, it was with an immediate conviction: The ivory might have been part of the plunder Ashurnasirpal carried back from the rich lands of the west, the hawk-headed guardian might once have stood at the portals of his palace at Kalhu, but they could not have been brought here during his reign or during that of his immediate successors; the Assyrian Empire in those days did not reach so far, not with any certainty of control; it would take another century of conquest for this to be established. Someone else then, someone later . . .

Fire had touched all of them; there was the evidence of the ash, the run of the bitumen, the clay tablet baked hard. But it could not be the same fire that had devastated Kalhu and signaled the end of Assyrian power. Their cities had gone up in flames, the inhabitants massacred by the invading Medes and Chaldeans with the fury of long hatred, a sort of ancestral revenge for all the centuries of Assyrian wealth and dominion. At a time of such chaos who would have thought to rescue such things from the conflagration, to bring them so far, all the way from the banks of the Tigris? To what purpose? No, they had been through some different fire.

He sat bolt upright in the bed. "Some different fire," he

muttered, the words coming without volition, as it seemed, almost as if uttered by someone else. It seemed to him, in the impenetrable darkness, as if the bitter ash of that distant conflagration were present to his nostrils. A scent of hatred and revenge and desolation. It was here that the burning had been; this had been a place of importance; only places of importance were worth the pillage and burning.

The intention followed so closely on this thought that it seemed always to have been there, in some weaker form, waiting for a fire such as this to harden it; he would go, in person and without delay, to Constantinople; he would see the Ambassador; he would explain the importance of these recent finds, the new scope of the excavation, the evidence of an Assyrian presence here, where none had been suspected, the possibility of valuable objects being found, the fame and prestige this would bring to the nation. The Ambassador would listen; he would bring pressure to bear, through the Foreign Office, on his German counterpart in London. The railway company would be induced to take a different route, perhaps keeping to the west of Ras el-Ain . . .

He groped for matches, found them, lit the lamp at his bedside, saw the flame flicker behind the glass, then grow into a perfect roseate globe as he turned up the brass rod that operated the wick. He was wide-awake and radiant with purpose. He felt a sudden need to tell Edith of his decision. He got up, crossed the room, holding the lamp in one hand. He tapped at the door that connected their two rooms, heard nothing, opened the door, and intruded head and lamp. He called his wife's name, saw her form stir under the bedclothes. "I'm sorry to wake you," he said. "I felt that I needed . . . I have decided something."

He advanced, set the lamp down on the floor, and sat on the edge of the bed, near the foot. "I didn't want to wait till morning," he said, feeling some compunction now as he saw her sit up, raise her hands to her hair, which she had untied for the night and reached down to her shoulders. The lamplight fell softly on her bare arms as she made this instinctive gesture, a response to exposure, in which, however, there was perfect precision, half asleep as she was. There was a bowl of flowers on the table beside her, long-stemmed dark blue anemones and the narcissus that came in early spring, single white flowers edged with crimson. Knowing her love for flowers, people who worked in the house would gather them on the stream banks and bring them for her. The shortness of the season made them precious to her. She arranged them herself and always perfectly.

"I'm sorry," he said again.

Edith drew the sheet up over her chest, as if cold. "What is it?" she said. "Is something wrong?"

"No, nothing wrong, it's just that I've come to a decision and I wanted to tell you about it."

"In the middle of the night?" There was a softness of tone in this, and it came to him with some surprise and a certain stirring of excitement that she might have misunderstood his purpose and not been displeased. She had always valued alacrity of feeling, setting it above what was cautious and considered, both in herself and in others; there had been little enough of it between them of late. But he knew that it had not been the sort of impulse she would value that had brought him here. Not impulse at all in fact: He had wanted to confide his decision to her so as to make it irrevocable, prevent him—under pain of her scorn—from changing his mind in the cold light of day. He would never be able to tell her this or she to imagine it, let alone sympathize. She could support strength with all the strength of her being, but she could not support weakness, not in men—in women it was to be expected.

"I wanted you to know of it," he said. "There are always other people round in the mornings."

Edith reached for the woolen wrap on the chair beside her and settled back against the pillow, actions that conveyed more clearly than any words could have done that she had revised her first idea of the purpose of his visit.

He told her then what his restraint had only allowed her to surmise before, his worries about the encroaching railway; he told her of the map Jehar had presented to him that very morning. It was easier to talk of it, now that the former paralysis of divided feeling was no more; she would not have understood how he or anyone could half desire defeat as a release from struggle. So as not to alarm her he said nothing about the financial difficulties that were facing him. Keeping his face at first turned away, he described the recent discoveries they had made, which pointed to something momentous, something that could make his name, make this site famous in the annals of Mesopotamian archaeology, bring great financial reward and an assured career in the future.

He had spoken with increasing passion, and now he turned and looked at her. In Constantinople were the blinkered ones, the British authorities who sat at their desks and allowed this monstrous thing to happen. Letters were no good. He would go in person; he would confront these people. He and the present ambassador had been at school together; it counted for something. He would make them see that it was not just a mound of earth that was in jeopardy but a part of the story of humanity. He would show them that he was no mere futile dabbler but someone to be reckoned with, someone who would not take this outrage lying down.

He raised his head and fixed her with his eyes. His voice was vibrant with the passion of his rage, released now after long repression. He saw that her eyes were bright and she was flushed.

"But it is splendid," she said, and quite unexpectedly, in the midst of his fury, he was carried back in memory to the May evening four years ago, when they had met for the first time.

He had talked about an excavation at Tell Barsip on the Euphrates, from which he had just returned. He had spoken with enthusiasm and had seen the warmth of this reflected in her face. Encouraged, he had confessed to her his intention of leading an expedition himself after these years as an assistant, and putting all he had into it. "But how absolutely splendid!" she had said. Looking at her across the table, at her bright eyes, her mouth that smiled upon him, he had felt they were both bathed in a visionary light. There were others there at the restaurant table, but they were in some area of dimness, excluded. Pagani's, the restaurant—all the rage in those days. They had been to hear a lecture at the Royal Geographical Society given by the American explorer Robert Peary, who had reached the North Pole in the previous year. She had been disappointed in Peary, he remembered now; he had not lived up to her expectations, he had spoken in an ordinary kind of way, making the whole thing sound more like a well-organized business trip than a feat of endurance. Indignation in her voice. It had occurred to Somerville later—considerably later, when that light no longer enveloped them—that he had been lucky in the occasion; he had served to repair this disappointment, restore her faith in the heroic ideal . . .

"You will prevail, I know it," she said. "You speak as you did when you first told me of your decision to give up that dreary business and venture everything on your dream of exploration and discovery." She sat forward a little now, and the wrap fell from her shoulders. "You are still that man. Nothing and no one can withstand you when you are truly yourself." She held out her arms to him. "My love, come here beside me."

Her body radiated heat; the skin of her face and arms was hot to his touch as if she were burning with his own fire of purpose. Her will, her wish for him to conquer and triumph, fastened on him now again, proof against all disappointment. But he knew, as she panted beneath him, as his own excitement mounted, that the man lying between her thighs had ceased very early in their life together to be truly himself with her and would never now be able to find the words to explain why this was so.

5.

"Yes," the Ambassador said, "he and I were at school together. In point of fact he fagged for me in my last year there. He reminded me of it in his telegram. Naturally, it makes a difference."

"Naturally." Lord Rampling looked straight before him through the widely opened windows of the veranda, across the ruffled, glittering expanse of water. The Bosporus was almost at its narrowest here, the landing stages and gardens of the houses opposite, on the Asian side, clearly visible. He knew which school it was, having spent some time prior to this meeting in reading a summary of the Ambassador's career, but he could not for the life of him see what difference it made. "In days gone by," he said, "in the old days of the Padishah, the ladies in their private boats would make assignations with their lovers across the water by using a system of signals based on the tilt of their parasols, left, right, straight up. Married women, you know—they had to be careful. I've always regarded it as an example of the way restrictions increase ingenuity, sharpen the brain and the senses. I don't know what the code was, of course, but I have always taken it for granted that the vertical position was crucial. You couldn't be more definite than that, could you?"

He could not remember now whether this signaling system had at some time in his long life of anecdotes been related to him or whether he had just invented it on the spur of the moment. His words had in any case been designed mainly to ruffle his guest, whose correctness of manner and orthodox official attitudes, so typical of British diplomats and the whole Foreign Office establishment, had irritated him from the start of their acquaintance. Glancing sideways, he saw that the Ambassador's long and rather horsey face had not managed much in the way of a smile. Good. Why did one go in for these puerile games? He sighed, thinking of his own parasol, which for a good many years now had been unreliable to say the least. It was a very audible sigh; these days random thoughts, whether disquieting or reassuring, brought out sounds from him, sighs, little grunts or groans, even chuckles. Never words, however—words he was always careful with.

"No indeed, definite enough, certainly." The Ambassador swallowed some of his vermouth. To a remark like that if uttered by an equal or subordinate, he would have made no reply and so delivered a snub. But it would be most unwise to risk offending this man, who held no office of state but was much more powerful and influential than himself, to say nothing of his hugely greater wealth. Rampling had more capacity for making trouble, if he chose, than almost anyone. Complicating the matter was the Ambassador's awareness that the other would not care much for his disapproval whether this was expressed in speech or silence. Or anyone else's, for that matter. There was the title, yes, but the fellow was simply not a gentleman.

"Imagine your feelings," Rampling said, "looking across the water, watching out for the right tilt."

"Wouldn't do to get it wrong," the Ambassador said. On the wall before him was a framed picture he had seen somewhere before, Britannia being handed the Crown of the Sea by someone he thought might be Neptune, with three allegorical figures in attendance, garish in the sunshine that filled the veranda. Commerce, Navigation . . . Reflected sunlight prevented him from reading the third. It was the first real day of spring, and a servant had been summoned to open the great bay windows that gave a view over the water. From where he was sitting he could see terns wheeling above the ruffles of the current, plunging down for fish. A fisherman's paradise. For a moment, oppressed by the physical presence of his host—the man seemed to take up all the space—he felt a sharp desire to be at his country place in Northumberland, in midstream, casting over the brown water. "I don't think I have ever seen another waterway so constantly in prey to currents as this one," he said.

"No, you see it more particularly here as the channel narrows. There is one tide of fresher, swifter water, coming down from the Black Sea, and another saltier and heavier, making an undercurrent in the opposite direction." Rampling smiled suddenly, a smile not unattractive but with something painful in the suddenness of it, a sort of jovial snarling. "Equally matched," he said. "One has dash, the other has weight. No winners, no losers."

"The markets of this city will never lack for fish, so much is certain."

No reply to this was forthcoming; Rampling was still gazing out across the stream. Not for the first time the Ambassador wondered how the man had known of Somerville's intended visit and why he had wanted to be present, issuing the invitation to luncheon at this ancient and beautiful wooden *yali* of his. People in the telegraph office? Someone at the embassy passing on information?

The Ambassador did not lack for a sense of his own worth; his career had brought him respect and authority and latterly a knighthood. But he could not overcome a certain feeling of awe as he glanced at his host's face in profile and the silence lengthened between them. No one knew for certain how old Rampling was; he claimed different ages at different times, sometimes wildly at odds with the official birthdate, which was 1835. No one knew how much he was worth either.

The Ambassador too had made inquiries preliminary to this meeting and had refreshed his knowledge of Rampling's business interests, those that were public and official. They were numerous. He was described in the press as "the shipping magnate," and there were grounds enough for this description: He was chairman and managing director of the Peninsular and Eastern Steamship Company, chairman and director of the British and Mesopotamian Steam Navigation Company, a director of the Steamship Owners' Coal Association and of the British and Oriental Marine Insurance Company. He had interests in various other commercial enterprises not directly concerned with shipping: He was vice president of the Suez Canal Company; he sat on the Council of the Ottoman Public Debt Administration. Then there was the more recent involvement in the petroleum industry. This was less clearly defined, but he was believed to have a substantial holding in the Anglo-Persian Oil Company, which owned 50 percent of the newly incorporated Turkish Petroleum Company.

The face gave little hint of the strain and anxiety that the control of such complex interests might be thought to bring about, or of any preternatural shrewdness. It was florid and equable, the dark, inquisitive eyes undimmed below disheveled eyebrows. The hair was thick still, though silvered now from the black it had been, and he wore it long. The Ambassador was aware that his own face showed more damage than this one, though he was a good thirty years younger. It was the clothes that gave the fellow away. Take that waistcoat, he thought. Velvet lapels, mother-of-pearl buttons, a trimming of gold thread along the seams. It was not the waistcoat of a gentleman. His watch chain was too thick and too golden. And the jacket, black velvet, hanging loose—he was wearing a smoking jacket to entertain people to luncheon!

"Somerville will be here fairly soon, I suppose," the Ambassador said. "We shall have to do what we can for him. I know you take the matter seriously, otherwise you would have not given it your valuable time." He had in fact been considerably surprised at the interest that Rampling was taking in what must be to him, after all, a minor matter; he was grateful too, aware that his own powers of intervention did not extend far.

Rampling turned his head to regard his guest, as if with sudden curiosity. "I haven't really arranged this for the sake of Somerville," he said after a moment. "Of course I know that you and he were at school together, and this makes a difference and

so on, but I must tell you frankly that it doesn't make much difference to me."

"But I understood you had decided to use your influence
on his behalf. Representing as you do the British bondholders in
the Ottoman Public Debt Administration, we thought you might
have a word or two with your German counterpart here in the
city. Verb sap, you know, a word to the wise."

Rampling was silent for a short while, invaded by a certain
sense of wonder. This inveterate belief in the old system, the net-
work of favors. A few words dropped in the right place, to the
right person. Could they not hear the marching feet? But no—a
bit of schoolboy Latin, a pat on the back, and everything would
be set right again, the world arrested in its collapse. "Nothing
can be done to help Somerville," he said. "In 1903, when the
Germans obtained the concession for the railway from Sultan
Abdul Hamid, they also acquired the right to operate mines
within a zone of twenty kilometers on either side of the line.
They can use the land as they like, whether it is owned by the Ottoman government or in private hands, for whatever they need
in the way of construction, quarries, gravel pits, sand, timber.
Free of charge, sir."

"I am familiar with the terms of the 1903 convention," the
Ambassador said rather stiffly.

"But do you realize what it means? The Germans know—we
all know—that there is oil in great quantities in Mesopotamia.
No drilling has been done yet, but they know it is there. They
have planned the route with this in mind. The other piece of
knowledge that we share with them is that war between us looks
ever more likely. Do you think, in these circumstances, in this

March of 1914, that they will agree to shift the route for the sake
of an obscure archaeologist without financial backing, working
on an excavation that has so far yielded precious little of interest? Yes, I have been into the thing, and believe me, his case is
hopeless. What inducement could we offer them? Mesopotamia
is riddled with archaeologists, British, French, German, American. They will all be running for cover before long. No good
appealing to the Turks. In the event of war they will almost certainly go in on the German side. In that case the line will be a
vital supply route for them, the only rapid way of transporting
men and matériel to defend their possessions adjoining the
Gulf."

The Ambassador had two views about the likelihood of the
war, one private and the other official; though quite different,
they were of equal value since both depended equally on the occasion and the company. "I wouldn't say that war is inevitable,"
he said. "The government does not take that view. Our relations
with Berlin and Vienna are cordial, and we continue to make
every effort that they should remain so. We all have much to gain
from this railway, which will open Mesopotamia to international
commerce. If you don't believe we can help Somerville, I find it
difficult . . . I mean, why have you—"

"Why have I invited you here? Well, as I say, it is not really
for Somerville's sake. I have other reasons, rather more important. I'd like to explain them to you; it's really why I wanted you
to come early."

"By all means."

"Still on the subject of oil, which I think you will agree
is more in the forefront than archaeology as things stand at

present—not much good trying to fuel our ships with potsherds and arrowheads, eh?"

"Er, no."

"I don't know if you have seen charts of the oil prospects in the vilayets of Baghdad and Mosul? I thought perhaps not. I have one with me, prepared on the basis of the most recent information we possess."

Without needing to rise, Rampling was able to reach to the small glass-topped table beside his chair and take up the single sheet of paper that lay there, now noticed for the first time by the Ambassador. "You will see the cluster of black dots," he said, passing over the paper, "thick in the middle, thin at both ends, going from Tikrit to Mosul on either side of the Tigris."

"I see them, yes."

"They are definitely ascertained prospects with evidence of extensive deposits. Westward from this no one has taken much of a look, but there are indications; there are swamps of pitch where the oil has leaked up onto the surface. The probabilities are strong that the oil fields continue here, particularly in the region between the Khabur and Belikh rivers." He paused a moment, fixing the Ambassador with a steady gaze. "That is precisely the area where your school chum is digging."

"We were not chums exactly," the Ambassador said with a certain caution. "I was already in the sixth form when he—"

"But he would be likely to think of you as a friendly presence, someone well disposed, wouldn't he? It is not only the school connection, important though we both know that is. You represent British authority here, you are His Majesty's accredited envoy to the Sublime Porte. He is likely to trust in what you say."

"I suppose so, yes."

"He would be less likely to trust me. I have no official standing. I have an aura of wealth, which makes things awkward, you know. And in any case, I'm not sufficiently British in my ways."

As if to illustrate this, he leaned forward and laid a hand on the Ambassador's knee, to the latter's acute embarrassment. To make matters worse, the fellow was wearing scent; he smelled of rosewater or something of the kind. "I am afraid I don't quite see where this is tending," he said.

"We want to send a man there, an expert in petroleum geology, to have a look around. The man we have in mind is an American named Elliott. He comes with first-rate testimonials from Standard Oil, with which he has been working in a position of trust for several years. He is one of the foremost experts in the field. I have talked to him on two occasions, and I am satisfied that he is just the man we need. He is in London at present, at an address known only to me. There are rival interests involved, you understand, we don't want anyone else to get wind of this appointment."

"I see, yes. Well, it sounds a very good idea."

"There are problems, however. He must have freedom of movement, you see. At the same time he must not attract any particular attention or have his activities watched by the Turkish authorities. I mean, he won't want to have a squad of gendarmes breathing down his neck, will he?"

"No, hardly, but I don't see—"

"He must go there in some other capacity, one that will not arouse any particular suspicion. As we were saying earlier, Mesopotamia is crawling with archaeologists, one more or less won't cause any comment whatever."

"You mean he should go in the guise of an archaeologist?"

"He must go as an archaeologist, as an assistant to Somerville."

"To the same site? But then Somerville will have to vouch for him. Why should he do that?"

Rampling leaned forward with a curiously gentle and lingering movement. For a moment the Ambassador thought he was going to have a hand on his knee again. Instead his host reached out and took the chart of the oil fields from his hands. "That is where you come in," he said. "You assure Somerville that you will exert every effort on his behalf and that you see a distinct possibility . . . no, a strong likelihood, that these efforts will bear fruit, that wheels will be set in motion both literally and figuratively to save his excavation."

There was a short silence, during which they could hear the screaming of the terns that plunged and plunged again into the seething shoals and never seemed gorged. Then the Ambassador said, "I see, yes. And in return for these assurances he will agree to pretend that this geologist has come as his assistant."

"Exactly."

"But that would mean deceiving the poor fellow, lying to him, sending him away with false hopes."

"In a sense, yes."

"In every sense, sir. I can't be expected to do it."

Rampling's sudden, painful-seeming, slightly snarling smile came and went. Nothing could better illustrate the great divide between the professional and the personal common to all career diplomats, constraining them to regard hypocrisy as a public virtue and a private vice. The Ambassador could not be expected

little farther down on this European side, to where the towers and walls of the Rumeli Hisar Fortress, built by Mehmet the Conqueror to control the straits and blockade the city, rose above the cypresses of the ancient cemetery. Not the first time these warring currents had decided the fate of empires. A year after this fortress was built Constantinople had fallen to the Osmanli Turks, and with it the thousand-year-old empire of the Byzantines. No accident he had built it here, where the Bosporus was narrowest, the currents at their strongest. What did the Turks call it? *Sheitan akintisi*, Satan's stream.

"We have much to lose," Rampling said. "Do you know the gross nominal value of Britain's stock of capital at present invested abroad?"

"No, not exactly."

"It is not far short of four billion pounds. Twice as much as France, three times as much as Germany. And much the greater part of it in distant lands vulnerable to attack, Asia, Africa, the Americas. Quite a lot to set at risk, isn't it?"

"Tell me," the Ambassador said, "why did you choose to inform me that Somerville has no prospect of success in getting the line shifted? You could have allowed me to go on thinking what I thought at the outset, that you were able to do something for him. Then I could have given him these assurances in good faith."

"But that would have meant deceiving you, wouldn't it? Unnecessary deception is entirely against my code of practice. It is immoral, it is messy, no ends are served by it. I paid you the compliment, as one of His Majesty's most respected envoys—a fact proved by your posting here, to this most crucial of embassies, at such a time—of telling you the truth. I have made it the rule of my life—"

But the Ambassador was never to learn Rampling's guiding principle because at this point he was interrupted by the entrance of a servant in red fez and white tunic, who announced in French that a Mr. Somerville had arrived and had been asked to wait. He was instructed to show the visitor in immediately.

It seemed to Somerville, at the time and in retrospect, that his whole experience of this visit, from the first moment of being admitted, was one of passing through zones of light that grew ever stronger. He had crossed a small tree-shaded courtyard, waited briefly in a shuttered anteroom, where a silver altar screen, a crucifix, carved wood panels of heraldic birds and beasts kept him company in the subdued light. Then he had followed the servant through a long and very spacious hall, which ran from front to back and in which the light grew fuller as the house opened out toward the water. He entered the veranda, confused at first by the radiant flood from the open windows, the sunlit expanse of the channel beyond. Two men, complete strangers, had risen at his entrance, one corpulent and gray-haired, the other tall and thin and immaculately suited, with glinting spectacles. That will be him, he thought; the other looked wrong somehow, dressed wrongly, too old. The deduction was confirmed a moment later, when the suited man advanced with outstretched hand. "Somerville," he said. "So good to see you after all these years."

6.

It was Rampling's definite impression that the luncheon had gone well. Hook, line, and sinker was how he expressed it to himself. He had felt no compunction, seeing Somerville's obvious joy at the assurances they had given him. Europe was on the edge of a conflict that would claim countless lives and in which Britain's survival as an imperial power was at stake; a railroad through a heap of antique rubble did not qualify for much regret in the scale of things. It was far from certain in any case whether the line would get so far before the outbreak of war, though he had taken care to make no mention of this to Somerville.

In fact he had never been in any doubt of the issue. He had found it diverting to seem eager to secure the Ambassador's agreement, to argue the matter with him, when both of them knew he had no choice. Rampling had sources of information at the embassy in Constantinople, and he knew of the recent memorandum, sent under the personal seal of the Foreign Secretary, to all diplomatic and consular officials in the Near East, instructing them diligently to obtain and promptly to forward any information regarding possible sources of mineral oil, a commodity of vital importance for Britain's present and future needs. So sure had he been that his design would succeed that the terms of Elliott's engagement—fee, expenses, indemnities—had all been agreed in London before he left. An excellent man, Elliott, a man after his own heart, qualified, dedicated, possessed with a crusading faith in the future of the petroleum industry.

After the departure of his guests, who had left together for Galata to have a good old chat, as the Ambassador put it, at the embassy, Rampling slept for half an hour. He had a faculty for dropping into sleep for a brief while at any time of day. On waking, he summoned his boatman and told him to get the launch up to the jetty. Byron, his Greek valet, who traveled everywhere with him, as did his private secretary, Thomas, and his bodyguard, an ex-wrestler of frightening aspect named Dikmen, laid out his clothes and helped him to dress. Byron knew his taste; he could be relied upon completely.

He dressed with his usual care: a pale green linen suit and a lavender-colored silk shirt very high in the neck. Tan shoes, a panama hat with a dark blue band, and an ebony cane completed the effect; he had a collection of canes and this time chose one with a silver handle in the shape of a wolf's head.

The launch took him down to the Galata quay in twenty minutes. Here, with Dikmen before him to ward off beggars and hotel agents, he found a cab to take him across the Golden Horn by the Pont Neuf, bargaining first with the driver, a process he always enjoyed; on this occasion he got the man down to fifteen piastres for the journey, the waiting, and the return.

The afternoon was mild; he was a little early. It was his usual practice to arrive some minutes late for appointments of this kind, so instead of proceeding directly to the street behind the Ministry of Commerce, where the Lynch Brothers had their Constantinople agency, he descended from the cab at the ministry building and made his way into the courtyard of the nearby Nuri Osmaniye Mosque, where he lingered for a while, Dikmen in close attendance.

The elm trees in the courtyard were in first leaf, and the pale buds glistened softly in the sunshine. Some men were crouching at the fountain, washing face and hands and feet before entering the mosque. But what took his eye and held it were the hundreds, perhaps thousands of strutting, gobbling pigeons in the paved area on his right. Against the slate-colored pavement their breasts looked vivid, blue almost. There was an old blind woman sitting on the edge of the curb with on her knees a tray piled with grain, which she gathered deftly and made into little packets and offered to passersby who might feel an impulse to feed the pigeons. Her fingers ruffled continuously in the grain; she buried her thin hands to the wrists in it, took it up in handfuls, poured it back in trickles into the tray, heaped it up in mounds, smoothed it down again. Rampling grew absorbed, watching her. As if she were counting gold, he thought, and indeed the grain was dark gold in color. No, not counting it, just caressing it, loving it—like a miser. Every so often she would pause to throw a handful into the mass or dislodge with a sweep of the arm any bird bold enough to settle on the edge of her tray.

He watched her for several minutes, and in this time her hands were never at rest. But it was the behavior of the pigeons that struck him most in the end because they seemed in a certain way to epitomize what he felt human societies might be capable of if totally subjected to the beneficial stimulus of having to compete for limited resources: They did not quarrel, that was the remarkable thing; any handful of grain that was thrown into the mass caused a local flurry of hopping and fluttering, but this lasted for seconds only. The birds were united; no discord, no dispute were allowed to get in the way—there was simply no time for it; in all that pullulation of creatures not a single second was wasted on acts of aggression; all was harmony and order—no wars, no territorial encroachments, just a never-ending scramble for life. Utopian really. Supplies would have to be strictly controlled, of course; that would be done by the people who made up the packets . . . The woman's eyes were blank and terrible; there was a discharge from them, as if white pebbles could weep. He gave Dikmen a five-piastre piece to put into the woman's hand and heard her mumbled blessing.

The office was on the third floor, and there was no lift. Rampling took the stairs slowly, Dikmen's hand at his elbow. Conservation of energy, he thought, as he felt his heartbeat quicken. Like the pigeons.

He left Dikmen in the outer office, where his massive build, shaven head, and drooping mustache caused visible perturbation to a thin clerk in a fez seated there behind the typewriter. Two men were waiting for him in a smaller room adjoining. One he knew already, the commercial agent Balakian, whose office this was and who greeted him with a low bow; the other was a representative of the Lynch Brothers, the nephew of a senior member of the firm, introduced to him now as Mr. John Saunders, who had come from Baghdad for this meeting.

An office boy appeared as if by magic, and he was sent down for coffee from the nearby bar with instructions from Balakian to lose no time on the way if he knew what was good for him, a severity that did nothing to disturb the boy's composure or quicken his movements, as he knew it to be merely assumed by his employer as a mark of respect to the visitor.

Little was said until the coffee arrived; by time-honored custom all semblance of haste in the broaching of business had to be avoided. Rampling was amused to see that portraits of King George and Lord Salisbury—the latter, bearded and heavy-lidded, looking directly down at him—had been hung on the office wall. He noticed also a loosely furled Union Jack on a short pole propped up behind the desk. Balakian did business with a wide variety of people, and he had a collection of portraits and flags, which he changed in accordance with the nationality and allegiance of his visitor.

Rampling was content to say little as they waited; it gave him an opportunity to rehearse in his mind the things he intended to say. He had a financial holding in the firm, a weekly steamer service operating between Baghdad and the port of Basra on the Shatt al Arab, under the name of the Euphrates and Tigris Steam Navigation Company. He knew, as did the directors of the company, whose sources of information were excellent—a member of the Lynch family sat in the House of

Commons—that it was now the aim of the Turkish government and the German railway company to divert the line from the Tigris to the Euphrates and take it beyond Baghdad, down the valley to Basra, thus increasing the threat to river traffic. It was a matter primarily of giving assurances to the Lynch Brothers of his continued support while at the same time committing himself as little as possible. It was the need for discretion that had made him choose Balakian's office, which was frequented by all manner of people, rather than his own house, for this meeting. The same need had made him prefer verbal to written assurances.

He had known that it would not be easy, and so it proved when the time for talking came. The firm had suffered something in the nature of a traumatic shock in 1903, when Sultan Abdul Hamid had granted the newly formed Baghdad Railway Company the right to construct modern port facilities at Baghdad, with the further prospect of extending the line to Basra and thence to a terminus on the Persian Gulf. In the eleven years that had elapsed since, the fear and rage aroused by this threat to the firm's fifty-year-old monopoly of the river trade from Baghdad to the Gulf had scarcely abated.

Rampling explained the terms of agreement that had been reached in the Anglo-German negotiations the previous month in London. They would know them already, but the positive aspects needed stressing.

"A contract was made with the railway company," he said. "It was signed by me as director of the British and Mesopotamian Navigation Company and witnessed by Herr von Kuhlmann of the German Embassy and Sir Eyre Crowe of the Foreign Office. In it were confirmed the exclusive rights of navigation by steamers and barges on the Tigris, Euphrates, and Shatt al Arab already granted to a new company to be formed by me, the Ottoman River Navigation Company, in which Mr. John Lynch will be one of the directors. It is true that Turkish capital has been offered, and has accepted, a fifty percent participation, but this is entirely without prejudice to the rights of the Lynch Brothers. In fact the firm has been granted the privilege of adding another steamer to their fleet with the sole proviso that it should fly the Turkish flag. Also, the firm and I in partnership together will be assigned by the railway company a forty percent participation in the proposed Ottoman Ports Company, with responsibilities for the construction of port and terminal facilities."

It was not a compelling argument, he knew; he himself had gained considerably from the recent convention, but there was no way of disguising the fact that the sun was setting on the firm of Lynch Brothers, that the railway would take away their time-honored privileges, reduce them to smaller fish in a pond that was getting bigger all the time.

"They will go back on it," Saunders said. "There will be further meetings, further agreements, further amendments to existing agreements. All this foreign capital coming in. You can't trust these people to keep their word."

"Turkish capital is foreign then?" Rampling's snarling smile came briefly. "Ours isn't, of course."

It was clear that Saunders found this not worth answering. "Those contracts are not worth the paper they are written on," he said. He was a tall, gaunt man with a waxed mustache and eyes that slanted downward slightly, giving his face a doglike look, faithful and sad.

Rampling was capable of a good deal of patience when his own interests were involved, but he felt a certain irritation rising in him now. "Let us be frank," he said. "You'll find they are worth something if you try to contravene them. That you are in danger from competition is true, but to a great extent it is your own fault. Your firm was founded back in the 1850s, you have had a virtual monopoly for more than half a century. It was a different world then, life was more leisurely; people were not in such a hurry. Things have quickened up, Mr. Saunders. In today's terms the service you are offering is inadequate, and that is to express it mildly. I have had recent reports on the matter. It is not uncommon for goods to stand for months on the wharfs of Baghdad and Basra waiting to be shipped. And the charges are unbelievably high. It costs more to send freight down the Shatt al Arab than it does from Baghdad to London. You know these things as well as I do."

"With all due respect, Lord Rampling, these questions of costs and delays are largely irrelevant."

"Irrelevant?" Rampling's unruly eyebrows rose in an expression that seemed one of genuine astonishment. He looked across at Balakian, whose soft brown eyes had noticeably widened.

"Or at least they are of minor importance. The exclusive privilege enjoyed by our company in the river trade is highly important to British commerce; that goes without saying, but it is of equal, and perhaps greater, importance to British prestige throughout the whole region. We *are* the river trade. We regard the custody of this privilege as our patriotic duty. The principal partners in the firm will not surrender it to a foreign power under any circumstances, and in this we have the backing of the government at home." Saunders's speech had quickened with the emotion of these words, but his face still kept its look of sad fidelity. "Over our dead bodies, sir," he said, "over our dead bodies."

Rampling took a deep breath, faintly rasping, clearly audible. It was not often that he was presented with the idea that exorbitant charges and unconscionable delays were elements adding to national prestige. But he knew better than to argue the matter; accusations of mismanagement and incompetence brought out a strain of patriotism in his fellow countrymen like almost nothing else. "Well," he said, "let us hope it won't come to that." There would be a large number of dead bodies in Mesopotamia before long; those of the senior partners in the firm of Lynch Brothers would not affect the balance much.

He paused for some moments longer to let the atmosphere of heroic sacrifice clear a little; then he said, "Let us look at the facts in an objective manner, Mr. Saunders. The Tigris is a very shallow river, and it winds about a great deal. Its course is subject to constant changes owing to floods and the formation of sandbanks and shoals and so on. Nothing new about this; it has always been so, but it is not ideally suited to boat traffic, as I am sure you will agree. It takes five days for a steamer to travel from Baghdad to Basra—and that is in favorable weather. The distance can be covered by rail in a single day, whatever the weather. Now there is a logic here, sir, and wrapping ourselves up in the Union Jack will not protect us from it."

"As I have said, sir, we have the backing of the government." Saunders's face had stiffened, and the line of his jaw had become more prominent. "Lord Curzon has denounced the railway as a threat to our empire in India, and he carries the majority of the House with him."

Rampling turned to the agent, who had taken no part in the discussion but gave every appearance of listening intently. Balakian represented various commercial enterprises, some known, some not, and in either case not necessarily friendly to the British cause. "Mr. Balakian," he said, "would you leave us in private for a few minutes? You understand, there are matters here that are not yet in the sphere of—"

"Of course."

If Balakian felt any disappointment, it did not show on his face. Rampling waited until the door had closed behind him before resuming. "It is a great mistake to place reliance on the speeches of politicians," he said. "Circumstances change and the speeches change with them, according to party advantage and political expedients. We must put our trust in the workings of money, Mr. Saunders, not in speeches. Banks and financial houses are not bound to do what the government tells them, and they are not obliged to tell the government what they are doing. They concentrate their energy on securing maximum profits, an aim much more steadfast than any political aim could be. As you know, I have a substantial holding in the firm of Lynch Brothers.

Do you think I will sell my shares because of the competition of the railway?"

In fact he was thinking seriously of selling and was keeping his eye on prices as the railway drew nearer. And the slight smile that he now saw appear on the other man's face indicated that his question had not been taken in the purely rhetorical sense that he had intended. "No, not at all," he said. "Far from it. It's no use trying to block the line or hinder it from going forward. Curzon can fulminate as much as he likes, but he hasn't got the power to do this, and he knows it. No, we must join the enterprise, but on our own terms. We must put British capital in it. The Germans are in sore need of an injection of capital—von Gwinner at the Deutsche Bank has been putting out feelers. I can tell you in confidence that I am part of a consortium, together with Morgan Grenfell and the Baring Brothers, which is exploring the possibility of gaining control of the line beyond Baghdad, together with all port facilities as far as the Gulf."

He paused on this, looking closely at the other man. Saunders did not strike him as highly intelligent, but he would faithfully report what had passed between them. And this was the message he should carry back with him to Baghdad. The advantages were obvious: continued protection for their trade on the Tigris; large profits to be made from their share in the construction of port facilities; political interests guaranteed by barred access to the Gulf for any foreign power.

Obvious, yes, but belief was needed first, and this had to be left to reflection. He said nothing more for the moment; too much urging too soon was always a sign of weakness. Balakian was invited back. Rampling refused more coffee and soon afterward got up to leave.

He was satisfied on the whole with the way things had gone, and this satisfaction persisted through the journey back to his house, survived a cocktail party at the Russian Embassy in the early evening, and was still with him at dinnertime. He dined alone and afterward went to his study to look at some reports that had been summarized by his secretary, concerning the competition between the Crédit Lyonnais and the Deutsche Palestine Bank in financing the trade in raw silk, hitherto a French monopoly. The French were increasingly worried by German encroachments in Syria. A good thing, of course—insecurity would make them more open to offers of joint financing, more yielding in the terms.

A fire of logs had been made for him, the evenings being still cold. He had his after-dinner brandy at his elbow; the fire was warm against his face; the armchair was deep. After a while his attention drifted from the reports, the pages fell loose over his stomach as he sat back. He thought briefly of asking one of his people to go down to the waterfront at Top Hane and find some woman for him. Tamas was the one he usually sent; Tamas knew what to look for: young, a bit on the fleshy side, with long hair. After a long and active career with women, including two marriages, three mistresses, and various affairs, he was reduced to a passive role now; he had no impulse to hurt the women, but they had to be ready to behave with abject obedience. He could still sometimes reach orgasm if they played their part well.

This evening, however, after some moments the flicker of desire died down. He was comfortable there. He extinguished the lamp at his side, looked down at the red heart of the fire, and settled into a mood of reflection. Things had gone well on the whole. He thought of the luncheon party now as something of a comedy, with the Ambassador's scruples melting away at the first hint of real trouble, and the ingenuous Somerville—he had actually seemed to believe they all shared his passion for the history of the Assyrian Empire. The line was unlikely to get very much farther before the outbreak of hostilities. We go on signing contracts and making speeches with the ground shifting under our feet, he thought. What else is there to do? We have to stay open for business.

The meeting at Balakian's office he felt somewhat less sure about, though still fairly sanguine. Whether the firm of Lynch Brothers survived or not was a matter of indifference to him, but the partners must be convinced that they would be protected, that the line would bring benefits to them. They had political influence in Britain; they formed part of the faction that opposed the extension of the railway. It was not altogether true what he had said to Saunders: British financial houses would not act in direct opposition to government policy. It was vital that the partners in the firm should be made to see that imperial and financial interests met and combined in this last stretch of the line.

Absolutely vital, he thought. He was growing sleepy. Native regiments from India could be transported and deployed in a matter of days. And afterward, emerging victorious, our base will be already secured for the occupation of southern Mesopotamia . . . Land of Hope and Glory. Great music—he liked marches. This great empire of ours. Mother of the harmonious pigeons. Our factories that clothe millions in every corner of the globe, our banking

houses that finance the businesses and control the trade of half the
world. Our great fleet, fueled now by oil. What was it Churchill had
said, in making that momentous decision? *Mastery itself is the prize.*
Prophetic words. He who owns the oil will own the world, he will
rule the sea and the land, he will rule his fellowmen. The day will
come when oil will be more desired, more sought after than gold.
I will live to see that day, God willing. But first there was need for reliable information—reliable and exclusive. Elliott would provide
that. Good man, Elliott. Highest recommendations. One of the
best petroleum geologists in the business. *Wider still and wider shall
thy bounds be set.* To include the vilayets of Baghdad and Mosul. And
all the oil east of the Euphrates . . .

His eyes closed and his mouth opened a little. He shifted in
his chair and the papers rustled to the floor. A struggling sigh
came from him and he slept. The fire, which he had allowed to
die down, smoldered for a while and seemed about to go out altogether. But by some process of self-renewal, almost as though
laboring for its own survival, the charred log shifted, settled
again, and owing to this small, barely noticeable movement, the
layer of ash beneath it was dislodged, sifted down through the
grate, leaving a red core of embers. The underside of the log began to glow, and then it took fire again and the flames pulsed
around the ends of it with an energy that seemed desperate almost. Light flickered over the man slumbering in the deep chair,
falling over his chest and legs, making him seem, for these few
moments, with his face in shadow and the human likeness obscured, like some beast of the jungle, barred and striped, at rest
in its lair.

7.

Somerville spent an extra day in Constantinople talking to colleagues at the Imperial Museum and examining some Hittite stamp seals recently discovered at Boğazköy in Anatolia, site of the ancient Hittite capital of Hattusas. There were also several sculptured reliefs from the King's Gate that he had not seen before.

It was late when he arrived back; his wife was already in bed and he did not want to disturb her. The following morning, before breakfast, was the first opportunity for them to talk together. Edith was still in her dressing gown. She had had tea served to her, but she was slow to wake in the mornings and still had the slightly bemused, sleepy-eyed look that he had always found voluptuous and touching at the same time.

"Well, they have given me assurances of help," he said. "I think I succeeded in convincing them of the importance of what we are doing here. I went into some detail about these recent finds, which point toward a substantial Assyrian presence."

"Them? Who were the others?"

"A man introduced to me as Baron Rampling was also there. In fact it was at his house that we met. He was very affable and hospitable."

"Rampling? The shipowner? What on earth was he doing there?" Surprise had taken the sleep from her eyes. "You didn't recognize him, you didn't know who he was?"

"No, why should I?"

It was now, with these words of his wife's, that the first misgivings came to him. The Ambassador, he now recalled, had said very little about Rampling in the course of their chat afterward, only that he was wealthy and had influence in high circles. The warmth of his reception, the cordiality of his old school friend, the genial attention paid to him by the obviously powerful man who was his host . . . And then the matter was of such overwhelming importance to him it had seemed natural that even a grand and titled personage should be prepared to help, should lend his attention to such a threat, such an injustice. Now this cold breath, where warmth should have been. It is you, he thought, looking at his wife's face. You take my faith away. Something close to hatred came into his heart for a moment, then was lost, merged in his doubt. "A beautiful house," he said. "One of those old wooden houses on the Bosporus, looking straight out across the water." He remembered how the light had grown stronger as he advanced, like an earnest of success.

"The gossip columns were full of his doings at one time," she said. John never read these things anyway, she knew that. "Daddy once acted for him, something to do with export permits. Said he is an absolute so-and-so, do anybody down that got in his way." Her adored father, after a highly successful career as a barrister, had recently been appointed a High Court judge. "I just can't imagine why a man like that should take an interest in archaeology," she said.

"He struck me as a fair-minded man. Very reasonable. We did a sort of deal."

He told her then of the agreement they had made, a quid pro quo really, he explained: the geologist, this dynamic American, to be given a cover for his activities, and the full weight of the Foreign Office, supported by the influence of Lord Rampling, to be brought to bear on the railway company. "Naturally," he said, "in this milieu of power politics, you have to give something if you want to get something, that is the way these things are conducted."

A reply rose to Edith's lips, caustic in nature, as she saw the look of worldly sagacity that had appeared on her husband's face, but she repressed it; there was really no point. "Well," she said in flat tones, "we shall have to hope for the best then, shan't we?"

And that was exactly it, she thought a little later as she dressed. John is the one who is doing the hoping, they have already got what they wanted, they will get this American here, who sounds absolutely dreadful, and we will have to put up with him at mealtimes and see him every day for goodness knows how long. This was all it had come to, the exaltation of the parting. A fire soon doused. If only there had been nothing required in exchange, if Rampling had been there for John's sake, instead of his own. Then he would have cut a dignified figure, whether or not they did anything about it. She herself did not care much about the railway, whether it went here or there. She had never understood how or why her husband had so convinced himself that the line would go bang smack into Tell Erdek. As far as she could see, there wasn't much to lose; John could go and dig somewhere else. She hadn't much in the way of historical imagination, and the finds they had made so far hadn't impressed her greatly; a bit of ivory, a fragment of stone, a few scratches on a clay tablet, a stump of a wall—it couldn't be thought to add up to anything very exciting. No, what mattered was the enterprise itself, the spirit of it, the going for what you wanted, the not being daunted. Again the thought came to her, unwelcome, painful even, but not to be held off: John was pathetic; he lacked what Daddy would have called a firm grip. That serious, slightly frowning air he had assumed, the man of the world pronouncing on power politics when he was really such a simpleton. She shouldn't have married him; she had been taken in by that early boldness of his, that visionary quality, giving up everything to follow the dream. He had not lived up to it; it was as though he had cheated her, broken the contract. She had seen Rampling's picture in the newspaper sometimes, elegant and portly, a big-nosed, bushy-eyebrowed, commanding face. Something predatory, almost savage, in the lines of the mouth. A brute of a man, Daddy had said. But someone who knew what he was doing, who went for what he wanted, who wouldn't have the wool pulled over his eyes.

The morning, she felt, had begun badly, and it was to continue in the same way. She and Patricia were still working to fit together the pieces of Seljuk pottery that had been found in promising quantity and quite close together, instead of in the usual scattering. She had reached a point in the process that she always rather enjoyed; some curved pieces from the neck of a jar were laid out before her on cardboard, and with the aid of rubber gloves and a small sponge on a stick she was applying a weak solution of hydrochloride acid to the surfaces. She was watching with the usual pleasure the melting away of the encrusted dirt, the magical emergence of the softly glowing green and blue glazes, when Patricia, sitting opposite to her at the table, said with characteristic abruptness, "I've decided what I would like to do when we go back home."

Well, Edith thought, that's a step in the right direction. That is, if one had to have a career; she herself had never felt the need for one other than that of support and companion to a man of purpose. But Patricia's restless wish for one, and her uncertainty about the choice, had cast a sort of drama over the business that irked Edith because it seemed so spurious.

"Oh, yes, what is it?" she said.

"I am going to work for the Women's Social and Political Union."

Edith stared, completely taken aback. Whatever she had been expecting, it was not this, the militant wing of the suffragette movement. She felt a gathering sense of outrage. It couldn't be a sudden decision, not a thing like that. The girl had kept quiet about her sympathies—a treacherous silence, it seemed to Edith now. "What," she said, "that appalling Pankhurst woman?"

Patricia laid down the piece she was holding, placing it very carefully on the table. "Mrs. Pankhurst is a very brave and dedicated woman," she said, in a voice that had the steadiness of conscious control.

"But how can they possibly think blowing up post offices and setting fire to theaters and doing wanton damage to private property can serve any purpose?"

"It compels attention," Patricia said.

"Attention to what?"

"Attention to the gross injustice of keeping women from participation in government by denying them the vote."

Edith attempted a smile designed to show Patricia that she was merely being humored in these views. But the smile didn't come well, and she felt the beginnings of an obscure distress. "Women are simply not fit for the rough-and-tumble of politics," she said.

"A lot depends on which women we are talking about. I saw something of the Fen villages while I was at Cambridge. The women there get a pretty good training in rough-and-tumble."

"Patricia, I must say that you astonish me. You are planning to marry, are you not?"

"Yes, when we go back to England."

"You are planning to marry and at the same time proposing to take part in a movement that will have for its only result an increased disharmony and antagonism between the sexes."

"Harold is entirely in favor of women being given the vote. We have discussed it. He is very progressive in his political views."

"Is he indeed?" Her respect for Palmer, already diminished, plummeted further on her hearing this. A traitor to his own sex. She thought of her father, home after the stress of the court-

room, the lines of strain on his face, her mother's care and support of him, her attention to him, which had not been servile or
demeaning, only loving. It was such a companion that she herself had wanted to be to her husband, had failed to be. But she
could not feel the failure to be her fault. What was there to support in John? Daddy had included them in his life; he had given
them a sense of the great world; he had returned from the field
of battle with triumphs and setbacks to relate, causes lost and
won. She felt the distress gather in her breast as she looked
across at Patricia. Once again she was visited by a sense of the
girl's duplicity. It was like looking at a stranger. As if seeing for
the first time the full mouth, unexpectedly sensuous in that bony
frame of the face, the jaw somewhat too prominent, the clear
eyes. Behind the face a life of thoughts, beliefs, intentions—a
cause, however wrong; this was the injury, this was the perfidy,
that she should have a cause.

"The world of politics and business and law has been made
by men," Edith said. "It is men who understand it. This is a time
when we should be united. Our empire is in peril, a firm grip
and a balanced judgment are needed, a *masculine* judgment. To
say that we should not have the vote is not to say that we are infe-
rior. We women have tenderness, insight, moral influence, we
can be strong in our own—" She stumbled on this, aware of unhappiness, afraid of betraying it. "These are things that belong in
the private sphere," she said.

"But surely these qualities of ours would be valuable in political life too," Patricia said in a gentler tone. She had heard the
quiver of feeling in the other woman's voice, sensed a distress
that seemed not entirely due to the topic of their talk but to

something more obscure, something there all the time. She had always felt a little in awe of Edith because of her beauty, her physical grace, her self-containment, which had some suggestion of sardonic judgment in it. Beside her, Patricia had felt plain and clumsy and untried, and this had caused her to be more intrusive with her opinions than she might otherwise have been. But now she had the advantage of happiness. Those in love are said to be self-absorbed, blind to the rest of the world, but in this first serious love of her life Patricia had become kinder and more noticing. "Surely they would be of benefit in our national life," she said. "The empire too. The influence of women, expressed through the vote, would make our institutions envied and imitated even more than they are now. We women could give so much. We should stand together instead of quarreling among ourselves." She smiled as she spoke and leaned forward with a sort of eagerness, as if she might reach out toward the older woman. She saw Edith's face stiffen into immobility, saw her draw back with a motion almost of wincing.

Somerville was aware of not having made the desired impression on his wife, aware of it with resignation, not any particular unhappiness. If she had any real sympathy for him in his plight, she would support him in his hope of success. It was too soon to be regarded as illusion; there was still a prospect in his own mind at least that the assurances made to him would be honored. It was beginning to seem to him now that Edith's good opinion was an elusive hare and that he was too busy to chase after it. And the news he got from Palmer after breakfast confirmed him in this feeling. They had continued the wall eastward, cutting deeper into the side of the mound in order to follow the line. The wall had continued, still with its base of stone, for some yards; then, only the day before, they had come upon the beginnings of a platform of some kind, opening inward from the wall and running along beside it at the same level. Impossible to make out the flooring; the area was covered with a debris of rubble from the collapsed walls of some later building.

"There seems to be a layer of ash under the rubble," Palmer said. "Pretty thick."

"We must get there for the start of the work." Somerville felt excitement gathering within him. "One of the foremen must be there all the time, no matter what else is going on, and only reliable people set to work there, no fools. They will have to clear the rubble without disturbing the ash, as far as it can be done. That section of the vertical trench will have to be widened so that the basket people can pass."

But it was he himself, all that day and the two following, who remained there to supervise the work. At the end of that time they had cleared an area roughly two yards by five, and next day the delicate task of sifting through the ash was begun. Almost at once they began to find fragments of bronze-plated furniture, chips of ivory, and smashed tablets.

Somerville found it physically impossible to quit the scene while the work was in progress or even to take his eyes off it. He left the house early, taking a sandwich and a flask of water with him, and remained there till the onset of darkness. At the end of three days, standing alone there after the workforce had dispersed, he found himself lifting his face to the darkening sky in a sort of beatitude of knowledge. There had been some huge conflagration here, still mysterious in origin, but what they were uncovering was the floor of an anteroom, probably one of a series of connecting rooms, and it had once been furnished with the costliest of materials, cedarwood and ebony and ivory and bronze, materials that could only belong in the palaces of the very wealthy, provincial governors, high-ranking military commanders, people of power and consequence.

In the days that followed, as the ash was cleared to reveal a floor of blackened brick and the remains of a stone doorway were discovered and the bronze hoops of what had been a heavy door and the beginnings of a passageway that lay beyond, practically all his waking moments were concentrated in the effort to make sense of what they had found, what they were finding. It had been a fascination with the Assyrian kingdom, inspired by the astounding discoveries of his boyhood hero Henry Layard at Nimrud and Nineveh, that had turned him to archaeology, first as an absorbing interest, then as a choice of career. In youth he had read everything he could lay his hands on, avidly and unsystematically; later he had studied more methodically, relating the empire of the Assyrians to the various others that had flourished and withered before and after it in the long course of Mesopotamian history. But it was the Assyrians who had made a conquest of his imagination, theirs the empire that had seemed to him a paradigm of all empires. A lust for power had inspired them from the first, an energy of conquest that had taken them from a narrow strip of land on the left bank of the Tigris to domination of practically all of the world they knew and to the development of a ruthless militarism that had made their army the most feared and efficient fighting machine that world had so far seen. Their wealth and splendor and cruelty, the hatred they had aroused, the fires of destruction that had marked their amazingly sudden collapse. How terrible—and how marvelous—to be Ashurbanibal or Sargon or Sennacherib, hunting the lion in a park specially made for you, driving your chariot over the corpses of your enemies, washing the blood from your weapons in the Great Sea.

Everything they had found so far could be seen as lying within a period of little more than two centuries, between the reigns of Ashurnasirpal II and Esarhaddon, the first embarking in the early ninth century on a program of ruthless expansion, the second presiding in the early seventh over the empire at its fullest extent, from Cilicia to Egypt, from the Taurus to the Persian Gulf. It was in the former's reign that a new kind of boasting appeared in the chronicles of victory, a vaunting of cruelty as an evidence of power. Echoes came to Somerville in the nights of his insomnia and colored his dreams. *Many I took as living captives. From some I cut off their noses, their ears and their fingers . . . Their youths and maidens I burned in the fire . . . Their warriors I consumed with thirst in the desert land . . .*

Some change in the human spirit here, not in the doing but in the telling, the pride, some ugly twist of soul toward a new idea of supremacy. How? From where? Why among these people at this time? Bred by conquest, like an appetite that grows from feeding? With the blessing of their god Ashur to lend them a sense of mission, bloodshed would become a form of devotion. Since Ashur was above all other gods and the king was his earthly embodiment, there would be a duty to impose his cult, carry light into dark places. The light they had carried had been cast by the flames of devastation. They too, the light bearers, had ended in that same fire.

It was in the evening, walking back from the mound to the expedition house, that the thought came to him, translated into conviction in the course of the next few steps. The weeping eyes of the lion, the compound of ash and clay so laboriously moved to reveal the curve of the beak, the braceleted wrist, now this layer of ash and the fragments muffled in it. The same fire, yes, but that was all they had in common. Because the ivory had come from elsewhere he had assumed the other things had too. But he had been wrong. They had not been brought here; they had been made here. And the demigod, the guardian spirit, could only have been made on the orders of a king and for a king's protection.

Amid the grime and smoke of the yards, always with an eye out for the uncle, his voice sometimes obscured by the hiss of steam or the clangor of shunting engines, Jehar continued to tell Ninanna about the paradise of Deir ez-Zor. She loved the repetition of details and never got tired of them, however familiar they were, and so he always began with the look of the place, the white minarets, the bridge over the river with its stone pillars resting in the water, the green island in the midst of the stream, the gardens and palm groves along the banks. He enlarged also on the fabulous fatness and sloth of the Pasha in Baghdad because this always made her laugh. The Pasha wore a fez with a gold tassel, and he smoked a hookah, and the rings on his fin-

gers got too tight and had to be filed off as they could not be removed in any other way. He ate halvah and baklava and cakes
made of rice and honey, and he got fatter and fatter. It took the
Pasha a long time just to raise an arm or turn his head. Jehar imitated, for the reward of her laughter, the palsied movements of
this legendary landlord, owner of the gardens of as-Salhijjeh on
the north side of the town, where they would rent their land and
prosper through his neglect.

Things he had seen on his travels, his plans for making
money, these too became part of the vision of life at Deir ez-Zor.
Lower down on the Euphrates was the town of Hit, surrounded
by swamps of the thick black tar they called bitumen. The principal occupations of the inhabitants of Hit were gathering the bitumen and building the boats they called *sahatir,* designed for
river traffic. The materials they used for making the boats were
wood and the pulp of the palm, and both the inside and the outside of the boat were coated with bitumen mixed with lime to
make it stick. He had never made such a boat, but love filled him
with confidence in his powers. He had seen it done; he knew
how to do it; he could make one in a week. A boat like this could
be sold for six Turkish pounds. You took it downriver and sold it
at Karbala or you crossed over to the Tigris by the canal and sold
it in Baghdad. You made a good profit, and this was because the
people of those towns did not have the bitumen close at hand.
There were also fields of it not far from where the Englishman
was digging for his treasure, but these were too far from the
Great River.

He had told her about this Englishman and his search
and his vast wealth—hundreds toiled at his command—and his

shorts and boots that made his legs look thin and his feet look big. He had told her too about the railway line that was heading for the place where the treasure was. The Englishman feared this line because he was one who always believed in his heart that he was a target for God's anger. Because of this secret belief, he had a constant need for news, now more than ever, as he was beginning to find things. And for news he was willing to pay.

She listened to him without always seeming to, busy as she was. The uncle had paid something and had been allowed to fence off a small piece of land adjoining the shoulder of a nearby siding; a dozen hens and a rooster lived together in this small space, fluttering and squawking in alarm at the occasional hissing sound of compressed air released by the locomotives. When Ninanna came out to tend to them Jehar was able to keep her in talk for a little while. Here in the open she felt less constraint; she smiled more often at Jehar and sometimes asked him questions. The black fields of Hit engaged her imagination. It was like Gehennem, the place of fire and torment where the damned were sent. What did they look like, the swamps of pitch? Did people live among them? Were there also some at Deir ez-Zor?

No, no, he told her. Deir ez-Zor was all white and green and golden. It was true that the pitch fields of Hit resembled what the Holy Writings said about Hell; they were black as far as the eye could see, and they steamed and bubbled in places with the heat lying within and below. But sometimes these black fields could look beautiful. There were salt springs among them, and the salt water mingled with the pitch and made rainbow colors around the edges of the spring. In the evening sunshine these colors glowed, and it was as if they were cast upward into the sky, like a promise of paradise.

Love aided native talent to make him supremely eloquent. She listened spellbound. Her lips, which were beautifully formed, parted a little with the interest of it, wonder passing to laughter without pain of thought. No one had ever talked to her like this, brought such pictures to her mind. They came to her sometimes at night as she drifted into sleep, the minarets, the stream, the palm groves, the fez with its gold tassel. Now there were these black fields that could be both ugly and beautiful. He was handsome too, with his level brows and pale eyes, and his talk was full of fire and promise.

The bitumen was scooped up with palm leaves, he told her, and stored in large pieces. It was diluted with lime and sent downstream on rafts. It could be sold at al-Felluge, and from there you could bring back grape honey and a kind of rice the people there called *tummen*. By this trade one could make a lot of money, and with this money they would buy land and plant palms. A hundred trees they would have . . .

Sometimes, in his desire to impress her with the wealth that would be theirs, he might go too much into detail and exhaust her powers of attention. He might be explaining that the people of al-Felluge needed the pitch for sealing and waterproofing the great straw jars that they then weighted with stones and hung on their waterwheels to make them turn and so irrigate their fields, and in the midst of his words he would see a sort of stillness settle over her face, and he would know she had lost her way somewhere in this chain of causes and effects. Then he would go back to the marvels of Deir ez-Zor and get lost in his turn amid the thickets of what was real, what was exaggerated, and what was invented. Amid the gardens that belonged to the fabulously slothful and permanently absent Pasha there was a spring, and the water came out of it with so much force that it bubbled and sang as it flowed. There were times when the water burst forth so strongly that fish came leaping out with it. If you waited by the well, no fish ever gushed out, however long you waited. But if you were passing at the right moment, you would have your supper provided for you. For this reason the spring was named Abu Simac, Father of Fishes, by the people who lived there.

8.

⬧

It was late in the morning and the sun was high when Mansur, who was her personal servant, came to tell Edith that strangers were approaching the house: three men, two on horseback, the third riding a camel. She followed the procedure laid down by Somerville in the event of visits during his absence, telling Mansur to summon two men, make sure they were armed, and wait with them inside the gate until these people were near enough to state their business and be clearly distinguished. She herself waited in the common room, whose windows gave a view across part of the courtyard but not the part that included the gate.

After a short while Mansur returned to say that the men were now two, the third having retired to the nearby village; it seemed he had acted as guide to the others. One of these was a white man; the other was an Arab, or at least spoke Arabic as if it were his own tongue, but he was not from these parts, he was a man of the city. "The other speak to him in English, tell him what he have to say," Mansur said, and smiled brilliantly, Edith was not sure why or whether there was any reason. He had not seen any arms about the Arab, but the white man had a rifle in his saddle holster and a revolver at his belt. "He say name Hellhot, sound like."

"You can open the gate to them," she said, accompanying this with a gesture of one unlocking and opening. She went to the hall, took her sun hat from the peg, put it on without looking in the mirror, then opened the door and stood waiting just outside it.

Elliott's eyes were strained from the hours of riding in a light stronger and harsher than he was used to, and sunlight was reflected from the white walls of the house, confusing him further. As he crossed the courtyard he saw a tall, full-breasted woman in a long white dress, her face shaded by the wide brim of her hat. She did not move as he approached. He removed his hat as he drew near. "Elliott, ma'am," he said. "This is my interpreter, Alawi."

His voice was deep, slightly nasal, with an accent she thought of vaguely as belonging to the American West, and it was drawling and sudden at the same time, as if his words were uttered on impulse.

"Edith Somerville." She extended her hand and felt it gripped with considerable firmness. The interpreter was retreating already, in company with Mansur, avoiding thus the undue familiarity of a handshake with the lady of the house.

This left the two of them standing together. "You will be the geologist," she said.

Sight restored, he was able to see that she was beautiful, the mouth full but delicate in its molding, the eyes a tawny color, set wide apart. "Your husband told you then?" he said.

"Yes, of course. Naturally he told me." He was very tall; she was aware of raising her eyes to his face. His head was still uncovered, and the thick fair hair glinted in the sunlight. The same glint of gold was on his face, and she saw now that there was a short bristle on his cheeks and jaws and around his mouth—he had not shaved, not that day, perhaps not the day before. His eyes were blue, and in the tanned face they had a steadiness of regard, an absence of shyness, that astonished her rather. "Well, come in," she said. Her mother's unfailing remedy for occasions of social strain came to her. "I expect you'd like some tea?"

"That would be just dandy."

Afterward she was to reproach herself at not having thought more about, inquired more closely into, his immediate needs; he would have been tired from the journey, he might have preferred to be shown immediately to the room that had been prepared for him, where he could wash away the dust of travel and rest for a while. But she had wanted to talk to him, perhaps listen to him rather, wanted it from the first.

"So you know I am a fake then," he said, with the same effect of suddenness, when they were seated together.

"Well, I know you are not an archaeologist." Anyone less like a fake it would have been difficult to imagine, she thought, as he sat there rather awkwardly, his long body inclined forward in his chair; with his straight regard, the irregular rhythms of his speech, at once drawling and impulsive-seeming, he bore sincerity with him like a lighted torch. "I suppose you are a genuine geologist?" she said.

He laughed at this. "You mean I might be something else? Two layers of disguise instead of only one? It wouldn't be so strange, I guess. Mesopotamia seems to be full of people engaged in some business that is not the one they tell the world about. No, nothing so interesting, I'm afraid. I'm just a feller that knows something about old stones. Correction, something about old stones that act as hosts to petroleum. Jailers would be a better word."

"What do you mean?"

"Well, there are some types of rock that keep the oil imprisoned." He smiled at her suddenly, an attractive smile, wide and exuberant. "You know, kind of like the genie that got trapped in the bottle. He's been there a very long time, millions of years. We want to let him out, let the poor devil get up to the air."

"So you can trap him all over again and put him in some other kind of bottle."

"No, ma'am, we don't aim to do that. Once you take the stopper out you can't put it back again—no one can." He raised large hands to make a shape in the air, a gesture that seemed almost worshipful to her, as if he were holding up a chalice full of blessings. His smile died, and there was suddenly a naked look of seriousness about his face, something rapt, as if he might be one of the apostles at the moment of being called. "He is right here below us, waiting for the word of release. It's not like the story. This genie isn't vindictive or vengeful, he is a benefactor, he is the greatest boon ever bestowed on the human race. He will bring prosperity and ease of life to millions of people who have never heard his name. He will light their lamps, warm their houses, drive their engines. This genie will be the harbinger of a golden age."

There was a quality of rhetoric in this, a rhythm in his words that seemed practiced. These were things he had said before. But the habit of talking in bursts, like pulses in a flow, saved him from seeming pompously oratorical. And she was attracted by the throb of the feeling in the words and the way they came out, not like a lesson learned and oft repeated but with a warmth that seemed natural to him.

He had lowered his hands now, and something of the smile had returned, though chastened. "I guess I'm talking too much, Mrs. Somerville," he said. "It's a bad habit of mine, especially when it comes to the subject of petroleum. We hardly know each other yet, and that makes it a whole lot worse. But I felt from the beginning you were a lady I could talk to."

This had come too easily, or perhaps too soon; some slight warning bell sounded in her mind. Despite this, she felt pleased by it. In accents she took care to make as neutral as possible, she said, "You are going to be here with us for some time, I believe. We don't stand much on formalities. Please call me Edith."

"My name is Alexander. My friends call me Alex."

This said, they sat and looked at each other for a moment or two. It came to Edith that something—anything—needed imperatively to be said. "But why have they sent you here? I mean, to this particular area?"

"The reasons are technical. Do you really want to hear them? Rule number one for visiting geologists pretending to be visiting archaeologists is to wait at least twenty-four hours before you start boring your hostess with stuff about rocks."

"No, really, I'd like to know."

"Right, here we go. At Hit on the Euphrates and a few miles

south of Mosul on the Tigris there are springs of bitumen coming up from belowground. Bitumen is a kind of tarry substance,
it is one of the components of petroleum. These springs, or
fountains you might call them, are dotted around for miles,
quite small, nine or ten inches across at most. The thing about
them is that the bitumen that comes out is almost pure, unlike
practically anywhere else in western Asia—in most other places
the bitumen comes out swimming on the back of the water, if
you get me. Now we already know there is oil there, we don't
know how much exactly, but we know it is a lot. We know that
for certain. But not very far from where we are sitting right now,
a few miles to the east, there is an extensive oil seep and a
number of fountains, some putting out salt water and bitumen
mixed, some putting out an almost pure bitumen. We have reports on it and some maps, but the area has never been properly
prospected for oil. It's going to be my job to have a good look
round and make some reports of a more detailed kind."

He paused here and looked at her for some moments in silence. She was interested, he could see it in her face; it was no
mere polite attention she was giving him. Wonderful eyes she
had, wide apart like a cat's. Easy to tell her things, easy to say
too much . . . He said, "I am working for the Turkish Petroleum
Company, which was formed two years ago in 1912. That is, I am
working for the British interests in the company." She would
know this already, from her husband. She would know who had
sent him. "We have to go carefully," he said. "The company has
not yet received a charter from the Turkish government. When
they get that, they will be first in the field. They need to know as

much as possible beforehand so as to keep a step ahead. That's where I come in."

"My husband told me that he had agreed with Lord Rampling, the financier, that you should come here."

"That is correct, yes. I don't know this Rampling personally, it's just a job of work, you know. I get a fee. I don't have anything to do with the financial side of it. They have just sent me here to follow up a few clues. I've been engaged in petroleum geology almost the whole of my working life."

Once again he paused and looked at her. The closeness of his regard, that blaze of sincerity, was unsettling, as if he were requiring responses not altogether clear from his words. As before, she felt driven into speech. "It seems like rather a hit-or-miss business to me," she said. "I mean, it's just the presence of the oil seep and these springs, isn't it? It could be just a very little oil, just a narrow little vein that has got gashed somehow and oozes up from close to the surface." Like a hemorrhage, she thought, oozing out, black instead of red, weakening the body, sapping mother earth. "I mean, over all that time even a trickle of oil would make quite a big swamp, wouldn't it?"

"Those are not the only things we have to go on. All those places I've been talking about—and this is true also of Dalaki, in Persia, where oil has been definitely discovered and drilling has begun—have one other thing in common. They are situated at the extreme edge of a gypsum foundation at the point where the gypsum is succeeded either by red sandstone or by fractured limestone, both of which are typical reservoir rocks."

Glancing at her face, he saw that a certain stillness had

descended on it and realized that she had failed to follow him in these details. "These are types of rock where the oil gets trapped," he said. "It's like the jar where the genie is kept prisoner. He is small when he is in the jar, that's because he's got these vast formations of sedimentary rock all around him. But once he is set free he swells up and gets huger and huger. If you could see a picture of the escaping genie in a storybook, it would look like a great cloud billowing up from the neck of the jar, filling all the sky. Instead of a cloud, think of a great flood of oil, like a million fountains all put together. Believe me, if you drill down through the walls of his prison, you will see how big he is, by jiminy you will!"

She would have asked him more. One cardinal piece of advice of her mother's, secretly scorned but somehow still operating within her, was always to ask men about their work, this being the best way of freeing their tongues and also, as a secondary advantage, of securing a reputation for intelligence. But this man's tongue needed no freeing. He was loquacious certainly, but this homely rhetoric of his turned everything into a story. She would have liked to go on with it a bit longer, though their tea was finished long ago. It was not like the genie, not really, because he was quite contained in his jar whereas the oil leaked all over the place, as it seemed. She did not understand how it could escape from these imprisoning rocks.

But manners prevailed now. She rang the little bell on the table beside her. "You must be tired," she said. "You will need a rest. Mansur will show you to your room. I will tell him to bring water. This is a sort of common room, where we are now. We generally gather here for a drink a little after sundown, when my husband and his assistant are back from the excavation."

But he must have slept long; he did not appear until it was nearly dark, just before dinner, when everyone else was assembled. Introductions were hardly over before they were on their way to the dining room. She had not failed to notice her husband's air of distraction and the shortness of his words to the newly arrived guest. She knew these for signs of excitement in him. And Palmer had a look of briskness about him, a sort of extra alertness, which meant the same thing. But at first neither of them made any mention of the day's work; the meal was half over before anyone spoke of it, and then it seemed that her husband was jolted into speech by a kind of rage.

Elliott proved no shyer in the enlarged company of the dinner table than he had been earlier over the teacups. The blaze of honesty, the hasty rhythms of his speech were the same. He was talking about the beginnings of the American oil industry and about a certain Colonel Drake, who wasn't a colonel at all, but a drifting and impoverished entrepreneur.

"He used the title to impress the local population, all the couple of hundred of 'em. This was in the 1860s, a lumber town called Titusville in northwest Pennsylvania. Everyone knew about the rock oil that came bubbling up from belowground near the town—there was a place in the hills there called Oil Creek. But no one thought of drilling for it—except this Colonel Drake."

Before that they had just scooped the oil from the surface or soaked rags in it then wrung them out. They might get four or five gallons a day like this—on a good day. That was how it had always been; that's what their fathers and grandfathers had done. They thought Drake was crazy, colonel or not.

"Sure, he was a fake," Elliott said, sitting back, smiling around the table. "But he was a man of vision, and that is kind of rare. He had no way of drilling for oil. He tried hiring salt drillers, but they turned out to be an unreliable body of men, they kept getting drunk or they just disappeared as soon as they had a few dollars in their pockets. So he set about constructing a steam engine to power the drill. But time was passing, the people back in New Haven who were financing him ran out of patience. They sent him a letter telling him to close down the operation. In the meantime he had found a driller, a man named Smith. He was a very big, strong guy. Everyone called him Uncle Billy Smith . . ."

Somerville listened with rising displeasure. The fellow was talking more than a newcomer should. But it was not this, the confidence, the manner too relaxed; it was not even the quality of attention being accorded him by Edith. He had come to the table with some momentous news of his own to announce, only to find the stage occupied by another, a stranger at that. And then, surely, someone here in the guise of an archaeologist should show an interest in the work they were doing, ask some questions, put himself in the position of listener, instead of droning on about oil. But he wasn't droning, of course, and that made it worse; he was a good talker, with an easy manner and a command of vivid detail, qualities Somerville knew to be lacking in himself, his own habit of repression showing more clearly perhaps in this than anything else, causing him always to downplay everything, to understate, to avoid the dramatic. And now here he was, with conclusive evidence that the site had been a residence of Assyrian kings, sitting here and listening to talk of this Uncle Billy.

"This was August 1859," Elliott said. "Drake had been there for more than two years already. The letter was delayed somehow, I like to think some angel of good fortune slowed it down. It still hadn't arrived on the Sunday morning when Uncle Billy went out to have a look at the well. They had been drilling at about seventy feet. When he looked down into the pipe, he saw a thick black liquid floating on the top of the water. He lowered a tin cup in it and drew up a sample." He paused for some moments. Then he said, "They had struck oil," and there was on his face that look of rapt attention, almost of awe, that had made Edith think that he resembled one of the apostles at the moment of the summons. "All they had to do was pump it out," he said. "I don't know if Uncle Billy danced a jig right there and then, but I sure would have done so in his shoes. The first oil well in the U.S. And that means anywhere. The day they started pumping was the day the letter came, telling Drake to close down. Who knows? If it had arrived a couple of days sooner, there might have been no Standard Oil, and Rockefeller would have had to find some other way to make his millions."

This final call on his sense of the miraculous was more than Somerville, irritated as he already was, could endure. "Well, Palmer," he said, cutting in brusquely and ruining the speculative silence that Elliott had intended as the crown of his story, "shall we give out our little bit of news? Not much perhaps, but at least it is about people who once lived in the world and not about commodities."

Quite why he called upon Palmer in this way was not altogether clear to him; Palmer himself seemed for the moment taken aback at the abruptness of it, recovering fairly soon, however, and restricting himself to his own part in the work. A clay tablet in good condition had been found near the remains of the stone doorway, and he had been able to decipher most of it.

"Baked hard," he said. "Nothing like a good blaze. It's in cuneiform and seems to be one of a series—we haven't found any others yet. It contains two clauses of an agreement or treaty—demands for the allegiance of the desert tribes east of the Euphrates."

"That is roughly the area where we are now." Somerville sat back and glanced around the table in what seemed, at least to Edith—and she disliked herself for the thought—a sort of paler imitation of Elliott's narrative style. "The tribes must have been causing trouble at the time," he said. "That might help us to date the tablet."

"The date is missing if there ever was one," Palmer said. "But the tablet bears the name of Esarhaddon, who was king of Assyria in the early seventh century B.C. It seems reasonable to suppose that the inscription was made here on his orders."

"He died in 670, on his way back from campaigning in Egypt, so the treaty must have been made well before that." Somerville waited a moment to lend dramatic weight. Then he said, "Taken with the other things we have uncovered, it is conclusive proof that Tell Erdek was a residence of the Assyrian kings for a very considerable period of time."

"It's really exciting," Patricia said. "Well, it is now anyway. Quite frankly, I was finding it fairly boring before."

She had spoken directly to Elliott with some vague idea of including him, making it up to him. With the increased sensibility that had come to her with love, she had felt distressed at the snub he had received. "I often go with them now," she added, rather lamely. "I had no idea it could be such fun."

Edith too had registered her husband's unmannerly brusqueness, the edge of contempt there had been in his words. It was unlike him. He was often distracted in manner and aloof-seeming, but this had been deliberate rudeness. Strange, when he was so clearly elated by these recent discoveries. But what was like him or unlike him she was no longer certain about; it was as if the structure of his character was loosening somehow into incongruous components. He looked exalted now, almost feverish, she thought, as he glanced about. She was about to repair the breach in manners by asking Elliott something more about oil, anything would do. But the American forestalled her. "I must take issue with you," he said, "in this matter of people and commodities. It seems to me you are taking the wrong view."

He was looking down the table at Somerville and on his face the blaze of sincerity seemed intensified. He had, Edith realized, been waiting all this while, all through the talk of Assyria, waiting to make this justified retort. She should have known he was not the man to take a thing like that lying down.

"Oh yes?" Somerville looked for a moment bemused, as if encountering some obstacle in a path he had thought was clear.

"It is a big mistake to separate the two. Gold is a commodity, people seek it and die for it. Tea is a commodity, hundreds of thousands of people in your British India get a living from it who would otherwise starve. In the African slave trade people were commodities, it was one and the same thing."

He paused briefly, aware of a distinct dislike for this cold fish he was addressing. "Yes, sir, one and the same thing. What you are digging up is commodities, as I understand it, bits of pots and so on. Is that people? It is all a long time ago in any case. Oil is a commodity, right, but it is the future of humanity, it will change the lives of millions. Millions of *people*, sir. It will change the face of the planet. It will flow like the milk and honey we are told of in the Good Book, a blessing to the children of earth. Now I ask you, what is this Esarhaddon guy compared to that?"

With a gesture only half conscious Somerville raised his fingers to his temples on either side. The heavy, blurting falls of the speech had sounded in his ears like the pistons of a machine working with a rhythm that was relentless, inexorable, like the pounding blows of a hammer on metal. That was the future this interloper stood for, with his odious rhetoric, a future that would see it as virtuous to obliterate the human past and substitute for human speech a hideous, universal hissing and clanking . . . A feeling of desolation rose in him, like nausea. He got up abruptly from his place at the table. "Excuse me," he said. "I need a breath of air."

Without pausing further he quitted the room, walked out

to the courtyard, and crossed to the gate, which he unbolted and passed through. He walked rapidly, wanting to put some distance between himself and the house, so that no one would be able to follow and find him.

As he walked, the agitation he had felt, the pounding of his nerves and the nausea that had come with it, grew less, and the silence of the night settled around him. After a while he stopped and stood still. He could feel that his hands were trembling slightly. There was no moon; but the night was clear, and the stars gave enough light to see by. There were lamps here and there in the village, and the distant sound of voices came to him. He felt no slightest kinship with the people of the place or with the land that stretched around him. All his ambition, all the passion of his nature were centered on the mound of earth that lay not far from him now; he could make out the dark shape of it, with its irregular crest, higher on the west side, where they had first started digging.

Kings of the royal line of Sargon had walked here. Once again the mystery of the fire came to him. It could not have been in Esarhaddon's time; so much was certain. The Assyrian Empire had been at its greatest extent in his reign, its power and authority unquestioned. One of the wisest of their kings, coming to the throne after the murder of his father, Sennacherib, the brutal and cowardly. Sennacherib had sacked Babylon and desecrated the temple of Marduk. He had been stabbed to death while at prayer, it was said by one of his sons—perhaps even this one, the youngest. Conflicting stories surrounded this distant murder; the truth would never be known now. Patricide or not, he had lived here; he had issued proclamations from here. But it had not been during his rule, this devastation. Whose then? And whose the hand that lit the fires?

He might not be given time to find the answers to these questions. No word had come from his old school friend or from Rampling. He had been a fool to believe them. It seemed to him now that this belief, his trust in them, even the rush of relief he had felt at their promises, in fact his whole behavior that afternoon in Constantinople, had been a sort of fabrication or display, designed to placate the demons of doubt that plagued him, not to drive them out. He had been his own dupe. And Elliott's presence was hateful to him because it was a constant witness to that fact.

9.

Rampling, at the moment Somerville was standing in the starlight, bitterly attributing deceit and falsehood to him, was in the dining room of the Hôtel d'Orient in Damascus, in the company of several others. And he too, in his own way, was occupied with the Baghdad Railway.

During the meal the conversation had been general. But now, over the coffee and the excellent Armenian brandy, to the strains of a trio dressed in Tyrolean hats and lederhosen playing tunes from *The Merry Widow* amid the Moorish arches, they came down to business. It was Donaldson, principal secretary at the Foreign Office, who began this shift toward a more serious tone. "We were wondering," he said, speaking in French, "whether you have given more consideration to the proposals of my government in regard to the joint financing of the railway south of Mosul."

Here was one who would end up with a perforated duodenum, Rampling thought, looking across at the pale, drawn face of the man who had spoken. Not yet forty and a knighthood already, a brilliant career foretold on every hand. So impatient of these social preliminaries, so eager to come down to brass tacks, as he would have put it, that he had done no more than pick at his dinner, had drunk only water when there was a first-rate wine of the country in plentiful supply. No capacity for enjoyment, no ease in company—a man would not go so very far without that, no matter what was prophesied for him. He himself had both, in good measure. He listened to the predictably cautious reply of Donaldson's French counterpart, Chapot. Yes, full consideration had been given to the British proposals, but very little could be done without Turkish agreement; the whole length of the projected line, all the way to Basra, ran through territories indisputably part of the Ottoman Empire . . .

"The Turks have everything to gain from the line." This came from Cullen, the British Resident at Baghdad.

"As consultant to the Turkish Ministry of Finance," Rampling said, "I can give absolute assurances that the British offer of a twenty percent participation in the enterprise will be guaranteed by the National Bank of Turkey, which as you know has recently been established by Sir Ernest Cassel with the express purpose of promoting investment of British capital in the Ottoman Empire."

It was to offer these assurances in his own voice and person that he was there at the table. He had been invited by the Asquith government, on very lavish terms, to take part. But it was not the fees and expenses that were his main reason for being there. Of course money was always desirable, however much of it one already had; it was through following this principle that he already had so much. But he had business of his own in Damascus, and the invitation had come as a convenient cover. In any case, he had no belief that there would be any concrete outcome from this meeting. There was a German director of the railway company at the table; but there was no Turkish representative, and this was because everyone knew that the Turks would make demands in return for concessions, and there was no concerted policy on this. Everyone also knew that the line south of Mosul would pass through some of the richest oil reserves so far ascertained in the Near East.

It would be just another in a long series of meetings. Most of the men there had traveled weary miles to attend; they would return home, submit their cautious, inconclusive, mendacious reports—further proof, if proof were needed, of the division and distrust that reigned among the powers of Europe. The only difference lay in the choice of meeting place. This Damascus hotel had been the brain wave of the Foreign Secretary himself: an informal atmosphere, bonhomie, a frank and free exchange of opinion. Then he goes and sends a man like Donaldson . . . No, threats to national interest might create international alliances, but these did not lessen the likelihood of war—rather the contrary. Only money might do this; below the patriotic bluster and the public pronouncements, money worked in silence to make partners of enemies, to form alliances of a different kind, too profitable to risk breaking.

The Tyrolean trio, whose smiles were wearing thin, had now embarked on excerpts from *Gypsy Love.* Rampling rose from the table and bade the company good night. He had done what was required of him; he could see no further need for his presence.

The following morning he embarked on his more private program. It was some years since he had last been in Damascus, a city he had always liked. He decided to set out from the hotel early enough to allow a stroll before the first of his appointments. He was accompanied by the fearsome Dikmen and by his secretary, Thomas, whom he did not trust completely—that would have been against his principles—but trusted more than anyone else. Thomas had been in his employment now for more than twenty years and had always proved the soul of discretion. With them was also a dragoman hired through the hotel, a Syrian who spoke French and English as well as his native Arabic; he would be useful in easing the way with small bribes if need be and would know the streets and which ones to keep clear of.

Rampling had dressed with his usual care in a suit of shantung silk of a very pale blue color and a pearl gray shirt, also of silk, with a fashionably narrow collar. On his head was a panama hat with a turned-up brim; in his right hand one of his silver-mounted canes; in his nostrils the occasional whiff of lavender from the handkerchief sprouting from his breast pocket.

It was a fine spring morning, still cool and pleasant. The apricot trees were in splendid flower in the gardens bordering the Barada. To the south lay the cone of Mount Hermon, the snow on its summit radiant in this early sunshine. They went some way toward the citadel, then crossed the stream by the little bridge at the beginning of Gayvet Avenue. As they walked, the dragoman, who announced his name as Richard and had a family to support, while shooing mendicant children out of their path, told Rampling a story he had told others before, thereby gaining goodwill and extra payment. The Prophet Muhammad, standing on the hill called Samaniyeh, gazing over the beauties of the city, had remarked that since there is only one Paradise, it should not be sought on earth and therefore he would not enter Damascus.

The offices of the Crédit Lyonnais lay just past the Palace Hotel. Rampling left Dikmen and Richard in the waiting room below and together with his secretary was shown up to the expensively appointed boardroom on the first floor. Awaiting him were the president of the bank in Syria, the manager of the Damascus branch, and a senior partner in the Imperial Ottoman Bank, which was largely under French control.

Armed with statistics provided by his secretary, Rampling spent two hours there, seeking by all means possible to allay the suspicions and quieten the fears of the French bankers. It was vital for his own interests and those he represented, both commercial and political, that French capital should be invested in the Baghdad Railway to an extent of 20 percent of the total holding. This would bring France to a parity with Britain and make them equal partners, and this in turn—and more important—would enable agreements to be reached about zones of influence in the territory traversed by the line. The grip of the Ottoman state on these territories was loosening from week to week.

He was given a courteous hearing, but it was no easy task that faced him. There was deep hostility to the railway on the part of certain French commercial interests. It was feared that this new line would divert traffic from the existing route across

Europe, thus seriously reducing the importance of the port of Marseilles and involving significant losses to French railways. Then there was the question of silk exports, which Rampling had studied while still in Constantinople. The powerful and influential silk manufacturers of Lyons were afraid that since the concession was after all in German hands, whatever the source of the capital invested, the railway would bring about a rise of German economic power in Turkey and threaten the supply of cheap raw silk from Syria, practically the whole of which had hitherto been consumed in French mills.

These were serious objections, and Rampling took care to give them due weight, while reiterating the argument, which he felt to be his strongest card, that those who established a financial interest in the line would thereby establish claims on the territories the line passed through at a time when the Ottoman Empire was disintegrating. There would, in short, be a day of reckoning, a division of the spoils.

Neither he nor the French mentioned the imminent threat of war, but it underlay everything that was said, as did the knowledge that their two nations were bound by treaty obligations and would be allies should war come about. To the victors would go the prizes, and the richest prize of all was Turkey in Asia, the wealth in minerals and fuel, largely untapped, the enormous potential for agricultural produce, the strategic importance for nations like their own that were seeking—naturally in a spirit of partnership and cooperation—an extension of colonial power.

How far he had succeeded it was not possible to tell from the impeccable courtesy of his hosts on parting. But he had spoken as an associate of the Morgan Grenfell group, which had close ties with French banking interests, and this would carry weight. He was, moreover, confident that his argument would carry the day, that his vision of the future was ultimately compelling: In this dangerous place that Europe had become, to protect your interests you must seek constantly to enlarge them; who held back, who played too safe, would fail and die, and the earth would cover him over.

He was some minutes late for his noon appointment, which was with Kruckman, one of the German directors of the railway company, who had been at their table the evening before and whom he had known for some years, though neither of them had given any indication of that in the course of the dinner, having made this arrangement to meet by telephone earlier in the day. An open-air meeting had been decided on, without any presence other than their own. There were in any case no formalities to go through, no papers, no signatures. Agreements in principle had already been made; it was no more than a chat really, a handshake, an expression of goodwill.

Very agreeable too, Rampling thought, with a certain sense of relief at there being no need to urge or persuade. The place they had chosen for their meeting was a small park between two of the gates in the old city walls, the Gate of Paradise and the Gate of Peace. The ground sloped upward gently, and from the summit of the mound they could look across to the dome and minarets of the Omayyid Mosque nearby and the gardens and orchards of Salihiyeh to the north. The midday sun was warm, and Rampling took off his jacket and gave it to Dikmen, walking some dozen yards behind them, to carry, having first asked him if his hands were clean.

Kruckman spoke passable English, and he was a friendly man, easy to talk to, combining joviality and cunning and a sort of cynical good-fellowship, qualities that Rampling always found congenial. In addition to being on the board of directors of the Baghdad Railway, he represented the Deutsche Bank in Syria and was a trusted associate of von Gwinner, the president of the bank.

Strolling together side by side in the spring sunshine, they said the necessary things, made the necessary assurances. Solidarity and common interest were what they both were concerned to express, sentiments somewhat forced on the German side, though naturally Kruckman gave no indication of this. Only the previous week, in London, his bank had finally been obliged to recognize southern Mesopotamia, as well as central and southern Persia, as exclusive fields of operation for the Anglo-Persian Oil Company, in which the British government had a controlling interest. This had opened the way for the formation of an Anglo-German syndicate to organize the newly formed Turkish Petroleum Company for the exploitation of the vilayets of Mosul and Baghdad. The controlling interest in this would still be British, through the National Bank of Turkey, in which Rampling had a substantial holding, but a 25 percent share would be offered to the Deutsche Bank. Agreement on this, a united front, was essential if they were to succeed in obtaining a charter from the Ottoman government.

Rampling returned to his hotel convinced that this accord would hold. The Germans had little choice; they had come too late into the field to gain any more commanding position; they must see that the best interests of German industry would be served by securing this quarter share. The potential profits were huge, and they constituted a force for peace, as he had not failed to point out to Kruckman. For who would want to hazard benefits like these on the doubtful outcome of war?

So cheered and invigorated was he by these thoughts, by his restored hope in the workings of capital, that he had decided to get some girl brought in to take her clothes off and do what she was told. But the packet that had been delivered by courier in his absence brought an abrupt end to this mood of celebration. It contained the information that the geologist Elliott had been closely watched while in London, a fact that he already knew, as it had been done on his orders. But the watching, it seemed, had not been careful enough. Elliott had succeeded at least once in escaping it—a proof of guilt in itself. He had visited the German Embassy. A security guard there, beset by gambling debts and in fear of bodily harm from his creditors, had come forward belatedly—and at a price. He had seen a handshake, heard a name. A meeting with a secretary at the embassy and two others not employed there, both Germans. He would have thought nothing of it, but next morning he had heard the name again. A man had come and asked him questions about visitors, politely, not like a policeman. He had said nothing at the time, not knowing the purpose of these questions, but the man had left a card with an address, an office just off the Strand. After some days it had occurred to him that this might be something he could sell . . .

It took Rampling no more than a few minutes to read this report. It took him less time to come to the only possible conclusion. Elliott had taken a risk in going so openly to the German

Embassy, but of course he could not afford to seem secretive to the Germans, could not afford to rouse suspicion that there might be competitors; they must believe, as he himself had been tricked into believing, that the American was serving only one master. Elliott must have realized he was being shadowed and succeeded in throwing his tracker off the scent somewhere not so very far from the embassy—hence the questioning next morning. He had gone calmly on to keep his appointment; the man had nerve, obviously. The detective agency had slipped up; it certainly would not receive the balance of its fee . . .

Something more drastic than this would have to be done about Elliott. Elliott had betrayed his trust. Elliott, no doubt for a substantial sum of money, had made a deal to report his findings also to the Deutsche Bank.

This was a day different from any other in Jehar's life, the day of his great idea, the day when he became, instead of a man who waited on the whims of others, one who shaped his own destiny.

For most of its course the day resembled all others that he spent at Jerablus. In the morning he found three hours' work hoisting coal in wicker baskets from the stockpile onto the waiting trucks, which were to carry it over the river and down the line. After this, standing in the yard at the kitchen doorway, hens scrabbling and stretching their necks nearby, two ragged men shouting in argument on the other side of the track, he watched Ninanna making coffee on the makeshift stove and added further details to the paradise of their future life together.

At Deir ez-Zor, he told her, beyond the lands of the fat and indolent Pasha, the banks of the Great River were well wooded and beautiful. That he had never set eyes on them did nothing to detract from the fullness of his description. There were wide meadowlands bounded by green hills, and the river wound among them, glittering in the sunshine. Yellow daisies grew there, and dark blue irises, and in the clear pools there were floating lily pads that gave off a scent of great sweetness. Just now, at this time of the year, the almond trees would be flowering, and in the strips of land adjoining the river the watermelons would be showing the first leaf, the seed leaf. In places the banks were steep and tangled with brushwood; wild boars littered there, and ducks took refuge, also the beautiful bird called the Aleppo plover. Red geese came to make their nests in these banks, where they were high and rocky. A man with a good rifle could provide his family with game all the year round. He, Jehar, had such a rifle, a bolt-action, breech-loading Enfield rifle of most recent design. He kept it hidden, wrapped in an oily rag, below the boards of the shack where he slept, but he did not tell Ninanna this, nor did he tell her how he had acquired it, which was by the ambush and murder, in company with some others, of a small contingent of Turkish troops. They were hated as occupiers, and hatred was just cause for killing and theft in Jehar's eyes, even if the hatred was borrowed for the occasion; he had no particular animosity toward the Turks, had merely coveted one of the rifles they were issued with. He was a crack shot, he told her; he could hit a piastre piece flung high in the air.

She listened to him with attention, keeping an eye on the pan, waiting to spoon in the coffee and the sugar when the water came to the boil. Sometimes, in the interest of the narrative, she would be in danger of forgetting her duties; she would look closely at him, her mouth a little open, her dark eyes full of wonder as she tried to picture these lands he spoke of, so different from the world of the yards that surrounded them, the flowery meadows, the shining stream, the birds flying overhead. She looked forward to his visits and tried in the midst of her tasks to make occasions for them. Jehar felt his power over her, and in the absence of touch between them it stirred his loins with a sense of conquest; it was as if by subjugating her with his words, he were laying hands on her body. He had been away for some days, but the story had reached such a plenitude of promise that it could be resumed at any time; it had no breaks in it and no beginning and no ending. And Ninanna knew that he brought the story to her as a tribute, an offering laid before a queen by a subject chieftain. She knew she had empire over Jehar, and the knowledge gave her a certain right to call him to account.

"I missed you," she said. And then, though she knew the answer: "Why did you go away?"

"I had to see the Englishman. I had to tell him . . . The line, they have started laying the track on the other side, beyond the bridge. They are almost halfway to the Belikh River."

She nodded. She had no interest at all in the progress of the line, whether it went here or there. "I missed you," she said again.

"I had to go. He gives me money for the information I bring him. I am his news bearer, I am the one he trusts. The money he gives me I put to the money I have saved already. When I have the hundred pounds, I will take it to your uncle and he will give you to me."

"Then we will be married and we will go to live at Deir ez-Zor."

"Yes."

"Will it be long?"

"No, not very long." This he tried to say with the ring of re-assurance in his voice. It was important that Ninanna should believe it. But in fact his stock was growing painfully slowly. He had lost weight in his efforts to save expenses on food. And lack of trust in the uncle was robbing him of sleep.

The work of the yards at Jerablus, the extension to Tchoban Bey, the building of the great steel bridge, the rail link to Alexandretta, the construction of storage depots and houses and offices for the employees of the company, all this had brought in its wake a great number of people, many of whom had no intention of seeking work on the line or doing honest work of any kind. Various nationalities commingled in this improvised township of canvas and tin canisters and scrap timber. Turk and Arab and Kurd rubbed shoulders here, along with an assortment of footloose Europeans and Americans, a good number of whom were fugitives from justice. However diverse in race and origin, all were driven by the same prospect of easy money. There were bars and gambling dens and makeshift stalls. Drunkenness and violence were common. There were also brothels. These were mostly for the benefit of the German railway employees and for off-duty Turkish noncommissioned officers, people with the money to pay. Mostly, but not entirely: a pocket picked, a purse snatched, a win at dice, some surplus of wages that did not go on drink—anyone might find himself waiting in line for his turn with one of the girls. It was a constant demand, there was a lot of money in it, and it was Jehar's growing fear that the uncle would grow tired of waiting for the bride-price and force Ninanna into whoredom. It was done commonly enough, and it didn't take long. She would be kept locked up for a while, violated a certain number of times free of charge . . . The first move the uncle made in this direction would be the last he ever made on earth. But what if the thing was done while he was away on the site of the excavation, carrying reports back to the Englishman? The uncle would not live to profit from it, but it might be too late to save Ninanna. Fears of this played tricks with his senses. As he lay awake, it sometimes seemed to him that amid the nighttime sounds of quarrel and riot he could hear Ninanna screaming.

These fears he sought to dispel by dwelling on those of another. "The Englishman is afraid of the railway," he said. "That is why he pays me for telling him that the line draws nearer. He expects only bad news. It is in keeping with his demon that the news should be bad. But he thinks that by paying he can somehow keep the line at bay. The line is like a fierce dog to him. Paying me is like throwing meat to it."

Ninanna's eyes widened as she looked at him. The threat of the line became real to her at that moment. The Englishman who was digging for treasure had joined the fat Pasha, creatures half real, half legendary. "How can that be?" she said. "The money, he gives to you, not to the people of the railway."

"It is how people think about money," he said. "And about time also. The Englishman is near to the finding of the treasure. He thinks that if he pays it might be granted him to possess the treasure before the line reaches him."

He told her then of the things he had learned on this last

visit of his: how they had started digging on the far side of the mound, the side that looked down over the German railway buildings; how they had found a wall and then rooms, palace apartments under a layer of ash. The wall continued; they would follow it. Perhaps they would go below this floor to a lower level, where the treasure might be; so far only fragments of small value had been found, but if they were granted some weeks more . . .

"He tries to hide it from me, to show nothing. This is because he thinks I am lesser than he. For that race it is a bad thing to reveal your feelings to a lesser person, they think it is a cause for shame—"

He was interrupted here; she had to leave, the coffee was cooling. Jehar was obliged to move away because she gave him a backward glance as she passed into the café, narrowing her eyes in a way that had become a signal between them, and he knew from this that the uncle had entered from the door on the other side.

But this day was not destined, like all the others, to end sadly for Jehar in longing for the girl and distrust of the uncle. It was like the finger of Allah, as he afterward thought of it, pointing him the way. Lately he had kept away from bars, not wishing to squander any of his savings. This evening, however, a certain mood of depression, a sense that he was losing his battle with circumstance, led him to a drinking place, no more than a shed, roughly timbered, roofed over with canvas, with a narrow bar, no space for seating and no one to serve you; customers had to jostle through the crowd to get to the counter. The drink was raki, made from crushed grain and fermented in open pans in the hot sun of the previous summer, raw to the taste and very potent.

The men surrounding him were of every kind, but there were some there who had a look in their eyes that he knew; they were men who had survived harsh toil but still lived with those who had not survived it, men who had worked on the line for years and given up their strength to it day by day, from the high Anatolian plateau to these banks of the Euphrates, through the Taurus and the Cilician Gates and the Amanus Mountains, where there were no natural passes, where the hills had to be pierced by blasting and tunneling. Many men had died in these ten years of labor—by falls in precipitous places, by sickness in that harsh climate, by accidents occurring in unloading the rails and sleepers or coupling the trucks, by attacks from mountain tribesmen hostile to the line. Two of the convicts released along with Jehar to work under the guns of the guards had died, one under a fall of rock, one when a shattered leg had turned gangrenous.

Perhaps it was recognizing this haggard companionship with death printed on some faces there that set Jehar talking now, with two drinks inside him and the third in his hand, set him telling a story of death to those standing near him. At least there was no other reason he was aware of.

It had happened during his early days of working on the railway. A charge of dynamite, a powerful charge designed to bring down a steep and rocky escarpment ahead of the line, had been laid. They used Armenian conscripts, Jehar said with a chuckle, because being subject to military law, they could be shot if they refused and because they were half starved and so light enough to be lowered down in a basket over the cliff face without the rope breaking. The fuse was shorter than it should have been, and it was shortened further by the charge having been set in the overhang on the farther side of the cliff. The Armenians had to light the fuse, then be hauled up and then run for their lives. Jehar acted it out, eyes staring, mouth open, arms working like pistons. But one of the two had stumbled and fallen and in falling done some hurt to his leg. The other—and this was the point of the story—instead of making good his escape, had paused to help his companion get to his feet and had tried to bring him to safety. This doomed, shambling run of the pair Jehar also acted, within the confines of the space allowed him by his listeners. But the charge had detonated; they were too close. Killed by the blast, stoned to death by flying splinters of rock— Jehar spread his hands; the manner of it was not important. The point was the folly of it, two men dying when only one needed to die.

He was smiling as he finished, warm with the raki, glad to be alive. But in fact he always felt some unease in the telling of this story, in spite of his chuckles and headshakes, because there was something in it that baffled him, something that defied common sense and mockery alike. The man had paused, but there had not been time for anything like decision; instinctively he had risked himself . . . Now, as he was raising his glass to drink, in that moment of indecision and unease, in the presence of a mystery, he felt the touch of Allah, and the idea came to him, at first like a distant strain of music, a promise of harmony. Then it came nearer, and it was a clash of cymbals, it was the song of a thousand throats. A hundred pounds, all at one stroke!

———

Somerville's insomnia became a settled condition during this period of discovery. He would fall asleep almost the moment that his head touched the pillow and sleep profoundly through the first part of the night, untroubled by any dreams vivid enough to remain with him on waking. Invariably he would open his eyes in the darkness, long before dawn, with the cold knowledge that sleep would not return to him.

This lack of sleep combined with his anxieties and the excitement of the discoveries they were making to give a quality of slight hallucinatory disorder to his days. From time to time he had a sense of movement at the edges of his vision, glimpses of some bright flickering motion, like small tongues of fire, seen from the corners of his eyes but never evident to his direct gaze. Sometimes he seemed to hear, in the far distance, beyond the verge of sight, a faint, repeated striking of metal on metal, and there were times when this became indistinguishable from the pulse of his own body.

In the hours of wakefulness, lying motionless while he waited for daylight, he elaborated the story he had begun to tell himself from the moment of finding the piece of carved ivory. This story began with the second Assyrian king to be called Ashurnasirpal, the first of them all to boast of his power to inflict suffering, the first to make this power the symbol and test of kingship, the first to aim not merely at conquest and plunder, as had his forebears, but at the permanent subjection of the conquered peoples, changing the very nature of the state, from one rich and strong within its borders and content to be so to one that gloried in dominion, ruthless in its greed for territory and vassalage, a policy that was to be followed by all his successors down to the last days, down to the fires in which the empire perished.

Mysterious in its workings this alchemy of empire, a change of chemistry in the body of the state, a thirst that once created was never slaked. He thought of the limestone statue of Ashurnasirpal, found in the temple of Ninurta at Kalhu, the hooked nose, the stony gaze, the rigid pose of the despot, the mace and curved spear in his hands. This king, early in the ninth century before Christ, invaded Syria, skirted Mount Lebanon, conquered the cities of the Great Sea, and brought back stores of booty, among which was an ivory plaque showing the lion of empire with its teeth embedded in the throat of a male victim, a Nubian, the throat offered in ultimate submission. That is why he took it. It had pleased him to take possession of this symbol of another's dominion, to take the power of it into himself. Like capturing the enemy's gods, another practice of the Assyrians. He had taken it back with him to Kalhu on the Tigris, a new palace, a new city, rich and splendid, built by slave labor to his order. There it had stayed for a period of time unknown. Who had brought it here? In the long line of kings that followed he had found record of one name only, Esarhaddon, who inherited the throne some two centuries later on the murder of his father, Sennacherib.

Sometime during his reign, probably sometime around 672, when he had proclaimed his son Ashurbanipal the legitimate heir to the throne—reasonable to suppose some degree of retirement after such a proclamation—this king had come here, had built himself a summer palace, here at Tell Erdek, where they were digging. My mound, he thought, the one I singled out. My instinct was right after all.

Certain things this king had brought with him, things perhaps that he had a particular fondness for or were in some way important to him. That would explain the presence of the ivory piece. Other things had been made here for the decoration of his palace or for his own protection, among them the carved relief of the guardian spirit. And—clinching piece of evidence—it was here that the tablets had been inscribed, those relating to his triumphs in Egypt and those dictating terms to the rebellious desert tribes.

So far everything held together. But Esarhaddon had not died here. He had fallen sick at Harran, on his way to another Egyptian campaign, and died there. So much was known for certain. Had his descendants continued to use this place? Perhaps his son and successor, Ashurbanipal, had come here in his turn. Erudite, ruthless—of all the rulers of Assyria, this one had been to Somerville's mind from his boyhood days the most awe-inspiring and, in a way he only half confessed to himself, enviable. It was he who had assembled the great library of cuneiform texts at Nineveh, thousands of tablets containing the whole range of Assyro-Babylonian knowledge. It was he who had subdued the rebel Arab tribes west of the Euphrates, a difficult desert war waged against elusive enemies, but he had conquered, he had cut them off from their wells, he had forced them to cut open their camels and quench their thirst with blood. From this he had gone on to devastate the land of the Elamites and sack their capital of Susa, putting a final end to

hostilities between the two nations that had lasted three thousand years. *Their bones I carried off to Assyria. I denied peace to their
shades. I deprived them of food gifts and libations of water . . .*

What implacable power was this, to punish his enemies beyond the grave and to believe, to actually believe, he had the
peace of their souls in his hands. In the year that Susa fell, 639
B.C., he was to outward view at the apex of power. From his magnificent palace at Nineveh he could look out at a world that
was prostrate at his feet. His storehouses were overflowing with
booty; his foes were conquered, the rebel chiefs dragged behind
his chariot or fastened to his gates with rings through their jaws
like dogs.

Yet the signs were there, if there had been any to read
them: Egypt was passing out of control; Babylonia was inflamed
with hatred and desire for revenge; his army was exhausted and
its ranks reduced by years of continuous fighting. And beyond
the Zagros Mountains, unsuspected, the growing power of the
Medes. Less than thirty years later, in the reign of his son, the Assyrian Empire had ceased altogether to exist. And it was this suddenness, this death in the midst of plenty, that made Assyria the
supreme symbol of the doom inherent in all dominion. Perhaps
this king, unaware of such doom, with no faculty for imagining
it, had rested here after his triumphs, here in this place where
they were digging. It was likely enough. The scraps of furniture
found in the ash, the rare woods and metals—a palace built at
such expense would not have been so soon abandoned. And
those who devastated it with fire would not have done so, surely,
if it had not been occupied by the hated Assyrian. But Ashurbanipal had not lived to see this devastation; he had died in 627, or

so it was generally believed. Then who had died here in the flames?

The questions revolved in his mind morning after morning as the light slowly strengthened in his room. He knew the answers could only be found by further search. And the railway was drawing nearer day by day.

Driven by these stresses, he took to walking out to the mound early, before it was fully light, as if he might notice something, perhaps some small clue hitherto overlooked. And some days after his dinner table argument with Elliott this actually happened, though the light that was shed was far from sudden.

It was close on sunrise when he reached the site, the time of morning when he had seen the dust of Jehar's party as it approached, heard from him that the bridge had finally spanned the river. But this time he did not pause to look westward toward the glittering streamlets of the Khabur and the distant fields of pitch but skirted the mound and climbed the long slope to the summit on the eastern side, where they had made the recent finds.

He had never stood here alone at this hour before, and the configuration of the land, in this early light, seemed strangely unfamiliar. The sheds and warehouses of the railway people seemed closer than ever this morning. The offices intended for the clerks and technicians, still no more than timber frames, lay beyond these, and beyond again lay the first houses of the village, half a mile away, suffused in a thin mist; he could make out lights here and there.

There were no lights, no sign of any human presence, in the railway buildings, no guard or caretaker to be seen anywhere, though he thought there must be one. The construction workers and those in charge of them would be asleep still in their billets in the village. Useless to deceive himself; worse than useless, stupid. The buildings were makeshift, but their proximity was not accidental: The Germans would know, none better, where the rails were to be laid . . . Once again, from somewhere far distant, far beyond the verge of sight, he seemed to hear the repeated sound of metal striking on metal. He raised his hands to his temples, which were throbbing slightly, and the sounds ceased as if he had closed his ears to them. At this moment the sun rose above the low hills at his back, and the first rays fell across the slopes of the mound, lower down, where the ground leveled. He saw then what he had never seen before, the rough shape of a circle, darker against the biscuit color of the earth, as if it still held within it the dampness of the night.

He did not these days altogether trust the evidence of his senses. If his sight could be troubled by that flickering, like flames or the moving teeth of a saw, it might also present him with shapes of shadow that were not truly there. He blinked hard, thinking it a trick of the slanting sunlight; he had walked over this slope a hundred times and seen nothing of this sort. But when he opened his eyes it was still there, quite clear in outline.

Like a man moving at some other's behest, he began to make his way down the slope. Where the ground leveled, where the rock lay below the earth, it had been. But already, before he reached the foot of the slope, he could make it out no longer, see no slightest indication of a shape designed, nonaccidental, among the whitish limestone that showed here and there like patches of pale scalp amid the yellowish mixture of sand and gravel. After perhaps ten minutes of fruitless search he returned to the summit, to the exact point where he had stood before. Strain his eyes as he might, he could see no sign of the shape; it had vanished as if it had never been.

Voices carried to him from the houses of the village. Elias and Halil would be here before long, and Palmer, probably accompanied by Patricia. Soon afterward the workpeople would begin to arrive. Once more he strained to see. There was nothing; the earth was a uniform brownish yellow, marked only by the outcrops of rock. He hesitated a moment longer, then began again to descend. As he did so he saw Elliott and three others come into view, mounted on horseback. They were heading, he knew, toward the fields of bitumen that lay some miles in a northerly direction, invisible from here, not yet touched by the sun. He watched them until they disappeared into the haze of morning.

10.

Each morning, armed with rifle and revolver, accompanied by his interpreter and two men from the village, also armed, Elliott set off on horseback for the fields of bitumen that glittered a somber welcome to him as he drew near. For a time that could not be measured, before there existed beings able to measure time, this seeping had continued: the slide of oil from below the sealing rock, the spreading acreage of swamp.

The source might be far away from the borders of the pitch; oil could migrate many miles before flanking the belt of shale or clay that held it trapped. He had to find clues to the direction of the flow, the whereabouts and porosity and depth of the underlying reservoir rock. Color was some indication of this, though far from entirely trustworthy; the fresher, more recent flow would be paler, sometimes yellowish against the darkly weathered older pitch.

He was proposing, with the help of his escort, who would lay aside their rifles to take up picks and shovels, to dig exploration wells and so obtain a cross section of the surface rock. Digging was not drilling; it was in keeping with his role of archaeologist. But for the time being, in these early days, he contented himself with the study of hand specimens and some scraping of the sedimentary limestone just below the surface. He kept a lookout for fault lines in the beds of sealing rock where oil or water might have gathered; over the millions of years since its formation, under the stress of pressure and heat, the rock would have buckled in places, crumpled into deep folds where oil or gas or a combination of the two might have accumulated.

He returned from these explorations with the eager anticipation of talking about them to Edith Somerville. He left for his fieldwork early in the morning, as soon as it was light, timing his return, as far as he possibly could, to arrive well before Somerville and Palmer were back from the excavation, which was generally well after sundown. Patricia nowadays almost always accompanied them, partly because she had become increasingly interested in the discoveries being made, mainly because she wanted to be where Palmer was. So usually—and it was a source of obscure disappointment to Edith and distinct vexation to Elliott if it proved otherwise—he would find her alone, and they would have an hour or so together.

It was remarkable, and might have been demonstrated on a graph, the rise in the frequency of their encounters, which both, however, still chose to regard as accidental, and in the amount of time these occupied. On one occasion he remained at the house for part of the morning to study the rock specimens he had brought back with him and make notes on them, and she brought coffee to him and they talked together while he drank it. Sometimes after dinner they would find themselves alone for a short while, though without conscious contrivance, on Edith's part at least—time for a smile to be exchanged and a few words to be spoken. But the regular time of their meeting was in the late afternoon; they would have tea together, just as on the day of Elliott's arrival. Quite soon this taking of tea together took on the quality of a ritual, with Elliott mainly talking and Edith mainly listening.

The preponderance was natural; he was by far the more loquacious. But he asked her questions about herself, and these she was usually reluctant to answer. Concerning her married life she said practically nothing at all, and he construed this restraint as a mark of discontent, though without really understanding it; she did not express energy of feeling through eager words or vivacity of manner like the American women he had known, but through a sort of charged reticence, which was new to him and full of erotic challenge. It was curious, it was intriguing, that she should seem less than happy without betraying the fact by any sort of remark save the most indirect. It was as if she were waiting with an assumption of nonchalance—and this could harden into hauteur if she was pressed too closely—for something, someone, to compel her to frankness, force an admission from her, make her expose herself to damage by declaring it.

About the years before, her girlhood, when she still lived with her parents, she would talk more, particularly about her father, the QC, his defense of the underdog, how much he had been admired and respected for his generosity and his passion for justice, how he never undertook a defense unless he firmly believed his client was innocent of the charge against him, how he would accept lower fees or even waive his fee altogether if he thought it was a deserving case.

He had got rich all the same, Elliott thought, with a skepticism that came mixed with immediate dislike for this phony philanthropist. Defending the underprivileged had paid off. She had been born to money; it was written all over her. She had never felt the ache of poverty and deprivation—not like himself, ragged-trousered and sometimes hungry, son of a settler on a homestead in Oregon. Naturally he gave no expression to these thoughts, even contriving nods of the head and looks of admiration. Concealment had always come naturally to him. He wanted her, and this gave him a tact that he might otherwise not have summoned, a tact indistinguishable in his mind from considerations of strategy, similar to the feeling that made him avoid glancing too frequently at the line of her bosom or the reclination of her limbs as she sat opposite him.

Her eyes shone when she spoke of her father and her life at home. Her mouth, which was wide but delicately molded, softened with tenderness, and she held her head up and looked to Elliott altogether beautiful and regal. Her father was a great storyteller in addition to everything else; he had told her a lot of stories when she was a little girl, he made them up as he went along, he could make anything into a story. There was one she remembered about a wolf called Cuthbert, who had a bad name, quite undeservedly.

"Well," Elliott said, "I guess wolves are much maligned." He had shot wolves as a boy, in winter, to keep them off the hogs, but he said nothing of this. He wondered whether she had sat in the QC's lap for these stories and how old she had been when they were discontinued. But these were not questions anyone could ask; and in any case she did not want those days, that paradise of an indulged childhood, from which he suspected she had never really emerged, subjected to questions; it was inviolable. Instead he talked to her about his activities of the day, though taking care to give nothing much away.

He began this way at least; but Edith had only a limited interest in source rock analysis, and the limits soon showed in a certain vacancy of expression that would descend on her. It was stories she liked—just as much as ever it seemed; it was the marvels of geology that made her face light up, and for this reward Elliott was more than ready to supply them. In North America, beneath the Great Plains, fossil remains of marine creatures had been found. Just imagine, five thousand miles from the sea, at altitudes of four thousand feet, they had found fossils of sea creatures, among them the giant reptile *Mosasaurus*. Had she heard tell of this unfriendly fellow? You can look today at the rock print of a monster that has been extinct for millions of years, that lived and feasted when these rocks were being formed on the floor of the sea. Imagine the power that tumbled these rocks from the seabed and thrust them up so high. At Los Angeles, where oil seeped to the surface and its volatile elements evaporated, a vast lake of pitch was formed and sheets of water gathered above it and the ancestors of Cuthbert the Wolf came to drink there and died there, trapped in the swamp of pitch. No one could tell how long this oil had been leaking. Among the skeletons they found while extracting the pitch were some belonging to *Smilodon*, the saber-toothed tiger, another ugly customer. *Smilodon* had ceased to inhabit the earth fifty thousand years ago . . .

Always, as he talked, his own sense of the miraculous came to him, informed all his words and gestures. To be here in this place at this time, to know oneself for the product of those inconceivably ancient travails of fostering earth . . . He was wooing the woman before him with marvels, this he knew, knew also that he was making headway, knew it from the quality of the attention she gave him, the way her eyes rested on his face as he related to her the phases of the globe, the gaseous, the liquid, the long consolidation. But he had no sense of exploiting this wonder of hers, because he so totally shared it; he was himself in thrall to these marvels, had been so from earliest manhood: the furnace at the heart of the world, the cataclysms of earthquakes and the secret paths of their vibration, the amazing tumult of volcanoes. When he described to Edith how the deposits of oil and gas had been formed from plants and creatures that had once been in the world, had lived and died and coagulated together for millions of years, and then for more millions had been subject to heat and pressure beyond human imagining, he was lost in the wonder of it, and she, needing always something less abstract, more touchable, thought of seaweed and eels and seahorses crushed into a paste, imagined some remote and mysterious animal breathing its last on the floor of the sea, adding its body to the great host of bodies that were slowly being squeezed and melted together to make the oil.

Elliott, the better to illustrate this long, hot grip of the rock, raised his hands and clenched his fists as if they too held that creative fire. His blue eyes burned; his voice came in bursts of rhetoric. Daimler, she heard him say. The first Mercedes. The Model T. A million registered automobiles in 1913, in the

United States alone. You could say good-bye to steam. It was fuel oil now, fuel oil in the boilers of the factories, trains, ships. He leaned toward her, his body tense with the vision of it. They were producing eighty million barrels a year now in the state of California. That vast and astounding upheaval, that unimaginable heat, designed by Providence to bring this great boon to humanity. A billion-dollar industry. Already the lives of millions of Americans had been transformed. It could happen here too, right here. The desert could be made to bloom, a new golden age ushered in. Where now there were just a few wandering characters on camels, living in tents and shooting at strangers, there would be highways, industries, spacious brick-built houses with front lawns and efficient plumbing and regular garbage disposal facilities.

Once more in London, in his Park Lane mansion, Rampling began to give serious consideration as to what to do about the traitorous Elliott.

There was much else to claim his attention at the time. A meeting was planned for early April to discuss among other things the further financing of the Baghdad Railway and the route it was to take. Germany and Russia and Austro-Hungary, as well as France, would be sending representatives to this, and the financial group Morgan Grenfell, of which he was an associate, would have a considerable part to play in the negotiations and needed to be well primed as to the conditions of British involvement. There were also to be preliminary discussions sometime in April at government level, between Britain and France, though very few knew of this and agreement about time and place had been delayed for reasons of secrecy, the subject being the delicate one of settling the territorial lines to be drawn between the two powers in the Near East in the event of war and consequent dismemberment of the Ottoman Empire. Some progress had been made: It was agreed in principle that the French should have Syria, and the British the land between the Two Rivers. But they were still at loggerheads over Mosul and the oil fields of northern Mesopotamia.

So he had enough to engage him without double-dealing geologists. But the business of Elliott's duplicity rankled with him. He had been hoodwinked; that was the only word for it. The thought was unwelcome to him. That he never fully trusted anybody did nothing to mitigate his displeasure, nor did the knowledge that there was no one to blame but himself; it was he who had made the appointment, there was no denying that, though of course there had been glowing recommendations. It was precisely the source of these recommendations that troubled him now; they had all come from high-ranking officials of Standard Oil. If Elliott was so much lacking in basic morality as to double his fee in this way, he might easily have tripled it by making some agreement with the Americans before leaving; if so, it would probably be with the Chester Group, which had lately been increasingly active in seeking concessions in the region. And then there was the further possibility that as an American he intended to favor these people by falsifying his reports to the others. With a delinquent character like that one could not be sure of anything.

It was a moral issue really. It was a question of what could be regarded as pardonable. There were degrees in everything, balance and moderation in good as in ill. But Elliott's turpitude went beyond all bounds. It was pardonable, it was even meritorious, for a man who was really a geologist to pose as an archaeologist in order to explore for oil on behalf of the British government. In lands not under British rule imposture was necessary before the activity could be carried out at all; and it was an activity that would bring profits to individuals, certainly, but that would ultimately add to the power and wealth of Britain, enhance her prestige, maintain her ability to rule the waves and enable her to extend the bounds of empire. These were worthy aims, and Elliott, though an American, had made them his own at the moment of accepting his fee and signing the contract. Quite otherwise were the greed and perfidy he had displayed in accepting a fee from the Deutsche Bank, and possibly also from an American cartel, to do the same job. This was to strike a blow at the foundations of commercial practice on which European civilization was based; the man had doubled, possibly trebled his reward while reducing practically to zero the value of his reports, even if they proved to be genuine; there was little advantage in obtaining advance information if it was to be shared among all the interested parties.

There was only one thing to do with Elliott, a solution urged equally by justice and logic. Too much was at stake to be sentimental about it. He would hardly have had time yet to do much in the way of compiling reports, let alone communicating them. If someone could be sent now, at once, he might get there in time. He could carry a letter under government seal, authorizing him to take into his care whatever notes the American had made, any maps or indications of findings. These once secured, he could arrange for something to happen to Elliott. The Arabs of the desert fringe were given to shooting at strangers; not much in the way of bribes would be needed. Or he could be shot and the Arabs given the blame. But who to employ in the business? Time would be saved if it were a local man, someone recruited by the British Resident at Baghdad, for example, or a professional assassin from Aleppo or Damascus. But this would leave too much to chance. No private agent could be fully trusted; being mercenary, he would be lacking in the spirit of service, probably, and without much in the way of patriotic feeling. Besides, there would be the danger of blackmail. Someone from the Secret Service, perhaps. But on what pretext, in what disguise could they get him to a remote archaeological site in Mesopotamia? And it would take too long to arrange things, to obtain his release; the red tape in that department could be measured in miles. No, it would have to be an army man, someone in military intelligence, used to taking orders, with a sense of honor, who knew Arabic, if possible knew the terrain, might even have been in the region before, someone whose arrival would not arouse much question.

He resolved to ask for the help of Johnny Westerfield at the Ministry of Defense, who owed him a favor from some years back when he had underwritten a deal between the ministry and a civil contractor for the sale of provisions to the army, five hundred tons of stewing steak, obtaining very favorable terms on the grounds, naturally not made public, that the meat had passed the date by which it was due to be consumed, though by less than a week, a purely technical matter.

Somerville was unable to investigate the mystery of the vanishing circle any further on the following day. It was the time of the month when the wages of the workpeople fell due, and the nearest banking agency they had been able to establish was at Shiritha, a full day's journey from Tell Erdek, necessitating a strong escort, an overnight stay, and a late return home next day.

After dinner on the day of his departure, Elliott walked about in the courtyard for a while in the light of the lanterns set in the walls. He smoked two cheroots in the course of this, and then he saw what he had been hoping to see. Edith came out, though it seemed she did not intend to linger there long; the night air was cool, and she still wore the white cotton dress she had worn at dinner, with nothing over her shoulders.

He came forward to meet her and spoke at once, without any preliminary greeting, as soon as he was near enough. "If you have a mind to ride out tonight, later on, there is something I think it would interest you to see."

"What is that?" she said.

"I'd like it to be a surprise. Will you come?"

"You mean, alone, just the two of us?"

"Yes."

Edith hesitated for a long moment, aware that her breathing had quickened. Then she laughed, but less certainly than she had intended and would have wished. "You can't be serious," she said, knowing he was. She could see little of his face, which was in shadow, but there was a lantern on the wall behind him, and light from it lay slantwise on his head and gleamed on his blond hair like a halo worn at a rakish angle. "You must be mad," she said. "In the middle of the night?" It was unprecedented, imprudent in just about every way it could be.

"You see it best in the dark," he said.

"It must be quite something."

He made no reply to this but stood there still and attentive. And this attentiveness of his, this silent waiting on her unwisdom, seemed suddenly to Edith like the waiting that had attended on her all her life and had always been disappointed, the gathering for a plunge she had never made. "In the middle of the night?" she said again. There would be people about, there was Hassan at the gate . . .

Some tutelary spirit, the god of schemers, kept Elliott from speech now. If he had tried to persuade her, if he had begun to urge his case, she would have found reasons for refusing. But he kept her in silence, and in this silence exhilaration swept through her. "Yes, all right," she said. "Why not?"

In the agitation of her feelings she barely comprehended the rest of what was said. They would meet at midnight in the compound beyond the courtyard, where the stables were. They could leave by the gate of the stockade that enclosed the compound. This gate was barred from inside by a wooden bolt. They would have to leave it unbolted, but no one would notice any difference, not at that hour. If they were quiet they would not be seen. She was to wear dark clothes, something to cover her head. It was a clear night; they would see well enough by starlight; he knew the way.

On this they parted. Edith waited through the time in her room. At intervals she thought she would not go, but each time, after the voice of caution, there came that slightly breathless, reckless sense that she was awaited, expected, not just by Elliott but by all the presences in the night outside. Well before midnight she changed into jodhpurs and a jersey of black wool and wrapped a dark scarf around her head. And after this change of clothes she had no more second thoughts about going.

Elliott was waiting in the compound. He had already saddled two horses, both blacks. He showed no sign of gladness that she had come, as if he had never been in any doubt about it. She saw that he had a rifle slung over his shoulder and a cartridge belt across his body. Together they led the horses out and, at a distance of some yards, mounted.

He had been right; the stars gave light enough to see the track. He rode ahead at an easy pace, she following behind. As the night closed around them, her excitement, the sense of escape, grew less; she was not afraid, but she felt the enormity of what she was doing, the departure from all custom and propriety.

The rhythm of the riding, the faint light in which no landmarks could be distinguished, combined to take from her all measurement of time. At one point she thought she could make out, in the distance, paler levels that might have been floodwater, and some time after this the need for silence lessened for a while because the outcry of frogs filled the spaces of the night, a sound at once multiple and single, like a vast, protracted belching after some unimaginably rich feast.

They veered away, began to mount a long slope toward higher ground. The clamor of the frogs grew less. Above her, above the crest of the rise, Edith saw that the sky was lit with a fan-shaped rose-violet glow. She could hear the frogs still, but the sound was different now, more murmurous, like a sort of droning or humming, seeming to rise and fall. The glow of light was low in the sky, and it too was not steady but dilated and shrank as if in time to this chorus. Elliott dismounted well below the summit at a ridge of rock where they could tether the horses. They went the rest of the way on foot, scrambling now and again, disturbing loose shale. She saw now that the flare in the sky varied in color also, though only slightly; there was a sort of pulsing or throbbing in it, from violet to saffron to pale rose. The sound was not being made by the frogs: it came from somewhere beyond the crest, it sounded like singing.

The ground flattened as they drew near the top. Elliott lay prone here, full length, and motioned her to do the same. From this position he began edging up the last few feet, and she followed him. The singing was louder now. The rocks they were looking down over were lit by a warmer light than could have come from the stars. She heard Elliott utter a low exclamation. He spoke close to her ear as she drew level with him: "Keep your head down. I didn't bargain for this."

She covered the last few inches and looked down. The breath caught in her throat. Below them the ground fell away steeply to a rocky plateau. Close to the center of this a cone of fire rose into the sky, gushing rainbow colors, showering fiery particles that lived only briefly. The amazing energy of the flames, the way they wavered and swayed to currents she could not feel took all her attention in the first moments, but then she saw that there were figures surrounding this pulsing column of light, moving in a circle, now forward, now back. Elliott spoke again, muttering close to her face: "I didn't bargain for people down there. I saw it in the daytime, there was nobody. Alawi learned of it and told me, that's my interpreter. Thank God I heard the singing, we might have had our heads blown off."

She scarcely heeded him. The sparks were like seeds, she thought, like a sperm of fire that died in the air. The people were dressed in white, and they were singing or chanting as they moved. The voices seemed to pulse in time to the flames, so that they were the same thing, voices and fire. It was like nothing she had ever seen before, a living thing, frightening and beautiful, with a shape that was constant yet endlessly blurred with change. She saw how it softened as it fused with the surrounding air, rose and fell back, ended in a zone that was neither fire nor sky, a co-rona of light.

"Fire worshipers, thrown in free of charge," Elliott said in low tones. "It is an escape of gas, you know."

His face was very close to her own; she felt the warm breath of his words on her cheek. The daring of it all, the dangers of the escapade, the shock of the fire, came to her now in a wave of re-action, made her tremulous, loosened her limbs. "I don't think I've ever seen anything so beautiful," she said. "How would it start? I mean, what would make it start to burn like that?"

"Anything could do it, any accidental spark. It comes out as a mixture of oil and gas—very inflammable. Or perhaps a flash of lightning. This one is quite recent, they tell me. They can go on forever, once they start. I thought you might like to see it." He paused a moment, then said, "Perhaps we'd better go, we are not so very safe here."

But she did not move and did not draw away from him and

after a moment he kissed her cheek and the side of her neck and she turned her face to him so as to be kissed on the mouth. She saw him move back to unsling the rifle and take off the cartridge belt. Then his arms were around her and she still saw the fire through closed eyes, and the beauty of the fire was in everything she felt and did.

11.

◈

"To tell you the truth, I am rather worried about Somerville,"
Palmer said. "He is behaving strangely, I can't make him out."

He and Patricia were sitting in the common room at opposite sides of the fireplace, where a fire of wood scraps and dried
camel dung was burning. They were grateful for it—the evenings
were cold still—and they were glad to be sitting here together,
talking companionably, with the house quiet around them and
no one else about. Also conducive to talk was the fact that they
were sitting at some distance apart; if too close together—and
alone—they would fall to embracing and kissing, and this was
good but also frustrating, as it could go no further for the time
being. Palmer, whose studies had not left him much time for girl-
friends in the past, had believed at first that this ache of unsatis-
fied desire was entirely his, entirely male, and he had admired
Patricia even more than before when she, in her capacity of
modern young woman who did not mince words, had informed
him that the symptoms might be different in women but were no

less physiological. Now, as he looked across at her, at the mobile features that changed with her thoughts, the generous mouth, the eyes full of life and intelligence, he thought once again how lucky he was. "It's very unsettling," he said, and for a moment or two he was not sure whether he meant his worries about Somerville or the desire to lay hands on Patricia.

"Why is that?"

"Well, his mind seems to be somewhere else half the time—he looks as if he is watching or listening to something. He is secretive too, in a way. I mean, take tonight for example. He comes back late from collecting the money for the wages. He's been riding all day and he is completely fagged out. Then he tells me he wants me to go with him to the mound at crack of dawn tomorrow morning because he wants me to look at something. He doesn't tell me what it is. All he will say is that he wants me to be up there, already standing up there at sunrise." He glanced at his watch. "That's about six hours' time," he said. "Hardly worth going to bed."

Patricia smiled at him. He didn't like early hours, she knew that, but it didn't matter because she didn't mind them. Once she was awake she wanted to be up and about. When they were living together, she would get up, she would start things moving . . . "I don't think he is very well," she said. "In his state of mind, I mean. He looks feverish to me, quite done up. He needs looking after, and Edith doesn't exactly excel in that department, does she?"

"Then there is this business of the line. He doesn't talk about it anymore, but he is convinced that the line is going to go smack through the dig. I mean, the Germans are not fools, are they? Why should they take on a gradient like that when they can

stay on the flat? I think he honestly believes that they are intending to use dynamite on it and flatten it out that way. Why should
they? What is to stop them going round the other side of the village? It's a matter of half a mile, if that. I just can't understand
why he is so pessimistic about it."

Patricia was silent for some moments. She was in love with
Harold, and she admired him too: his steadiness, his kindness of
heart, his brand of vigilant skepticism, a sort of critical acuteness
in which there was no malice, the lightness with which he bore
his very considerable learning. But *pessimism,* at a time when
Freud and his circle in Vienna were publishing papers on patho-
logical states both individual and collective! No, she couldn't let
it pass. She wanted him to be a success, and she was ready to help
him. But she also wanted to be a success herself, and success began at home, like charity: It lay in the freedom to differ, even to
reprove and correct, and this was something that had to be established early.

"I know you are fond of John," she said. "You got on well
from the start, didn't you? I think your concern for him is making you take a rather superficial view." She saw some startlement
come into his eyes; it could not be often that he was accused of
this. "It's natural enough," she said quickly. "It makes you reluctant to think that there might be something more seriously amiss
with him. I mean, when you talk about pessimism, you are imply-
ing it is a sort of mood, something he can be jollied out of. But
this is something more than that: He has convinced himself without much in the way of evidence. That's another way of describing obsession. You can't be so easily jollied out of an obsession,
can you?"

"You mean he believes he is a victim preordained, that the bomb is aimed at him?"

"Something like that. I don't know how people get into that state, it's a mystery of the psyche."

Palmer reflected for a while. "I think you are probably right," he said, much to her relief without animosity. "Right about me and about John. I hadn't wanted to think along those lines because it amounts to saying that in his heart he actually wants to be wiped out, and that is slightly mad."

"Not so much that he wants it, but he feels that it is certain to happen, that something has been set in motion that can only end in destruction, that it gathers pace whatever anyone can do and it's coming straight for him. I don't know if you would call it mad. A lot of people in Europe must be feeling like that these days."

There was a look on her face now that Palmer recognized, combative, ready to deal with hecklers—her speechy look, as he called it to himself. He didn't dislike it, it belonged to her, but it brought out a spirit of contradiction in him; he had a constitutional distrust of large statements. Patricia saw him screw up his mouth and narrow his eyes in an expression she was destined to see quite often. "I think you are piling it on a bit," he said. "John Somerville as the soul of Europe?"

"You think it is far-fetched? Perhaps you are right. But John is a sensitive man, and it must be distressing to be living at a time when people like him—and like you too—people trying to put things together, make sense of things, add to the sense of human community, are facing a contrary spirit of dismemberment and destructiveness that is terribly strong and pervasive. It is a kind of brutality that goes under the name of realism, and it is alive and well in Britain. You can call it the spirit of commerce, or the spirit of empire, or the élan vital. At Cambridge I made a special study of the Whig administrations of the mid-nineteenth century and their dealings with Belgium and Russia, and what Lord Palmerston said during his time as Foreign Secretary has always stayed in my mind. I've forgotten a lot of the stuff but not that. 'There are no longer permanent principles, only permanent interests, and we pursue these to the exclusion of all else.' That's more than half a century ago, but nothing has changed."

Her face, which was normally pale, had flushed with the warmth of the fire and the force of her feelings. "Except that the politicians are more hypocritical now," she said. "At least he was honest. I mean, a railway can serve permanent interests, but it is hard to see how archaeology can."

"Unless a museum is a permanent interest," Palmer said. "Must get to bed. Perhaps the first rays of tomorrow's sun will bring some enlightenment. I love you, and that serves an interest that I hope will be permanent."

Not much later, taciturn, unshaven, rather disheveled-looking, he was there by Somerville's side at the summit of the mound. He had needed to be roused from sleep and he felt stupid and he was missing his morning coffee, which there had been no time for. And in this state of discomposure, which the walk there had done little to improve, his concern for Somerville found expression in feelings of irritation. He was fed up, he told himself, with these vagaries, with what seemed increasingly erratic behavior on the other's part, the irregular hours he kept, his wanderings about the place, his nonappearance at meals, his frequent habit of raising his head as if listening to something, some distant sound. They were onto something here, Palmer knew that. These latest discoveries could lead to something really important. Already they had broken new ground; they would be able to demonstrate that this had been an Assyrian township, that the great king Esarhaddon had issued proclamations from here at the apex of Assyrian power. If they were given time to go on, if they were able to finish the season's digging, more, much more, might be found. They should be getting on with it in proper order instead of standing here in the cold morning air waiting for some occult revelation.

He turned his head to look at his companion in a way that was deliberately interrogative, though without saying anything. The German railway buildings lay directly below them, still seeming half shrouded in night. There had been no unusual activity there of late, no sign that the track was imminently expected. After all, he reasoned, construction of the line had begun in 1903, and that was eleven years ago now. The work had been subject to long delays from the very beginning; surely they could expect to have three months more to work on the site. If more inscriptions of that degree of importance were found, and he was able to decipher them, he might make a name for himself here. All the same, he would be glad when the time came to return to England. Somerville was no longer a comfortable man to work with. And then there was Patricia; they were planning to marry in the autumn.

Still no words were exchanged between them. Somerville

stood without moving, looking straight before him down the slope. We are like two devotees, Palmer thought, waiting for the sun god to give us a sign. Hereabouts Assyrian priests would have stood, waiting with their incantation to the sun. He had risen every day, all through their lives, yet still he needed to be begged to return once more and illuminate the life of mankind . . .

The light was changing, warming, though the sun was not yet visible, as if the sky were in a glow of expectation. This took on a brief ruddiness as the rim showed, then drained paler. Then there was no color at all, only a spreading brightness.

Utu in Babylonian; Shamash in Akkadian—it was under this name that the Assyrians would have prayed to him. Palmer remembered phrases from the Great Hymn to the sun god. *Dispeller of darkness, brightener of gloom, all monsters of the deep behold his light.*

"There," Somerville said loudly. He pointed down the slope. "I knew it." There was exultation in his voice. "Down there, where the ground levels."

Palmer looked where the finger pointed and saw a shape roughly circular, four or five feet in diameter, perceptibly darker than the surrounding earth, as if still retaining some damp of night.

"You go down," Somerville said urgently. "I'll stay up here and keep it in view. You won't see it from close, but I'll give you directions from here. Put a pile of gravel or small stones, anything you can get hold of, in the center. We'll have to be quick, we only have about ten minutes."

Palmer did as instructed. He could see nothing when he got down there. The circular shape had vanished completely; the earth was one indeterminate yellow-brown, caked with drought. He looked up to where Somerville stood above him, on the summit, shouting already. He strained his ears to listen.

"Come forward towards me," Somerville shouted. "About six paces. *Six paces.* Good God, what kind of paces are those? Now a little to your right. To your *right,* man, directly to your right. Stop!" He held up his right arm like a policeman stopping traffic. "You're there," he shouted. "Mark the spot."

By the time Palmer had made a pyramid of stones and retraced his steps to the summit the outlines of the shape were no longer so clear. And in the succeeding minutes they disappeared altogether, leaving the two of them looking down at a small heap of stones.

"We must set a guard there," Somerville said. "We must make sure no one displaces the stones before we can get to work."

"Get to work? How do you mean? It might be accidental. The circle is a shape you find in nature. A subsidence of the ground, some operation of water below the surface—"

"It is only when the sun's rays fall at a certain angle. And then only for a few minutes. At all other times the ground looks entirely uniform. What shape in nature would behave like that?"

"I don't understand what makes it visible at all, I mean ever. Why does the earth inside the circle look darker?"

"They must have gone straight down, through everything in their way."

In this early sunshine Somerville did not look at all well. His face had thinned over these recent days, his eyes seemed deeper in his head and had an unusual fixity of expression.

Doubts about his chief's state of mind returned to Palmer. "Who do you mean?" he said.

"The people doing the digging. Somewhere below they had to go through rock. They would have used baskets to pass the chips and splinters up to the surface as they went deeper, just as we do now. Then, when they filled up the pit again, some of this rock stuff must have been left round the mouth."

"I still don't see—"

"The stone from underground would have been darker. After three millennia, in spite of the weathering, it is still darker. Very slightly, of course, but the rays of the sun, when they fall at a certain angle, bring out the darker tint." Somerville paused for a moment and when he spoke again it seemed with a conscious effort to keep his voice dispassionate. "I can think of only one reason why people should want to dig vertically down like that. What we are looking at is the mouth of a tomb shaft."

On the evening before he left Jerablus for Tell Erdek, his great idea grown more compelling and brilliant, irresistible, as he hoped, to the Englishman, worth every gurush of the hundred gold pounds he intended to ask for, Jehar tried to tell Ninanna how much he desired her and how much he suffered for her sake, by means of a story—the best way, he had found, of making an impression on her mind. He chose a time when business was slack and she was at the yard door getting a breath of air and the uncle was busy in his shack, with the door bolted, counting the takings. There were not many places inside this shack where things might be hidden; Jehar suspected that the uncle did as he

himself did with his rifle and kept the money concealed somewhere under the loose boards that covered the floor. He had
sometimes thought of breaking in and trying to find it, but not
any longer now; his new idea was far better.

Ninanna had taken off her long calico apron and thrown
back the scarf she wore over her hair while serving. The sun was
low and shone directly onto her as she stood there, gleaming on
her hair and brows and on the long-skirted cotton dress that was
loose at the waist but still revealed the shapeliness and sturdi-
ness of her body, the surge of her breasts and the curve of her
hips. The light that shone on her came through manifold impu-
rities of air—the acrid haze of the steam, the fumes of kerosene
lamps in the cabins of the engines, the smoldering heaps of refuse here and there along the sidings—but in Jehar's eyes it lay
on her like a primal blessing, like the light of God on the first
woman.

The story he told her was that of Kerem, the handsome son
of the Shah of Ispahan, who fell in love with the daughter of an
Armenian priest, a beautiful girl indeed and unfortunate in her
father, as the story would show. No, he was not her father, he was
her uncle . . . Jehar paused here, nodding significantly. "An evil
man," he said.

"What was the girl's name?"

"Her name was Aslihan. The priest, being a fanatical Christian, did not want her to marry a Muslim, even though Kerem
was a prince. But he was too afraid to refuse, so he gave his consent and named the wedding day. When the day came, there was
a royal procession through the city, with banners of crimson silk

and the music of golden trumpets. All the people of the town, dressed in their best, joined in this procession."

He paused again here, to enlarge upon the splendor of the procession, the sumptuous clothes, the richly caparisoned horses, swaying his head and spreading his hands to indicate the pomp of it all. But Ninanna, though not a girl much troubled by thought as such, was becoming more and more sensitive to stories, and she already had a premonition of the doom hanging over this match, a doom made all the more grievous for these colorful preliminaries.

"Something bad happened," she said.

"Kerem stopped the procession when they drew near the priest's house and went on alone to claim his bride. But he found the house deserted, all the doors swinging open. The priest had taken Aslihan and fled with her, no one knew where."

He made a break here for the sake of dramatic effect, and she waited in stillness, knowing this could not be the end of the story. "He went to look for her," she said at last.

"Yes, you are right. It is what I would have done in his place, though not a prince, not by birth at least. I would go to the ends of the earth for you, I would dare anything. Now this Kerem was a poet, a singer. He began to sing to the belongings of his beloved, her sandals, her embroidery frame, the coverlet of her divan, and they sang back to him. He wandered far and wide with his lute in the simple dress of a minstrel, asking news of Aslihan from hills and clouds and flying birds, and they answered him in song. After many adventures he found her in a town in Anatolia, a town called Sivas. He sang to the chief people of that town, and they were enchanted by his singing. They forced the uncle to give his niece to Kerem in marriage. But he was in league with Shaitan and versed in black arts. He fashioned a gown for Aslihan to wear on her wedding night with buttons that went from the neck right down to the hem of her skirt. Once she had put this gown on these buttons could not be opened, not by any means, not by anyone at all. Kerem took his magic lute and sang to the buttons, and in this way he succeeded in persuading them to open, one after the other, down to the bottom. But before he could remove the gown the top buttons started closing up again."

At this point Jehar looked at Ninanna in a lingering and expressive manner. "It was torture," he said. "It went on like that all night." All his own torment was in these words, all the times he had watched the girl moving about, the straight shoulders, the sway of the buttocks, the clear gaze of her eyes that would widen in wonder or laughter. How often he had cursed his own constancy, the fixity of his desire, just as Kerem must have done in his long search. Well, he had his idea now; the money would be his; *he* would not burn to death.

"The first light of dawn entered the bedchamber and he still had not succeeded in opening the gown. All night the fever of love had been burning in his veins and now it started turning to real flames. He gave one last sigh, fire burst from his mouth, his heart was burned to a cinder, and his whole body turned to ashes."

———

At a distance of one mile or so from where he thought the seepage of oil began, Elliott came upon a roughly circular, slightly sunken area of mingled earth and gravel, where the ground had apparently fallen in over a hollowed space below, whether natural or man-made. It seemed to be a fairly recent subsidence; the filling was compacted but still loose enough to be broken and shifted without too much trouble by the men with him, who, to add to the semblance of archaeological research, carried picks and shovels and grappling hooks and had leather baskets strapped to their backs.

After some hours of work they had succeeded in clearing a pit down to a depth of seven feet. It was narrow—no more than a yard or so across—but easily wide enough for a man to climb down into it, which Elliott now proceeded to do. It afforded him what he had been seeking for, a cross section of the rock formation immediately below the surface, to a shallow depth only, of course, and lacking in dimension, but possibly offering some clues nevertheless.

He was standing at the edge of the subsidence with his face against a wall of fractured limestone. The men had cleared away the earth and gravel that had lain against this, leaving it intact, though the picks had struck against it here and there, chipping a little of the surface and leaving whitish scars. Rock of this sort would be permeable enough to form a storage reservoir for oil, but the knowledge of this was no help in itself. The presence of oil could not be deduced merely from the presence of suitable reservoir rock. That would be too easy, Elliott thought; life is not like that.

His four companions stood looking down at him as if he were their captive. He became aware of a certain dampness in his feet. Glancing down, he saw that he was standing in a thin stream of water only just deep enough to lap against the uppers of his boots; a trickle of water was flowing down into this from a fissure low in the rock face against which he was standing, coming from goodness knew where, probably from a source far distant; this region of limestone would be riddled with underground watercourses—it was probably water that had caused this ground to subside in the first place.

There was a smell here, difficult to identify, not an earth smell. The stream at his feet, though very shallow, had a definite current; it disappeared into the rock at his back. The water was slightly milky in appearance. On an impulse he crouched down and wet his hands with it. He sniffed it first, then licked his wet fingers; it was heavily charged with salt. Nothing so surprising in that; the whole of this desert steppe between the tributaries of the Euphrates was dotted with salt springs.

He began hoisting himself up, seeking a toehold in the rock the more easily to do so. Two of the men came forward to help him. As he clambered out he saw something he had not noticed before, perhaps because the light had changed, perhaps because he was looking from a point slightly lower than usual. Immediately before him there was a rise in the ground, a very slight swelling that continued into the distance. It was not so much the incline itself—it was barely perceptible—as the look of smoothness in this slow curve, a look of uniformity, despite the greatness of the extent—two miles at least, he thought. It had the unbroken, organic appearance of a curve in some vast and sparse-haired human cranium.

When he was on his feet and standing straight, he looked again. The lay of the land seemed more fortuitous now, the rocks more scattered and random, but the sense of a single shape was still there. Through Alawi he gave the men instructions to build a pyramid of stones, high enough to be seen at a good distance.

12.

◈

The presence at Tell Erdek of a newcomer, another archaeologist, was naturally reported to Fahir Bey, the Ottoman commissioner who was following the progress of the excavation. Also reported to him, in considerable detail, were the movements and activities of this newcomer, and they did not strike him as altogether consonant with those of a bona fide archaeologist, at least not of the kind he had observed at work before. This man was wandering far and wide; he was spending all his time in areas where there were no configurations of ground that might indicate previous human habitation. The men who accompanied him had been separately questioned, though not the interpreter—that would merely have served to put the American on his guard; they professed not to know what he was seeking, and this might be true. He was paying them well, it was enough. Fahir felt sure, however, that one or two well-chosen questions would be sufficient to establish whether he was what he claimed to be; with this end in view he chose a day to ride over and make the newcomer's acquaintance.

By a rather singular coincidence the day he chose was also the day when Major Manning made a reappearance, accompanied as before by an escort of Shammar tribesmen, mounted and armed. He was still occupied with surveying and mapping the region, he explained, now officially commissioned to do so by Sir William Wilcox, in preparation for the important and extensive irrigation projects this great engineer had been appointed, with the full approval of the Ottoman government, to carry out in Mesopotamia.

So this evening, as darkness fell and the lamps were lit, it was, with the sole exception of Elliott, the same company that had sat down to dinner on the evening of the day when the piece of carved stone had been found, that depicting the guardian spirit of the Assyrian kings, which had first turned Somerville's attention to the eastern side of the mound, where they were digging now.

Fahir lost no time in expressing his doubts directly to the one who was the cause of them, a policy in the main determined by his paradoxical position of being able to admonish, even to threaten, and at the same time feeling essentially powerless. Mesopotamia was full of foreign spies and impostors, who should all be sent packing. But his government felt it unwise to offend the United States or the European powers, even in small matters—and what seemed small might not prove to be so—because the former had made large investments in Anatolia and the latter, by an agreement among them, determined the level of customs duties on imported goods and Turkey desperately needed an increase in these to help shore up her ailing finances. That his country, with its vast imperial possessions—one of the greatest and most enduring empires the world had ever seen—could not set its own customs dues and was regularly blackmailed on this account was a source of private humiliation and rage to Fahir, though he took care not to let this show when he was in the midst of infidel foreigners. As a member of the Young Turk movement he was an infidel himself, but a Muslim infidel, which was something very different to his mind.

His feelings of resentment, as always, took the form of a rather elaborate courtesy. "They tell me," he said, in his careful English, looking down the table at the American, "that you spend much time examining the surface of the ground. May I ask what it is that you are so earnestly searching for?"

"Sure you may," Elliott said amiably. "Surface indications are of first importance. The surface offers valuable clues as to where it might be profitable to start digging."

This seemed for a moment to Somerville, sitting at the head of the table, so audacious a statement of Elliott's true aims that his breath caught a little. He was not sure he had heard properly; the accent was not always easy, words of two syllables sometimes came out as only one. Had he said "drilling"? The last thing he wanted was for the man to be unmasked now; it would seem to Fahir that by acting as host to one he knew for an impostor he had made himself a partner in the illegal enterprise, which, in a certain way, of course, was true. Then, in addition to the inexorable advance of the railway, which plagued his days and haunted his nights and from which his only relief was the excitement of the discoveries they were making, there would be a squad of Turkish soldiers posted on the site, watching every move, getting in the way. But no look of triumph, no change at all had appeared on Fahir's face. His head was still inclined forward in the attitude of courteous attentiveness that always seemed ironic in him, like a parody.

"Well, yes," he said now, "forgive my ignorance, but what kind of clues would be so valuable? We have understood from our friend Somerville that this Tell Erdek was the site of an Assyrian royal palace in the time of the Sargon dynasty. Are you looking for further evidence of this?"

"No, sir, not at all," Elliott said. "I am not an Assyriologist. My colleagues"—and here he smiled benignly at Somerville—"sometimes tend to think the Assyrian presence in this region the only thing of interest, but there were other empires that preceded theirs. My area of expertise is the Hittite kingdom in the Late Bronze and Early Iron ages. Of course, it is well known that this kingdom was centered in Hattusas, which the Hittites knew as Hattusha, the site of the present village of Boğazköy in central Anatolia. Now that is a long way from here, a very long way. But it has to be borne in mind that at its fullest extent, in about 1180 B.C., their empire included most of Syria and all of Mesopotamia, down to Babylon. That is a very considerable extent, sir, very considerable. In fact the Hittites were here first—it was the Assyrians who took over from them. There are Hittite remains scattered all over this region."

He had spoken with an air of authority that secretly astonished everyone at the table but his questioner. Fahir raised his head. His face had lost all expression. He still persisted, however. "And what kind of remains would signify the presence of these Hittites?"

"Well now, that's a mighty interesting question. Some consider the Hittites to be the first people to work with iron and thus the first to enter the Iron Age. This is disputed, but obviously any surface traces that could bear it out would be of immense importance. Then again, they were famous for their skill in building and using war chariots. The period when they went from sheathing the wood in bronze to sheathing it in iron is fairly reliably dated, but reinforcing evidence is always desirable. The smallest scrap of metal can be vital in indicating where to take a closer look. Then there are fragments of clay tablets that often lie quite close to the surface. They may bear traces of inscriptions. The Hittites spoke an Indo-European language, as I am sure you know."

"Yes, of course," Fahir said. "May I ask who is employing you and financing these investigations? This is not mere idle curiosity on my part, you understand. I am required to furnish information of this sort in the reports I send to my superiors."

Elliott smiled and nodded with an appearance of full understanding. "I am fortunate enough to have ample funds of my own," he said. "I can indulge my passion independently. I consider it a great privilege and a great responsibility to be able to shed light on the past, to serve the interest of truth, to strive to add something to the sum total of human knowledge. An understanding of the past is of vital importance, not only for the way we live our lives now but for the way future generations will live theirs. As someone wiser than I has said, if we ignore the lessons of the past, we will be condemned to repeat our mistakes."

A silence followed on this, rather prolonged, broken by Major Manning, who spoke now for the first time and was clearly as unafraid of anticlimax as he was of practically everything else.

"There's a lot of stuff very close to the surface," he said. "For part of the way down here I followed the railway. The gravel they use for the bed of the track is full of broken pots."

He looked directly at the American as he spoke and gave him one of his thin, infrequent smiles, clearly friendly in intent. His words turned the talk toward the progress of the railway, and Fahir for one seemed glad of this. He had spoken to various people, including the German advance party near the excavation site. The general opinion was that the line would reach the site and pass beyond it within a fortnight.

Edith saw the lines of tension gather in her husband's face as he listened. But her regard dwelled mainly on Elliott, who was silent now and whose face wore a slightly amused expression. He was pleased with himself; he had come through with flying colors. Well before he got here he had chosen this limited field of knowledge, studied it, memorized some salient facts. He had really performed very well, she thought. Such care, such attention to detail, could only be admired. Daddy would have given the same sort of consideration to one of his cases. But it was not quite admiration that she felt now as she looked at him. The care he had taken had been in support of falsehood, a pack of lies, in fact. Was that the difference? But Alex was a man of vision, a man of fire. He was striving to unlock the secrets of the earth, Pluto's kingdom. Once embarked on a necessary deception he would bear it out, make it good, rejoice in the triumph of prevailing. Was not this better than to be like John, the victim of deception, the poor dupe?

Thus she struggled to preserve the idealism of the man who had made the gift of fire to her, but could not succeed altogether, not while his face still held that look of satisfaction. And it was this failure that gave a certain coldness to her manner when the time came to say good night to him.

In bed, before sleep came, she went on thinking about it. She heard her husband moving about in the next room and tried to fight off the pity for him that came with the memory of his face, so drawn with anxiety, at the dinner table. She had always hated the emotion of pity, when she felt it for others, when she felt herself the object of it; it was this that had made her draw back from Patricia, the note of pity she had heard, or thought she had heard, during their argument about voting rights for women. Pity was negative; it was defeat . . . She thought again of that little smile on Alex's face. It was more than relief at having passed the test; he had *enjoyed* outwitting Fahir.

He had been so earnest, so fervent. That blaze of sincerity in the blue eyes, that straight, unwavering regard, the voice that came in blurts, like the very throes of truth. But what struck her most in retrospect was the way he had spoken about the future of humanity, the benefits that would come to future generations. Not from oil this time but from a knowledge of Hittite war chariots. He had spoken with a conviction that had nothing to do with his knowledge of archaeology, was independent of it. It was as if, at a certain point, the mantle of prophecy fell on him, and then knowledge or ignorance, truth or falsehood didn't matter any longer. She remembered how he had clenched his fists as he spoke of the hot embrace of the rock, a sacred fire in a past so remote she couldn't imagine it, and how the same passionate awe had throbbed in his voice when he went on to speak about the present and the future, the statistics of production, the profits to be made. The same fire . . . It was in the puzzlement of this that she finally passed into sleep.

Elliott had noticed the more distant manner, the way her eyes did not quite meet his own when she bade him good night. He did not trouble himself too much as to what the cause might be; it could not be anything to do with him, he felt sure of that; he had been brilliant at the table, he had held his nerve, she should have been impressed. Women were subject to moods; the fact was well known. However, he took it for a sign that they would not be meeting that night; she would not be coming to him, entering his room and joining him in bed, hot with her own stealth and eagerness—it was quite a while since he had had a woman so ardent.

All the same, he did not mind, tonight, if she did not come. In a way he was glad of it. He wanted to have time to himself on this, one of the most important days of his life, as he felt it to be, a highlight in his career. His victory in the game with Fahir, that triumphant parade of knowledge, had been a sort of celebration, in a minor key, of the momentous discovery he had made earlier that day, about which, naturally, he had said nothing to anybody.

They had returned to the pyramid of stones on the following day. He had gone over that shallow rise, which was roughly oval in shape and covered something like a mile from north to south and perhaps half of that at its maximum width. As he tramped back and forth, the conviction had grown in him that it formed a single geological structure. His work party, who he knew had long ago decided that he was mad, he left to their own devices. His excitement had grown at the thought of what this formation might be. He had felt neither weariness nor any discomfort from the sun. Then today, in late afternoon, when the sun's rays were slanting low and shadows were long, he had ridden to a point some two miles beyond where the sweep ended. Here the ground rose fairly sharply to a rocky shelf. It was no more than a hundred feet in height, but standing here and looking back the way he had come, with the sun's rays slanting across, he saw beyond any doubt that it was a single unit he had been traversing, a single shape, a diapir.

How long he had stood there, as the realization came to him, he could not afterward recollect. Some massive formation of the rock had been forced up to pierce the surface, hardly perceptibly, like the slightest protrusion of the tongue between the lips. No, not quite like that: It had no crest or peak; it was a single shallow dome, the cap of rock that had formed over it. He remembered the water charged with salt, the taste of it on his fingers, the prevalence of salt springs everywhere. This great cylindrical mass pushing up from below, piercing the surface, could it be rock salt?

Conviction had grown as he thought about the dimensions of the thing. If it was a mile across on the surface, it could be five or six miles in depth below. Salt, being lighter in density than the surrounding rocks, was often forced up, but very rarely in quantities like this. He had read about salt domes but never seen one. They had been observed in various places, the Gulf of Mexico, the Zagros Mountains, southern Persia. But no prospecting had been done yet, none that he knew of. After the millions of years of heating and compression that had molded the dome and forced it up, the salt, in its rise, would have wrenched out of shape the strata containing the petroleum, forming perfect traps . . .

The excitement that had seized him in the afternoon as he stood looking down returned to him now, set him pacing backward and forward in his room. As always, a sense of the miraculous attended on him—the nearest he ever came to ethical feeling, though it transcended all notions of right or wrong. How many millions of years, how many floods and evaporations in the shallow sea that had once been Mesopotamia had gone to form these vast deposits of salt? In its slow, irresistible journey up to the surface, the salt would bend the layers of rock above it, bend them upward, forming pockets where oil and gas would collect, trapped along the flanks of the cone, between the salt and the enclosing rock. The dome-shaped cap of rock forced up to the surface, this could have formed a reservoir above the salt, where oil might gather. A lake of oil, not far below, easy to get at. Closer examination would be needed, but this would explain the oil seep, the swamps of bitumen . . .

He was disturbed in this excited reverie by a light tapping at his door. His first thought was that Edith had decided to visit him after all. But it was too early for this. He opened the door to find the British major at the threshold. Manning looked neat and spruce in a white shirt and white shorts and white stockings that rose just below the knee. There was about him a slight odor of what Elliott thought might be disinfectant soap.

"I hope it's not too late for a visit," he said, "but I am a great believer in prompt action."

"I guess that's the military training." Elliott stood aside for the major to enter. What kind of action could he mean? Perhaps it was hair lotion or the sort of thing one put on one's face after shaving. Could the major have shaved before coming to pay this visit? Could some glance or word of his own have been misunderstood, misinterpreted? The British picked up some kinky habits at those schools of theirs, that was common knowledge. The clipped mode of speech, the mannerism, noticed at dinner, of tightening the lips, causing the carefully trimmed, gingerish mustache to bristle slightly—was there some wrestling with impulse going on there? Better get him sitting down as soon as possible.

"Have a seat," he said, pointing to one of the two upright chairs at opposite sides of a small table, all the seating there was in the room. "Would you care for a drink? I've still got some of the Scotch left that I brought with me from London."

"Thank you, just a spot."

"Water?"

"No thanks, just as it comes."

Manning watched the American as he poured out the drinks. A tall man, steady-handed, moving easily on his feet, with a direct and open regard and a sort of shine about him, as if the light fastened on him, favored him in some way. No telling from appearances. That unblushing reference to London, scene of his treachery. This was the traitor who was working for two conflicting interests, two countries on the verge of war, and taking payment from both. Such baseness was hardly conceivable; it was beneath contempt. He felt more than ready to carry out the orders he had received; he felt it as a mission. He was on duty; it was why he had taken pains with his appearance, shaving and dressing carefully before his visit. "Well, cheerio, down the hatch," he said, raising his glass to Elliott, who had taken the chair opposite.

"Your very good health, sir," Elliott said, managing to infuse this accustomed phrase with accents of deep and heartfelt sincerity.

"Won't beat about the bush, don't believe in it, never have," Manning said. "I am the bearer of a letter from Lord Rampling, authorizing me to collect your interim report and convey it back to London."

"Interim report? I haven't made an interim report. I wasn't asked to make an interim report, not at this early stage. There must be some mistake."

"No mistake." Manning's right hand went to the breast pocket on the left side, unfastened the button, drew out a sealed envelope, and laid it on the table.

"No, I don't mean to doubt the genuineness of the letter . . ." Elliott paused a moment or two, then said more slowly: "No, I meant some confusion about the nature of my instructions." Looking across the table, he saw the major's mouth tighten in that slightly lopsided involuntary grimace. "I've not been here long enough to make a comprehensive report," he said. "All I've got are notes. How come you have been saddled with this business?"

"Well, by chance really. I was due to leave for Mesopotamia anyway. I know Arabic, and I know this region well. It seemed a good idea, you know, to pick up any papers you might have as I was passing by."

"Are you working for Lord Rampling?"

"Good heavens, no. I am a military man. I have specialized in cartography, and I have been detailed to carry out surveys and make contour maps of the region between the Belikh and the Khabur, preliminary to a major irrigation project to be carried out under Sir William Wilcox. You will have heard of him, no doubt."

"The engineer, yes."

"That's a very mild way of putting it. He is an international authority."

"Well, I don't know much about irrigation."

"The Wise Men come from the West now, you know. Once they came from the East, now they come from the West. I am quoting Sir William when I say that."

"Meaning he is one of the Wise Men?"

"Yes, so he is. And among the nations Britain is foremost in irrigation technology. We lead the world. In the absence of a report the letter authorizes me to take whatever notes you have so far accumulated."

Elliott made no immediate reply to this. Like most tricksters he was distrustful, and a certain suspicion had entered his mind while Manning was quoting the words of the wise Sir William. He had the definite impression that the major was acting a part and that he was not—unlike himself—a very good actor. The attempt at a friendly, easy manner had not succeeded. Of course, this did not necessarily mean that he was up to something; such attempts on the major's part would probably never be successful, whatever the circumstances, perpetually defeated in advance by the stiff movements of shoulders and head, the occasional nervous twitch of the face. All the same, there were things here that didn't quite add up. Manning seemed to want him to believe that picking up the papers was a casual matter, something he had been asked to do in passing, as a convenience, in the course of other business. If that was so, why the haste, why this visit rather unconventionally late on the first evening of the major's arrival?

"A little more Scotch?" he said.

"Just a drop. It's very good. Malt, isn't it?"

"Yes, that's right. Twelve years old. I see you know something about whiskey." Could the major be a fake? He was almost too good to be true, but that might be the reason he had been chosen. Like a double bluff . . . Could he be working for some other oil interests? The d'Arcy Group, for example, or Shell, or the newly formed French combine, the CFP. In that case, it would make good sense for them to try to get whatever information they could; it would save them time, put them a step ahead. "Perhaps I'd better see the letter," he said. "Not that I doubt your word, of course, but Rampling has placed a great deal of trust in me, not only in my capacity but in my prudence."

"Of course."

The wax seal had an official imprint; Rampling's sprawling signature lay below a clear and explicit authorization of the bearer to take possession of all written records so far made. Nothing obviously wrong with the letter, but there wouldn't be, would there? How could he know whether it was genuine? Easy enough to stick a bit of red wax on the flap. That stamp would be lying about on the desks of a hundred offices in Whitehall.

He had no specimen of Rampling's signature. His contract was with the Turkish Petroleum Company; Rampling's name appeared nowhere on it.

"I must keep possession of the letter," Manning said, holding out his hand for it, "until such time as the notes are handed over. The notes would suffice. In the absence of an interim report, I mean. They would help us to form a picture of the progress you have made to date." Notes, reports, it didn't really matter. His orders referred only to written records; once he had those, he would shoot Elliott, and that would be that, he could leave with a sense of duty done. No sign of guilt or confusion on the fellow's face, a hardened scoundrel if ever there was one.

"How can I make the report if I haven't got the notes?" Elliott said. "In any case, the notes by themselves would be of no use to anyone, they are only comprehensible to me. I use my own system of personal symbols. For the sake of security, you know. It's a kind of code. It wouldn't do for these papers to fall into the wrong hands, would it?"

"No, certainly not. How much time would you need? To get them into shape, I mean."

Elliott narrowed his eyes with an appearance of considering. "Well," he said, "to tell you the truth, there have been some important indications recently, just in the last few days, in fact, but I can't commit myself to a definite opinion without further checking. Then I would have to make a full summary of all the findings in the form of a written report, incorporating the maps and sketches I have made. I should say it will be a week at least before I am in a position to hand anything over."

"I see, yes."

Manning said nothing further for a while but stared down at his glass with a slightly frowning expression. In certain ways he was not the right choice for an assignment of this sort. He was too emotional, for one thing. And he had a rigid cast of mind that made him easily thrown out by the unexpected. He had not foreseen this present setback, and there was no provision for it in his orders. He had envisaged it as a cut-and-dried transaction: Convinced by the letter, Elliott would hand over his papers without demur; then, in the course of the next day or two, there would be an opportunity to follow him out to some lonely place, preferably at a time when he was busily occupied and therefore not on the lookout, and shoot him, making it look like the work of some trigger-happy Bedouin tribesman. He was an army Grade A marksman, and he was confident that in open ground with an unrestricted view he could kill Elliott with a single shot at four hundred yards. Now there was this complication. But it sounded as if the American was onto something. It was a patriotic duty to make sure that any information of value got back to the mother country. He could keep a close watch on this treacherous geologist, make sure no approaches were made to him by a third party. "All right then," he said. "There's no great hurry. I have a roving commission. I can afford to wait a few days."

"I sure am glad to hear you say that."

On this, Manning finished his drink, patted his mustache with a handkerchief he kept in the sleeve of his shirt, and stood up to take his leave with the best he could manage in the way of a smile.

For quite some time after his departure, Elliott remained where he was, standing motionless in the middle of the room. A new and more disquieting thought had struck him even as the door closed on the major. Supposing the letter was genuine, after all. In that case, what could it mean to be asking him for notes and reports at such an early stage? No previous mention had been made of any such requirements. It came back to his mind, but in a different light now, that attempt on Manning's part at an offhand manner, falsified by the haste and urgency he had not been accomplished enough to conceal. Had they got on to him somehow? He knew he had been watched in London, watched and followed. But he thought he had thrown pursuit off for long enough to call at the German Embassy undetected. Perhaps he had been mistaken in this . . .

If so, his whole security, in fact his best chance of staying alive, lay in keeping possession of the papers; he was glad now that he had spoken of recent important developments, not yet written up. Until they were satisfied that they knew what he knew, however much or little it was, and had the evidence in their hands, he was safe enough. After that they would want to stop him talking, make sure he did not pass anything on to the Germans. The stakes were too high; they would not want to take chances. In fact he had never had any intention of passing on anything of value either to the Germans or to the British. All the capital he possessed and all he had been able to borrow was invested in the Chester Group, an American combine very interested in exploiting deposits of oil in Mesopotamia. He was acting for them; it was to them that he would make his report. This had been agreed before he had left the United States for London.

The major would have his orders. A bonehead, but his finger would be steady enough on the trigger. "I can shoot too," he said aloud, very softly. The major would not realize he suspected anything. With the advantage of surprise he would have a good chance of putting a bullet into Manning before Manning put one into him. Or perhaps the major would arrange an alibi, bribe some local tribesman, make it seem like a casual murder in the course of a casual robbery, the sort of thing that happened here from time to time. He thought not, however. Manning would regard killing him as a patriotic duty; he would want to keep things in his own hands.

In the meantime what to do with the notes and sketches he had made already? He would keep his door locked and the window, which also gave onto the courtyard, secured. This would strengthen the impression in Manning's mind, if he made an attempt to enter the room and search, that the papers were valuable.

But the fastenings of the window were flimsy, and his bedside drawer, in which the papers were kept, had no lock. He would not keep them here; he would take them to Edith and ask her to keep them for him. He would say he was afraid of robbery by rival interests. He would say that Manning was in the pay of the Russians and that they were dangerous people. He would hint that his own life was in danger, not seeming too much afraid, of course, so as to stand the test of heroism in her eyes. He would swear her to secrecy. She was given to notions of high enterprise. She would jump at this sort of romantic involvement. She would swallow it wholesale if he pitched it up enough. Besides, it was partly true . . .

———

The shaft went straight down, and it was deep. They had to widen the mouth considerably and dig two lateral trenches, one on either side, so as to convey away more easily the filling of earth and stone chips. On the fourth day of digging, the deeper of these trenches, which sloped down to a depth of twelve feet, revealed the crown of a brick vault. Since they had started digging from a point lower down, they were already below the level of the palace apartments, but there was so far no trace of fire. They did not attempt to clear the roof from above for fear of damage, but continued down the shaft, the work becoming slower and more laborious as they went lower. Roughly eight feet farther down they came upon what Somerville had wanted so much to find that he had hardly dared to hope for it, the beginning of a stone stairway projecting outward from the vertical line of the shaft in the direction of the vaulted ceiling, roughly the height of a man below this. There was no doubt in his mind now. It was a vaulted tomb of traditional construction; the stairs would lead to an anteroom.

The deeper of the trenches had to be enlarged further, made into a pit, so as to give access to the head of the steps, which were heaped over with rubble. On the afternoon of the day when the first two steps were uncovered, Somerville and Palmer together, both in a state of considerable elation, were directing this work of enlargement, which it was thought would take some further days, and Jehar was watching both men from a point carefully chosen, about fifty yards away. He was waiting for a suitable moment.

Since first setting eyes on Ninanna he had been constantly

surprised by his ability to wait. Before that he had always lived in the present moment, his lusts and rages and his need to survive always directed at what was there before him, as opportunity or necessity. Even now he had no real sense of the future as a progression in time, a sequence of days during which people aged and changed. The future he waited for was an improved state of being, a sort of readjustment of the present, no more than a step from the railway yards at Jerablus and the watchful and miserly uncle to the wondrous land of Deir ez-Zor, immediate prosperity in the river trade, and unrestricted enjoyment of Ninanna's beauties.

He brought the same spirit of patience to his dealings with the Englishman. The idea that had possessed his mind almost to the exclusion of all else since that night in the bar when he had related the story of the two Armenian conscripts, he had not gone running to the *khwaja* with it at the first opportunity, brilliant as it was. No, he had watched and waited for the right moment.

It came now. He had known about the discovery of the tomb shaft; the work of excavating it was already under way when he arrived. He had known when they had uncovered the section of brick vaulting, but still he had waited. Now, today, they had come upon the beginnings of a stairway, leading down. There could only be one reason for steps under the ground: They led to a burial place. It was there that the treasure would lie; soon now the *khwaja* would be feasting his eyes on it.

Somerville was alone when he saw Jehar approach, Palmer having gone some distance off to take measurements, and he was lost still in the discoveries they had made that day. Stone steps, a vaulted chamber—it gave every sign of being the entrance to a royal tomb.

"Yes, what is it?" he said. He spoke sharply, reluctant to leave this elation of discovery for the ugly shapes of danger and doubt he knew from experience this messenger would bring. Jehar was a carrier of anguish and a vendor of it.

"Lord, I have come from the track of the railway. It is getting close, they have reached the village of Arattu. The people say that within one week they will reach Ras el-Ain."

He paused a moment, then said, "They will come through this way, they will smash the tell." He drove the fist of his right hand into the palm of his left to make a smacking sound of impact. "Much crushing and damage," he said, "many ancient and valuable things all smashed up. Also, the people here, below us here, they will start soon, maybe in two or three days, to transport the rails and sleepers and links they have been storing in their sheds here, to the railhead at Arattu and to some other places. The purpose of this is to avoid delays in continuing the line. This I have been told by very trustworthy people, whose word cannot for one single moment be doubted."

For some moments Somerville regarded the man before him without speaking. He did not believe this last statement, did not believe, in fact, that Jehar numbered any trustworthy people among his acquaintance. It had been the flourish of the habitual liar, the sort of bravura that would always give Jehar away and that he would never be able to resist. But that the Germans below would start moving materials to the railhead very soon, any day now, was entirely probable, certain, in fact. A sudden weariness descended on him, replacing the elation of earlier. Only a few short weeks had elapsed since he had appointed Jehar as his messenger on the scant qualifications of speaking some German and having worked on the railway in the mountains of Anatolia. But it seemed a lifetime now that he had been anguished by the news Jehar brought him and by the very sight of his face, with its light eyes and straight brows and fiercely serious expression—a fanatical face, but with an unsettling innocence in it too . . . "Well," he said, "we'll have to hope for the best. I'm tired of paying you to bring me bad news. I've had enough of it. In fact we can consider our agreement at an end from this hour forth."

Jehar drew a breath. His moment had come. "No," he said, "Jehar brings you good news this time, news of the best. He brings you no less than the solution to this problem of the railway. I, in my time of working on the line in Turkey, became very familiar with dynamite."

"Did you indeed?" Jehar's face wore a look he had never seen on it before, an expression of great happiness, almost of beatitude. It came to Somerville that he might be under the influence of hashish. "Dynamite, eh?"

"It is true, please believe me. I used it every single day. The Germans, they have dynamite in a shed below us here. I have watched, I have seen it. It is used to make gravel for the bed of the track. This shed is kept locked, but a lock can be broken. I also have experience of breaking locks."

"Are you actually proposing to steal their dynamite? Apart from being a crime, what good would it do? I can only think that you are joking."

"Lord, the joke will be against them. We will blow up their

sheds before they can start transporting the rails. We will use their own dynamite to do it, that is a good joke, no? It will be much better than blowing up the track. The line cannot proceed without these materials. It will take them weeks to replace them, as many weeks as it took to bring them here. If you will promise Jehar one hundred gold pounds, he will do this for you, he will save your treasure. You have but to say the word, and it is done."

13.

Somerville could never afterward recollect the exact words with which he had rejected this outrageous proposal; he knew only that they had been angry and emphatic. The proposal itself, on the other hand, remained in his mind with total clarity: all the circumstances of it; Jehar's words and the eagerness with which he had uttered them; the look of joy his face had worn. All this remained vividly present to him in the time that followed, as he supervised the work of clearing the steps that were now seen to give access to a vaulted chamber.

It was during this period too that further visitors arrived, unexpected and unannounced, all on the same day, first a Swedish couple, man and wife, who smilingly introduced themselves as seekers after truth and were members of the Society for Biblical Research, which had links all over the world, they said. They were always grateful, as they also said, for the generous hospitality they had invariably found on their travels. They had come from Abu Kemal on the Euphrates, where there was a

Swedish mission house. Then, some hours later, a Swiss journalist arrived. He had been commissioned to write an article about Mesopotamian archaeology and in particular about the men and women engaged in it, the successors to the great figures of the mid-nineteenth century, Botta, Layard, Rassam. He was hoping, he said, to interview Somerville and anyone else who cared to talk to him at Tell Erdek. He had a camera, and he was proposing to include photographs in his article—photographs of the people and the places.

It was thus a strange and ill-assorted company that sat down to dinner that evening, the newcomers in their different ways adding to the incongruities already existing, the Swedish couple effusive in manner and frequently exchanging smiles, the softly spoken, gentle-mannered Swiss waiting patiently for the time when Somerville, who grew more and more secretive as his discoveries promised to be important, would grant him an interview. A certain atmosphere of constraint hung over the table, with the major seeming more stiff and bristling even than usual, Elliott silent and preoccupied, Somerville prey to a temptation still unadmitted, Edith absorbed in thoughts of how appearances could deceive: Who could have ever suspected that Major Manning, such a perfect type of British army officer, as she had thought, could be in the pay of a foreign power and working against the interests of his own country, was little better than a spy, in fact. And the Russians, of all people, so backward and savage.

It was the major who, whether advertently or not, brought an increased vivacity into the conversation. "I don't really see where all this research business comes in," he said, addressing the Swedish couple, who had asked if the seating plan could be changed so as to allow them to sit side by side—something, they explained, they always liked to do no matter what the company. "I mean, either you are a believer or not. It's a question of faith, not proof." He had spoken in his characteristically clipped manner, though rather more irascibly than usual; he was feeling the strain of keeping up a constant watch for false moves on Elliott's part, and he had, in any case, a rooted aversion to missionaries of any persuasion, regarding them basically as troublemakers who unsettled the subject peoples and made the colonies more difficult to govern. "Look at India," he was fond of saying. "Look at the Siege of Lucknow and the Black Hole of Calcutta. That's what comes of busybodies meddling with people's beliefs."

"Excuse me, if I may ask, since you have raised the subject, are you yourself a believer?" This came from the husband, whose name was Johansson.

"Certainly I am," Manning said. "God and the King."

It was a remark of such baseness, made worse by the fact that for some reason the major had glanced toward Alex as he spoke, that Edith could not forbear a look of contempt in his direction, though she did not think he noticed this and after the first moment hoped he hadn't; she had been sworn to secrecy, which meant of course behaving normally toward this wretched man.

"Well, I am glad," Johansson said. "But it is our view, as members of the society, that faith in the message of salvation contained in the Scriptures is strengthened by showing beyond question that the facts are as related there."

"Not the truth, that is absolute," Mrs. Johansson said, "but our belief, our readiness to accept that truth."

"Exactly, my dear," Johansson said. "You do well to make the distinction." The two exchanged a loving smile. They were dissimilar in appearance, though clearly identical in their views and in the excellent quality of their English. Johansson had a slow and weighty manner and a heavy, crumpled-looking face, rather appealing, with some fugitive likeness to a teddy bear in it, one that had been knocked about a bit but not in any spirit of malice. His wife was sharper of face and quicker of movement. Her hair was very fair and rather neglected-looking; strands from it escaped the containing band and fell forward over her brows; from time to time she made a sudden birdlike, preening movement, raising both hands as if to clear her vision.

"We too are archaeologists," Johansson said, smiling at Somerville. "We are biblical archaeologists. Let me give you an example. On the eastern side of the island of Malta, on the Munxar Reef, members of our society have found the anchor stocks of the grain ship from Alexandria in which St. Paul and the Apostle Luke were voyaging when they were shipwrecked off this island, thus demonstrating the truth of the account as related in Acts Twenty-seven."

Mrs. Johansson raised her head and parted her hair on her brow and spoke toward the ceiling: " 'Then fearing lest we should have fallen upon rocks, they cast four anchors out of the stern . . .' " Her expression, solemnly exalted while she uttered the words, grew severe as she came to the end of them. "There are those," she said, "and unfortunately there are members of

the society among them, who try to belittle the importance of
this discovery by insisting that the shipwreck took place off the
coast of Dalmatia. They have no case, they have found no anchor
stocks."

"Then take Sodom and Gomorrah and the Cities of the
Plain," Johansson said. "Members of our society have located
these cities, all five of them. They have found balls of brimstone
embedded in a wide area of ash near the Dead Sea. Now, if you
consult a dictionary, you will find that 'brimstone' is another word
for sulfur. Golf-sized sulfur balls with burn marks all around them!
You could not have a clearer truth of the words in Genesis Nine-
teen. No doubt you are familiar with them? 'Then the Lord rained
brimstone and fire on Sodom and Gomorrah . . .' Chemical analysis of these balls has revealed that the brimstone is composed of
ninety-six to ninety-eight percent sulfur, with traces of magnesium, a substance that creates an extremely high temperature
burn. This is the only place on the earth where you can find this
percentage of pure sulfur in a round ball." He looked around the
table, and his likeness to a battered teddy bear deepened as he
broke into an upward-curving smile. "*Quod erat demonstrandum*,"
he said.

"The sulfur was probably ordered up from hell," Patricia
said in low tones to Palmer, who was sitting opposite her. As often happens, this remark, which was not really intended to be
heard by the Johanssons, released feelings of irritation in Patricia that had been building up all through this talk of the fire-
bombed cities. "Do you really mean to say," she said loudly and
furiously, "that you think God put the magnesium in the mixture

to make it burn hotter? I can't believe that people spend time and money and go to all that trouble in a futile attempt to prove the truth of a myth, and a pretty nasty little myth at that."

Johansson's smile was now full of tolerance and understanding. "We can only guess at God's purposes, we cannot know them. When we speak of myth, we are acknowledging that fact. It is a confession of our ignorance."

"It was a warning," his wife said, directing a look of kindly reproof toward Patricia. "A warning that this rain of fire will one day be visited again on the wicked."

"As long as it is clear who the wicked are," Palmer said. "I mean, a lot of people who weren't particularly wicked must have gone up in smoke too." He had spoken mildly, with some vague idea of reducing the emotional level—Patricia was looking distinctly cross at having been called ignorant.

"It is not clear to us, but it is clear to God," Johansson said.

"That must be terrible for him," Somerville said. "All the darkness of all the hearts in the world." He was conscious as he spoke of the darkness he had harbored in his own heart since Jehar's proposal. Neither Johansson nor his wife seemed in any way put out by the obduracy they were encountering. Of course, he thought, they are the ones that have the proof.

"Just one black heart would be enough to go on with," Edith said, taking care not to look at the major again.

"God bears this burden of the soul's darkness through our Lord Jesus." Johansson's face had returned to gravity. " 'Surely he hath borne our griefs, and carried our sorrows.' "

" 'And with his stripes we are healed,' " Mrs. Johansson said.

"Statistically though," Palmer said, "it is unlikely that every single inhabitant of these cities deserved to have fireballs rained on him. Unless of course by wicked we mean simply those who are in line for firebombing, come what may."

The Swiss, whose name was Spahl, spoke now for practically the first time. "It is interesting, what you say. But Malta, the Dead Sea, these are places far away. May I ask why you are here, what in this place you are doing?"

The Johanssons looked at each other and smiled, a smile of affectionate complicity. "There is no harm to speak of it now," Mrs. Johansson said. "Now that we have the lease."

"For fifteen years now my wife and I are engaged in one single quest," Johansson said. "And that is to discover the exact site of the Garden of Eden. We have devoted all our time and efforts to it. I tell you now, with a full heart, that our efforts have at last been crowned with success."

"Over the years we became convinced that it lay in Mesopotamia," his wife said. "On grounds of climatic conditions first of all. The description of the plants in the Garden is very suggestive of a tract of land lacking in rainfall, to which irrigation has been brought. 'And out of the ground made the Lord God to grow every tree that is pleasant to the sight.' He did not send rain to make the trees grow."

"Also there is the fact," Johansson said, "that Adam and Eve, when detected in their sin, had nowhere to hide but among the trees God had made to grow. Outside the Garden the land was bare, there was no other vegetation. We lost much time searching at Kurna, where Arab tradition places the Tree, but this was a great mistake. Kurna is in the south, where the floods are heavy, much of the time it is swampland. Would the Lord God have set our first parents down in a swamp?"

The Johanssons paused on this question to exchange a smile in which all such mistakes and disappointments were dissolved in joy. No one else at the table said anything.

"We believed for a while that it might have been at Aman on the Euphrates," Johansson said, "but in the end it was the evidence of the four rivers that convinced us. 'And a river went out of Eden to water the garden; and from thence it was parted, and became into four heads.' Four is a symbolic number, it stands for the four quarters of the world. Once we had understood this, we realized that the earthly paradise must have been set dead in the center of the known world. After that it was only necessary to identify the four rivers. They are the Tigris, the Euphrates, the Nile, and the Persian Gulf. We had some uncertainty about this last, but it is a narrow inlet, it can be regarded as a river. Now, if you join the mouths of these rivers with ruled lines, with the Nile and the Gulf at the base, you will get a perfect equilateral triangle. And if, within this triangle, you bisect the Belikh and Khabur rivers at exactly the same latitude, you will form a perfect diamond shape. At the very center of this diamond, the one unique and indisputable place, that is where the Garden was."

The Johanssons sat back in one identical movement and smiled one identical smile of triumph around the table. For an appreciable while nobody spoke. Then Palmer, with a certain sensation of coming up for air, said, "And you have identified the spot, you say? The actual bit of ground, I mean."

"We inspect it tomorrow," Johansson said.

"It is not far distant then?"

"It is less than a mile from this very place where we are seated. It is between this house and the little hill where you are digging. That is close to where the railway will pass, but it will not touch the sacred place where the Garden was."

"How can you be sure of that?" Somerville said, not knowing, in his own quandary, whether to envy or pity such blithe confidence.

"Because, my dear sir, my wife and I, on behalf of the Society for Biblical Research, have obtained a lease of the site to the extent of four acres of ground. Let me tell you now of our further design. We intend, naturally with the blessing and financial backing of the society, to build a beautiful hotel surrounded by gardens on this site, and we will call this hotel the Garden of Eden."

"Or the Paradise Hotel," his wife said, with sudden sharpness; it was clear that there had been some disagreement between them on this matter.

"It will be a great success. People will come here from all the four quarters of the world; the railway will bring them. It will be a sort of pilgrimage, you see, being built in such a sacred place. And it will be unique in all the world. A luxury hotel that will also have a spiritual atmosphere. We are proposing to incorporate a mission house and a chapel with a minister of the church in permanent attendance. How happy it makes us that we can speak of this now, now we have the lease."

Once again, as in his earlier question, the Swiss showed himself interested in immediate, practical matters. "And this lease that you have," he said, in his soft, slightly purring voice, "this lease, from whom you have obtained it?"

"Why, from the Ottoman government, of course. It bears the stamp of a high official at the Ministry of the Interior. They have granted us a lease of ninety-nine years."

Elliott quitted the table shortly after this. He was grinning to himself as he made his way to his room. The Johanssons had provided some light relief, much needed. They looked so happy, which made it funnier. Someone at the Ministry of the Interior had made a tidy little sum. All the same, it wasn't such a bad idea; there would be plenty of people ready to shell out for luxury with a spiritual atmosphere. The waters of Jordan coming from the shower—nicely warmed up. Especially honeymooners, he thought. Quite a kick in it, having your nuptial couch directly over the spot where Adam and Eve had theirs. Of course, they didn't have long to enjoy it before being kicked out . . . The lease wasn't worth much. The Ottoman government might have legal title, but they had no firm hold on the region and if war broke out those who came off best would have the say-so and it was pretty unlikely to be the Turks. But of course it was not just the Johanssons; the agreement was with these biblical research people, an international organization with members in every country of Europe and the United States. It would survive the war. It was like oil: Common interest, common profit, these would survive any upheaval. A multinational, multilingual luxury hotel with a spiritual atmosphere and spacious honeymoon suites—and a lake of oil not far away.

He had decided against locking his door when he was inside the room and awake. It gave the wrong message; he wanted to appear confident that Manning would keep his word and allow him the time they had agreed on. However, he kept his revolver always within reach, in the drawer of his table or under his pillow. And while he slept he kept the door locked.

He had cause for self-congratulation this evening, in spite of his troubles. He had completed his investigations, more or less; he had sufficient evidence. It was only necessary now for him to get out of here and back home with a whole skin.

He had been since early in the morning on the site of what he was now convinced was a gravity-induced, piercement salt dome, a vast pillar of Cenozoic and Mesozoic salt something like three hundred million years old, which had traveled through several miles of sedimentary rock to reach the surface. Everything had confirmed it. The caprock was composed of limestone, anhydrite, and traces of calcite over a large part of its surface, the result of groundwater interacting with the salt and causing mineral changes. A good deal of the calcite had dissolved through this exposure to water, forming cavernous expanses; he had discovered the existence of a system of linked caves not far below the surface, and he was now sure that these were filled with oil.

This promised extremely well in regard to the amount of oil trapped in the flanks of the dome; he had reason now to think it was there in vast quantities. But when a zone like this one was penetrated by the drill, the oil would come out fast and furious; there was danger of a gusher that could be sudden and violent in the initial stage, before it could be brought under con-

trol. This would make the operation more difficult and dangerous—and more expensive. The risk was increased by the difference in pressure between the strata that had been broken and
pushed upward in the slow rise of the salt and the shallower
strata these had penetrated. This meant there would be overpressured layers—floaters, as they were called—near the surface,
and these posed a threat of violent outflow when attempts were
made to drill through them.

All this would go down in his report, the one that neither
the British nor the Germans would see. He would describe the
site and give the exact location; he would specify the risks and
give his estimate of the quantities; he would include sketches
and diagrams and notes of depth and densities. And this report
he would carry with him at all times. It would be with him on the
morning, coming soon, when he rode out with his helpers as if
for another day combing the ground, carrying with him the few
possessions he would need. And it would be there, still with him,
when he dismissed these men and paid them and made his way
on horseback, accompanied only by Alawi, to Lataku, where the
boats left for Cyprus and Smyrna. Here he would say good-bye to
Alawi and give over the horses to him. Only in the evening would
his presence be missed, and he would be well on his way by
then . . .

He was disturbed in these reflections by a light tapping at
his door. His first thought was that Manning had taken it into his
head to come and inquire into the progress he was making with
his report. No attempt was made to turn the handle, so it could
not be Edith. "Who is it?" he called through the door.

"It is I, Spahl."

Elliott opened the door to find the Swiss smiling on the threshold, a smile that looked as if it had been there already, prepared in advance.

"I hope you will forgive this lateness of hour," Spahl said. "I wanted to lose no time."

Elliott smiled and held the door open. He said, "I will have to come clean with you right from the start. I never give interviews after ten o'clock in the evening."

"Ha-ha, no," Spahl said as he entered the room. "It is not for that I am coming." He was a big man, heavily built, but he moved very lightly, Elliott noticed now, and with short steps. He looked very carefully about him as he advanced into the room. "No, it is for business," he said.

"Have a seat." Elliott pointed to one of the two upright chairs at the table, the one on the opposite side to the drawer where his revolver lay. "Would you care for a drink? I've still got some of the Scotch that I brought from London with me."

"Thank you, yes."

"Water with it?"

"No, I like it straight, as you Americans say. Why make crooked what is made to be straight? That is a joke I am making."

"Well, I agree with you. Your very good health, sir."

"Gesundheit!"

"I was wondering," Elliott said, "just out of curiosity, you know, which paper do you work for?"

"I work for this one or that one. I am freelance."

"Freelance, eh? I see, yes."

"But it is not for the newspaper I come to see you. For the newspaper it is to talk with archaeologists, not geologists, that is my purpose."

These words cleared any doubt remaining in Elliott's mind as to the true nature and purpose of his visitor. "Naturally," he said. "We are a lesser breed altogether."

"Ha-ha. Lesser breed, very good. You Americans have a sense of humor very special. My good chap, I do not want to take up your time, so I will come to the point without delaying more. I am carrying a letter from Herr Kruckman of the Deutsche Bank giving me authority to collect the reports that so far you have made and take them back with me to Berlin when I return. Herr Kruckman is a close friend of your Lord Rampling, they have many interests in common."

"You mean Zurich, I suppose."

"Eh? No, no, I am stationed in Berlin."

By this time Elliott was feeling constrained to keep to the lines of the dialogue as far as he could remember them, as if there were an audience somewhere that expected it of him, having enjoyed the first performance. "I have not made any reports as yet," he said. "It was not part of my commission to make reports at this stage. There must be some mistake."

"No, there is no mistake. I have the letter here." Spahl's hand went to the inside pocket of his coat.

"I don't need to see the letter; I have no doubt it is genuine. I mean some mistake in the instructions, some misunderstanding about the terms on which I was employed."

"If reports you do not have, it will be enough to take your notes and papers."

"How is it that you were landed with this job?"

"Landed? Oh, yes, to land from a ship. It is an accident. They know I am leaving for Mesopotamia to do the article, they know I am traveling here in this region—"

"I see, yes. It seemed a good idea for you to pick up the papers as you were passing by."

"Exactly, yes." Spahl shot a sharp glance around the room. "You have them here, the notes?"

Elliott explained—he was more fluent now than on the first occasion—that he had notes, yes, but for reasons of security he had used a private language of symbols that no one else could possibly decipher. He would need some days in order to summarize these in the form of a report and add some important facts that had come to light recently and had not been written up yet.

He watched Spahl considering, guessed at the calculations going on behind those small, sharp eyes. And it was now, in these few moments, while he was hoping Spahl would understand that he had to be kept alive, at least until the report was made, that the idea came to him for a radical departure from the script. It was a difficult decision to make; Manning was keeping a watch on all his movements; it was almost certain that he would already know about this nighttime visit. He would have guessed immediately what Spahl was up to. He would have decided to kill Spahl to make sure no private arrangements were made, no privileged information passed on to him. Spahl would be a sitting duck; he could have no idea that the major was any other than he seemed. Was that more, or less, dangerous to himself? If they were both in the know, it might give him a breathing space. And there was a chance that one of them would succeed in killing the other, thus halving the opposition.

"Let us say three days then," Spahl said.

"Agreed. It is odd, you know, an odd coincidence, but Major Manning, the British officer you met at dinner, he came tapping at my door at just this time two or three nights ago, and he too was carrying a letter that authorized him to collect my papers and take them back with him. We had a conversation very similar to the one I've had with you. Similar in some ways, at least. He wanted to take the papers to London, not Berlin."

The way his visitor took this news confirmed Elliott's first impression that it was a dangerous man he had to deal with. He made no comment, showed no emotion. After some moments of silence he said, "Three days then, it is agreed," and shortly after this he got up and took his leave.

When the door was safely locked behind him, Elliott sat down at his table and began to compile his report. He had made notes and sketches over these last few days; they were the only papers he had of any value, those concerning the salt dome, the mineral constitution of the disk cap, estimates of the quantity of oil in the upfolds of rock and the closeness to the surface and consequent risks of drilling. The report would contain only the essentials; folded into an envelope, it would remain on his person day and night until he could get clear. The notes he would destroy.

It became ever clearer to him as he worked that his original escape plan would have to be abandoned. He could not just ride out one morning and go on riding; it was too risky. There were two of them now; they would be watching each other, but they would also be watching him. At a distance, unseen, waiting for a chance to pick him off . . . It might not be so, but he could not take the chance. Both were in their ways opponents to be respected, the fanatical major with his highly developed sense of duty, Spahl with that soft-footed, watchful, professional look about him—a Secret Service man probably. A freelance, he had said. *I'll bet you are.*

He was beginning to doubt the wisdom of describing his earlier notes—still in the custody of Edith—as being comprehensible to no one but to himself. This gave him no protection, rather the opposite. He could make a false report, but that would not save him either. False or not, as soon as it was handed over his hours would be numbered. His only safety lay in these few days of grace, the belief on their part that he had knowledge of value. He must use the time to his advantage; he must somehow find a way of taking the initiative.

It was true, as Elliott had surmised, that the major had kept his room under watch, witnessed Spahl's visit to him, and come to the only possible conclusion. But Manning had done more than this: He had kept all the other rooms under observation too, which was made easier by the fact that the house was built in the local style; though some of the rooms were interconnecting, they were all entered from the courtyard. On the day following his talk with Elliott he had seen him return from his day's work in late afternoon, seen him emerge with a jacket over his arm— suspicious in itself at this hour of the day—seen him make his way to the common room, which Mrs. Somerville had entered sometime before. They had remained there together for an hour, a fact that already raised some questions in the major's mind. When they returned to their respective rooms, one ten minutes after the other, Elliott still had his jacket, but Mrs. Somerville was now carrying a cardboard folder.

He continued to keep them under observation. On the next day too they had tea together at the same time; also on the day following. This led to certain conclusions on the major's part, which condensed into a deepening contempt for the treacherous geologist. The scoundrel had somehow inveigled himself into the good graces of the lady of the house and in an effort to save his own skin had made her the depositary of his papers, thus abusing her trust and putting her in danger of harm. Thinking of this, the major could hardly find words in his mind for it. The fellow deserved to be strung up. Well, he promised himself grimly, he couldn't be the hangman, but he would be the next best thing; he would be a one-man firing squad when the time came, though he might have to deal with the odious, soft-voiced Swiss first.

He saw it as a clear duty to warn Mrs. Somerville, even though it meant a breach of his instructions, which were to preserve strict secrecy. An opportunity for this came when he found her sitting alone in the workroom, cleaning and assembling some pieces of ceramic. But he had not gone far with the relation of Elliott's contemptible behavior when he found himself being regarded with eyes of fury and scorn.

"How dare you." It was the last straw; she could contain herself no longer; such insolence was not to be borne. "How could you be so base, to hide behind this appearance of an officer and

gentleman, to come here to me, a woman, to try to make a fool of me, to lay your own treachery at another man's door, one who is worth twenty of you? Alex has told me everything. I know you are not what you seem. I know you are in the pay of the Russians."

The major had brown eyes, amber in shade, something like the color of marmalade. They were open now to their widest extent, and his jaw had slackened as he regarded his hostess. "In the pay of the Russians? He told you that?" His face was smoothed out. Astonishment had dispelled all sign of the nervous mannerism that twisted his mouth from time to time. He seemed about to speak but then fell silent. After a moment or two a strange, uncertain smile came to his face, one in which incredulity struggled with reluctant amusement. "By God, that's rich," he said.

It was the smile that did it, more than the words that followed. That and the doubts that had been gathering in her mind for some time now, doubts about that fiery sincerity that Alex seemed to exude from every pore. But mainly it was the smile. Astonishment could be faked, but a smile like that never. Except perhaps by some superbly gifted actor, and the major was not that; he was too unmistakably the genuine article. Unless he had all this while, ever since his arrival, been acting the part of the genuine article, which Edith could not believe. The reasoning that had led Elliott to distrust the major led Edith now to believe him. It was Alex who was the actor. It was Alex who was in the pay of a foreign power, the Germans, the major was telling her now, Britain's great enemy; that was why he had wanted to hide the papers. It was Alex who had done what she had just been furiously accusing the major of doing, even worse, because he had come as a lover, a more heinous offense, he had lied to her and deceived her and laid the blame on another man . . .

Conviction of this, when it came, was total. And the distress of it brought sudden tears to her eyes. She could not listen to the major any longer, and she asked him to leave her, but in tones that told him he was believed. When he had gone the tears came faster. How could she have been so foolish, how could she have believed that a man like Major Manning was a hired assassin? It was someone else Alex was worried about; naturally he had not told her who. But it didn't matter anymore; he could sink or swim as far as she was concerned. She had felt contempt for John because he had been Rampling's dupe, and now she had been Elliott's. That is the truth, she thought through her tears. No good trying to hide away from it. She and John were alike; they belonged in the army of the gullible. It is because we are believers, she whispered to herself, and the thought calmed her tears. He and I, together in this, perhaps we should try to believe each other.

She felt soothed at this thought, though less than fully convinced by it. And it was followed by a strange feeling of relief. The major was genuine, and that meant that everything else was too, all the things that Alex's lies had made her doubt, the honor of the British Army, the values of loyalty and devotion to duty, the foundations on which the British Empire was built. She would never forget the night of the fire, but she knew Alex now for what he was, a man who used fire to warm himself and fuel his lies and burn other people with.

"I can't say I'm sorry that the Johanssons have gone," Patricia said.

"They got on your nerves rather, didn't they?"

"Well, didn't they get on yours? Darling, your glasses could do with a bit of a clean."

Palmer took off his glasses, which were often dusty owing to his habit of rooting about among dusty things, and, peering closely at them, fumbled in his pockets for a handkerchief, failed to find one, and gave the lenses a brisk rub on the front of his shirt. "I didn't take them all that seriously," he said. Patricia took things pretty seriously—he knew that—or she didn't take them at all. She was feeling sorry now for having spoken so crossly to the Swedish couple, instead of being worldly and ironical.

"I suppose it sounds ill natured," she said, "but I think it was that rather awful joy of theirs that got me down most of all. I mean, they were totally out of reach. Neither of them has any sense of metaphor. I'm a member of the Anglican Church, I go to communion, but I can spot a myth when I see one. We all aim at happiness, I suppose, but I wouldn't want to find mine in a literal belief in some vengeful brute up in the sky raining fireballs down on whole populations."

"They are happy in each other, more than in anything else, I think. Talk about common interests. Hand in hand they have discovered the earthly paradise. It's enough to put a smile on anyone's face, isn't it? Personally, what I find really surprising, and somehow depressing, is the refusal to make comparisons, to allow the mind a bit of room. They will labor to prove the Genesis version of the Deluge, for example—I daresay that members of the Society for Biblical Research are combing Mount Ararat at this very moment, looking for fragments of the rudder. What they will never do is sit down quietly somewhere and read a bit of comparative mythology. They won't say to themselves: Well now, this story already existed in both Sumerian and Babylonian as early as 2000 B.C. The names are different, of course—God is called Ea and Noah is called Uta-napishtim—but the instructions are all there: Build a boat, fashion it so-and-so, bring all seeds of life into it, and so on. I haven't got the text here with me but I have it at home, it's in volume four of Rawlinson's *Cuneiform Inscriptions of Western Asia.* I'll show it to you when we are back in England, if you like."

Patricia smiled at him. "I'll look forward to that," she said, and rarely had she meant anything more profoundly. Sumerian mythology and working for the vote and friends by the fireside and a glass of sherry and the house they shared together . . .

"Take this Garden of Eden business," Palmer said, warmed and encouraged. She was interested in what he said; she approved of him—he had never felt so much approved of. "They have found similar accounts in Sumerian records, strikingly similar accounts actually. The whole story of an earthly paradise belongs to the mythology of the ancient Near East. I mean, the term itself derives from the Akkadian *edinu,* which was borrowed in its turn from the Sumerian *eden.* In the Sumerian story there occurs the word *Nin-ti,* Lady of the Rib. There are some variations, naturally. There were eight fruits forbidden to the Sumerian pair, and instead of a serpent the seducer was a fox."

"It's the same thing, though, isn't it? Whether they were tempted by a fox or a snake, it's still about the danger of human overreaching, wanting to be like the gods, wanting to know more than we should."

"Notions of paradise differ," Palmer said. "The Johanssons think of it in terms of an apple tree inside a diamond inside a triangle. Some see it in terms of speedboats. My idea of it is bound up with knowing more, not less. You with me day by day, a regular income, a reasonably spacious house in Bloomsbury, not too far from the British Museum . . ."

14.

॰

They were helped in reaching the lower steps by the discovery of a natural cave where the limestone had split and shifted owing to the operation of underground streams. Miraculously, as it seemed, the water had bypassed the tomb.

There were six steps altogether, descending steeply. Then, after a space of four feet, three broader steps that mounted to the doorway, fallen in and ruinous, of an entrance chamber. At once, just beyond the threshold, they began to make finds, various bowls and drinking vessels of alabaster and pottery, needed for feasting in the life to come. They were beneath the roof of the vault now. This had held up through the millennia, and the stone floor beneath was clear. There was a limestone statuette lying against the wall, a seated figure, upturned.

Further work was suspended while Palmer took photographs with the aid of lamps. For a moment, while he did this, there was no one with him, Somerville and Elias and the group engaged in clearing the threshold having returned to the surface, where Somerville told them to remain for the time being. He was possessed now by fears, which he recognized as irrational but could not help, that someone, anyone, would do some irreparably clumsy thing, somehow interrupt and violate this miraculous sequence that had started with the first sight of the descending steps, had led to this threshold, would lead across the floor of the anteroom, through the fallen masonry that blocked the entrance beyond, and so into the burial chamber itself and the royal sarcophagus he believed would lie there. The sight of Jehar, standing some distance off, did nothing to reassure him. It was obvious that Jehar had not taken no for an answer; he haunted the site, a ubiquitous presence, always alone, always watching.

Palmer did not touch the statuette, which was grotesquely tumbled from the sitting position, skirted knees raised, head lying back, rather like a large white beetle that had been overturned and could not get itself right again. But he looked closely at it, more closely than he had had leisure for up to now. And he played the narrow beam of his torch over it, the better to do this. And in so doing he noticed what neither he nor Somerville had noticed previously: There was the stylized symbol of a spade thinly incised along the forward base.

Somerville, descending alone, found his assistant on his knees, as if in prayer. "The spade," Palmer said, and he shone his torch on it again for Somerville's benefit. "This can't be Assyrian work."

"Why not?" There was no note of dissent in this, only a simple question. Palmer knew more about this sort of thing than he did. "It doesn't look so very much like a spade, more like a hooded figure," he said.

"It's the Babylonian symbol for a spade."

"Babylonian? What is it doing here then?"

"It must have been placed here to guard the entrance to the tomb." Palmer squatted to take another look. "There's no doubt about it," he said after a moment. He looked up at Somerville, and the beam of his torch cast a partial light over the lower part of his face, giving him a curiously disembodied look. "The spade is the sacred symbol of Marduk, the Great God of the Babylonians."

"A captured god," Somerville said. "Yes, there are precedents for it in Assyrian practice. It would make sense if you had your back to the wall, if the Babylonians were at the gates and your own gods had failed, to use the enemy's god for protection."

"A very ancient and potent god," Palmer said. "He doesn't look so impressive at the moment, does he, doing a knees-up like that? I suppose we can put him upright now."

The statuette, though no more than a foot tall, was surprisingly heavy. A considerable effort was needed to raise it, very carefully, and set it upright against the wall. At once, in this restored position, it reasserted its elemental power, head thrust forward, hands on knees, transformed into an object of terror and devotion.

"Yes," Palmer said. "You can see it, can't you? He wasn't one to cross. The sculptor, whoever it was, must have been in fear and trembling when he made him." He got up and took some steps farther into the chamber, toward the entrance to the larger chamber beyond, which was blocked off by double stone doors and a fall of masonry across the entrance. "If he was there, where he is now, against the wall, anyone making for the tomb would have had to cross the path of his gaze and so incur his curse. Like a kind of psychic burglar alarm."

"His eyes are made of pitch," Somerville said. "Like the lion's. But they have not been touched by fire. If it was so, if Marduk was installed here as a last-ditch defense against any who would come to violate the tomb, it must have been close to the end, it must have been in the last—"

He was interrupted by a sudden exclamation. "Come and look at this," Palmer said. He was standing close to the blocked doorway, gazing upward. Part of the wall on one side had fallen across the entrance, but the stone lintel above it was still in place, and the beam of Palmer's torch was resting steadily on this.

"What is it?" Somerville moved to Palmer's side and looked up at the lintel. After a moment he made out the marks of incisions on the stone. It was cuneiform script, Assyrian.

"They chiseled the signs into the stone. Pretty deep, aren't they? They wanted the message to last."

"Can you make it out?"

"I don't think it's a text, it looks like just a single name. Hang on a minute . . ." When he spoke again the pitch of his voice was higher, charged with a tone of protest. "Can't be," he said. "Must be a fake of some kind, a theft of identity. If they can borrow the power of a god, I suppose they can borrow the power of a king too."

"What king?"

Palmer lowered the torch. "The name up there is Sin-shar-ishkun," he said. "There can't be any mistake. The first syllable refers to the god Sin, who appointed him *shar,* or king."

"There was only one king of that name," Somerville said. "He died in the flames when the Babylonians and Medes took Nineveh in 612 and put the city to the fire." He made a gesture toward the doorway and the chamber beyond. "It's in the Chaldean chronicles. Whoever is in there must be an impostor. Look, it's getting late now, I don't think it would be advisable to go any further today. We'll get them to make a barrier to block off the entrance to this anteroom, keep out the light, keep people out too. Planks lashed together will do. We'll set a guard of four men to stay at the top of the shaft. I'll stay with them if you will send someone with provisions for me. Tomorrow morning we'll clear the doorway and try to shift the doors. With any luck, they will still turn on their pivots. It won't take more than two or three hours. Then we'll see who is inside there."

"No reason why you should do the whole night. You need sleep just like the rest of us. I'll come to relieve you around two A.M."

In the heightened state of his nerves—and with the knowledge that his assistant disliked any disturbance of his sleep—this offer brought a prickle of tears to Somerville's eyes. He was reluctant to accept, however, reluctant to leave the scene even for the space of an hour. But Palmer insisted and in the end prevailed.

———

Manning had not told Edith the whole truth, by any means: He had limited himself to the American's duplicity, he had naturally said nothing about his own designs once the report was secured, and he had said nothing that might cause her to suspect that Spahl was on the same quest. Such knowledge was useless to her, he had reasoned, and might even be dangerous, causing her to do or say the wrong thing. He was not a man with a great play of mind, but he had seen from the way she took the news—first the rage, then the tears—that there had been something going on between her and Elliott, that the swine had been taking advantage of her. Hell hath no fury, he had said to himself sagely, and he took care not to fan the flames.

Consequently, Edith, in deciding what to do with the papers that had been so falsely entrusted to her, had no idea that Alex was in any real danger. She wanted to show her contempt for his behavior and to make sure he understood that all was over between them. After some thought she decided to return the papers to him publicly, with as many spectators present as possible to add to his discomfiture. On the morning following the major's revelations she rose somewhat earlier than usual and took more trouble with her toilette, arranging her hair carefully and putting some color on her cheeks. She chose a dress that she knew to be becoming, one that fitted close but not so much as to be vulgarly flaunting. When she felt sufficiently ceremonious and prepared for the scene she made her way to the courtyard, Elliott's folder under her arm.

She found everyone but Palmer seated at the breakfast table; he was still at the site, and Patricia was proposing shortly to take him a thermos flask of tea and stay there with him until Somerville returned to relieve him. It was a good occasion, with everyone present like this; in fact during these days there had been what seemed an increased sociability among them; Elliott in particular was never seen alone but always in the company not only of the major but of the Swiss journalist.

She was put off her stride a little by the sight of her husband at the table; he was rarely at meals now, and she had somehow not envisaged him as a witness. Might he not think it strange, seeing her dressed and made up like this, seeing this rejection of Elliott's papers along with Elliott himself? But it was too late now to hold back. Holding herself very straight, as she had been taught to do as a child when reciting poetry or acting the queen in pageants—she had always had the queen's part— Edith walked to the place where the American was sitting and dropped the file with deliberate carelessness on the table beside him. "I have no further use for these," she said—or for you either, her tone and looks implied.

But she had forgotten, in the hurt to her feelings, quite a number of things. She had forgotten that Elliott was still officially an archaeologist, that the major would be obliged, in company, to pretend to believe this, that the Swiss would believe it anyway, that it was important for her husband's credit and his relations with the Turkish authorities that it should be generally believed. These things came to her, all in a rush, in the silence that followed. Elliott had not moved. She felt the color rise to her face. She looked across at her husband with a sort of entreaty, conscious suddenly of how much she cared that his name and his ambitions should be protected. But he did not meet her gaze; he seemed abstracted, hardly aware of what was happening.

It was Manning who saved the situation, for which she was always to be grateful to him. "Your notes about the Hittites, Elliott, I suppose," he said. "Have you found any evidence of those bronze-sheathed war chariots you were talking about the other evening?"

Elliott rose from the table, keeping a loose and careless hold of the file. He did not glance at Edith but looked steadily at the major. After a moment he nodded. "There are indications," he said. "Certainly there are indications. I am compiling a report." A sudden smile came to his face, exuberant, full of confidence. He looked with his usual unwavering frankness at the major and Spahl, who were both now standing. "In fact," he said, "I have already compiled it. It is on my person at present. I am proposing to carry it on me at all times—to avoid losing it, you know. When I return home, I am hoping to publish it in the *American Journal of Oriental Research*." He turned toward Edith then, but still without looking directly at her. "These notes are no good to anyone," he said. "They never were." And as he spoke he dropped the file back on the table with a gesture very similar to hers.

He was moving toward the door, closely followed by Manning and Spahl, when Somerville, seeming to emerge from some species of daydream, addressed the whole company: "I'd like to invite you all to come over to the excavation site at midday today. We will have cleared the entrance to the burial chamber by then. There is every sign that the tomb has not been disturbed. We expect to find a sarcophagus inside, perhaps more than one. I want you to be witnesses of what promises to be a momentous discovery. I am sure that you as a colleague"—and here he looked at Elliott—"will want to be present."

"Certainly," Elliott said.

"I too," Major Manning said. "Sounds dashed interesting."

"This in my article will find a place," Spahl said.

Somerville looked at his wife, noticing that she looked particularly attractive this morning. "I know I can count on you to be there."

"Of course."

The invitation issued, Somerville remained where he was, watching the others leave the table, Edith too. She had eaten nothing; she had not so much as sat down at the table, unusual with her, she always enjoyed breakfast. He himself had eaten very little. He had been punctually relieved by his assistant, but he had not succeeded in sleeping much afterward. He was overwrought, and the talk he had had with Palmer before leaving for the house had added to the tension of expectation he was living under. Palmer had not been able to sleep either, and lying awake, waiting to return to the site, he had remembered something. The series of Chaldean chronicles that began in 616 B.C. were an invaluable record of the last days of the Assyrian kingdom and provided a detailed account of the destruction of Nineveh by the Chaldeans and Medes in alliance in 612. There were omissions in them, of course, and defacements of the text, and one of these last had come to his mind and assumed particular significance as he lay there. He had tried to bring the passage to mind but had not been able to remember much but the date. *A*

strong attack they made against the city and in the month of Ab . . .
Then he had remembered, with sudden excitement, that the
words referring to the king's death had been bracketed off in the
translation and queried as uncertain. *On that day Sin-shar-ishkun,*
the Assyrian king [was killed?] . . . Some accidental damage to the
face of the text, just at this point, a chance in a thousand? Or
some uncertainty on the part of the scribe? Was there some alternative version, some knowledge possessed by only a few? In any
case, in the absence of more evidence, that he had died there
was an assumption, no more than that. He was thought to have
perished in the flames because nothing more was heard of him
after the destruction of the city. But no proof had ever been offered; the body had never been identified.

This fact—the uncertainty that lay over the king's death—
he had mentioned to Somerville, and they had talked about it
for a little while. It was in Somerville's mind now, to the exclusion of all else, as he watched the others leave the breakfast
table, saw the houseboys enter to clear away the dishes. And it
was still there a little later as he walked back to the mound, an essential element in what was becoming to his mind a marvelous
story.

On the way he went over the official version of events as far
as he knew them. The father of Sin-shar-ishkun was Ashurbanipal, the learned and ruthless, the last great king of Assyria,
hunter of lions, creator of the vast library of cuneiform texts at
Nineveh. He died in 627, and Kandalanu, the puppet king he installed at Babylon, died in the same year, which had led some to
believe, and Somerville among them, that this monarch never

existed, that Kandalanu was a throne name and it was Ashurbanipal himself who was worshiped at Babylon in a form of a statue
named Kandalanu.

A not uncommon practice for the Assyrian kings to create
alternative selves—it was what he now believed Sin-shar-ishkun
to have done. In 623, on the death of his brother, he had become king of Assyria, the last of the line. Eleven years of desperate fighting against the growing power of the Medes, the
destruction of Ashur, the home of their gods, the meeting of
Nabopolassar the Chaldean and Cyaxares the Mede below the
walls of the devastated city, the agreement they made there to divide the dying empire of the Assyrians between them. From that
point on they were to fight side by side, and Assyria was doomed.
Then the final battle, the final siege, and the defective text that
Palmer had remembered.

His excitement increased as he drew nearer the mound.
Today might see the answer to the enigma contained in the
chronicles. A totally new light on the last years of the Assyrian
kingdom. If so, he would go down in the annals of archaeology,
and Palmer with him; he would join company with the great
ones of the past, so much revered, Layard, Rassam, George
Smith. He would be famous; he would be in demand; he would
never again lack for financial backing.

He found Palmer sitting hand in hand with Patricia at the
entrance to the vertical shaft. Hardly a hundred yards beyond
them, the tin roofs of the German sheds gleamed in the early
sunshine. The workpeople were arriving, and the two foremen
stood talking together at some distance from the shaft, obviously
wanting not to intrude on the young couple. Fortified by the tea

Patricia had brought him and by her company, Palmer declared that he would stay on and see the progress of the work. Patricia too wanted to stay. Only one group of six, composed of the workmen Somerville trusted most, under the pickman who had found the stone carving of the Guardian, was set to work on clearing the rubble that lay over the entrance to the tomb and opening the stone doors. The rest of the people, directed by the foremen, were set to work higher up on the side of the mound, one party continuing to trace the course of the wall, the other taking up the flooring of the ash-covered platform they had found.

By midmorning the rubble had been cleared. The six men were enough to make the stone doors swing open on their iron pivots. Somerville sent them up to the surface and stationed Elias at the mouth of the shaft with instructions to wait there for the people of the house and allow no one else to come down. Then—and only then—he and Palmer, armed with lamps from the anteroom, stepped over the broken brick that still lay strewn over the threshold and entered the chamber.

Set longways against the wall that faced them as they entered, and occupying most of the wall—there was scarcely room for a man to stand at either end—was a terra-cotta sarcophagus three or four feet in height, closed with a slightly beveled lid, also of terra-cotta. In the walls on either side were shallow alcoves containing carved alabaster vases of closely similar design. Otherwise the room was bare.

Somerville halted in the middle of the room, held back in these first moments by a sort of superstition from proceeding farther, as if haste might seem disrespectful to the presences

here. He held his lamp up toward the ceiling. "It's a perfect bar-
rel vault," he said. "These bricks were set by people who knew
what they were doing. Shaft, steps, anteroom, burial chamber—
he must have had it built long before, maybe years before. He
wanted to be ready for the end, when it came."

"There's an inscription." Palmer had not been so reluctant
to approach the sarcophagus. He was crouching forward now,
looking closely at the foot.

"Can you read it?"

"I think so, yes. Take me a bit of time. The terra-cotta is in
good condition, good as new, almost."

"Is there a name?"

"Hang on a minute. There's an invocation to the gods at
the beginning and the usual curse on anyone who comes to disturb the tomb. The name of the occupant should be somewhere
between. Yes, here it is, two names." He paused here for further
scrutiny, a pause that seemed long to Somerville. "One of them
is Sin-shar-ishkun," he said at last. "I can't make out the other
just yet. It's a woman's name."

The rush of relief these words released in Somerville made
him unsure he could control his voice if he tried to speak. He
fell to studying the lid of the sarcophagus. It was sealed with
bitumen, he saw now. "We'll need a sharp, thin-bladed knife,"
he said, restored to self-control by this practical consideration.
"Preferably with a serrated edge. Would you go up and ask Elias
to find one for us?"

He made no further attempt to examine the sarcophagus
while he waited but stood without moving in the center of the
room, feeling the silence of the place settle over him. Two

names. It was unusual; in fact he had never heard before of an Assyrian king and his consort laid in the same coffin or even in the same tomb. The royal women were buried at home below the domestic wing of the palace; the kings were customarily taken to Ashur, dwelling place of the father-god, for burial. But the city had gone up in flames, and the god Ashur made captive and led away on a cart in 614; it had been the first of the Assyrian power centers to fall. The tomb must have been built well after that. He could not recall the name of Sin-shar-ishkun's queen; perhaps he had never known it.

When Palmer returned with Patricia, they were accompanied by Edith. A few minutes later Elliott, Manning, and Spahl arrived; it seemed that these three had walked over together. Somerville waited until everyone was assembled and the lamps were set around the wall. Then he set to work with the knife Palmer had brought. It was easier than he had thought, there was hardly need for sawing; the bitumen was brittle, the seals parted one after the other as Elliott and Spahl, standing on either side of him, eased up the lid very slightly at the points where the knife was inserted.

"We are ready to take the lid off now," Somerville said. "It will probably need four of us at least. I'd just like to say a few words first. I wanted you to be present so that if questioned about the authenticity of these proceedings you will be able to give eyewitness accounts. Mr. Spahl, in particular, as a journalist of considerable standing, might be willing to bring the discovery before a wide readership, might even be glad to be the first to do so."

"Indeed yes," Spahl said. "A scoop of big proportions, my paper will be greatly pleased."

"I feel it is important for you to be informed of the facts, as far as Palmer and I have been able to establish them. The name on the sarcophagus is the same as that over the doorway to the tomb, it is the name of the last king in the line of Sargon, effectively the last king of Assyria. There is a name alongside it, a woman's name."

"I can manage to make it out now," Palmer said. "It is Lattalia."

Somerville went on to speak of the doubts that hung over the final fate of this king, the time and place of his supposed death. He told them of his own first belief that this must be an impostor. "Impostors were not uncommon in ancient Assyria," he said, "especially in times of crisis or extreme danger, when the king might temporarily bestow his identity—and his name—on another. There are precedents for this, historically documented. If you will bear with me a few minutes longer, I will tell you what I think might have happened. In the summer of 612 B.C. the Assyrian Empire was in its death throes. Ashur, the religious capital, had been destroyed two years earlier. Now the siege was tightening around Nineveh, the administrative heart, the seat of government. Sin-shar-ishkun, whose name is on this sarcophagus, decided to give that name to someone else. The true name of the man he chose is not recorded anywhere as far as I know. I think it probable that he was some high military commander—a reasonable choice at a time like that."

He paused on this and smiled a little. He had visibly relaxed in posture as he talked; it was now as if he were delivering a lecture to a group of students. None of his hearers had made the slightest sound or the slightest shift of position. None of them had taken their eyes from him. He is in command of us, Edith thought. As if we were children, listening to wonders. Such different kinds of people, yet we are all in the grip of his words, in the grip of this story he is telling. She had never seen her husband as a man with a gift for storytelling. And it was more than that, much more: His voice was quiet, but there was authority in his words, a kind of power emanated from him. And there was nothing assumed, nothing theatrical; he was entirely himself.

"So for a while there was a king in Nineveh who was not the true king. The true king escaped the siege, fled here with the belongings he valued most. Among these was a statuette of Marduk, the god of the Babylonian enemy, who he hoped might protect him. With him came queen and concubines, servants and guards, followers ready to cast their lot with him. We know now that this place was a residence, probably a summer palace, of the Assyrian kings, at least for a century or so—since the time of Esarhaddon. We have found definite proof of this. So here the king lived quietly under his borrowed name for some time longer, perhaps some years, far to the west of the Assyrian heartlands on the Tigris. This vaulted tomb and the sarcophagus were made ready on his orders, and when the time came for him to be laid to rest, he had Marduk installed in the entrance chamber as a guardian. Perhaps we can try raising the lid now. There is no room behind it, but if Elliott and Manning can take the sides, the rest of us can try to lift it from the front and rest it back against the wall."

It took all five of the men, straining with the effort and the need for care, to raise the lid and get it propped securely resting on its edge. In this combined effort, and in the wonderment of

looking down into the coffin—they were the first to do this—
these men were as one, bound together in a common sentiment
for the first time and the last.

Edith and Patricia came forward now and joined the men,
and all stood close together there, looking down. The two skeletons lay side by side. They had died, or been laid in death, on
their backs; the caverns where their eyes had been seemed in
that inconstant light of the lamps to have retained some power
of seeing, to be returning the gaze of the spectators. The flesh
had long gone, but the framework of bone was perfectly pre-
served; no hand had touched it. Only the teeth were ruinous.

"They have been lying here for about twenty-five hundred
years," Somerville said, breaking the long silence. She had been
shorter than her burial companion by a foot at least, but the two
skulls were on an exact level, he noticed now. As if they had lain
with faces close, he thought. But of course they must have died
outside the coffin. Perhaps the king gave orders that they should
be laid with their faces touching. "Queen or concubine, no way
of knowing for the moment," he said. There was a shared headrest of what looked like filigree gold lying beneath the skulls.
The dust of their decay lay around them, and a scattering of
beads from the necklace she had worn, more than one necklace
probably. The beads were numerous and of different types and
coloring; he caught the glint of gold among them. Other jewelry
he saw in this first quick, surveying glance: fibulae, armlets, a
pendant with a thin chain. There were three rings on the man's
right forefinger. Priceless, these objects. He felt a surge of pro-
tectiveness almost violent in its nature. The others were standing

too close; he would have liked to shift them away. "We'll get a covering made," he said to Palmer.

It was Patricia, striving in typical fashion to combat the awe that had descended on her, who came up now with a question that brought them back from the violated privacy of these bones to time and event. "The man he gave his name to," she said. "What became of him?"

"It is not known," Somerville said. "Nothing in this room will tell us. I can only say what I think might have happened. The man who took the king's name was not happy with it. He was a man with high ambition. He did not want to be identified for all time to come with a defeated monarch. So he gave himself a new name, Ashur-uballit, a very illustrious one in the annals of Assyrian history. The first king of that name had freed his country from foreign domination, freed his people from the tribute they had been paying to the Mitanni, and been hailed as king of the universe by a grateful people. This army officer, whose true name has not survived, thought the adopted name would act as a sort of talisman, a guarantee of success. Like capturing a flag or appropriating an emblem of another empire or using an enemy god as guardian because he has proved a stronger god than your own."

"A good move," Elliott said, speaking for the first time. "I admire that guy. Desperate situations call for desperate remedies, isn't that what they say? He wouldn't accept defeat, he kept his nerve. In my opinion, that was a man who deserved to make good and succeed in life."

Yes, you tricky devil, Manning thought as he glanced at

Elliott and sought to guess whereabouts on his person the report might be. You would admire a trickster, wouldn't you? "But did this king actually exist?" he said to Somerville, with a sense of returning to decent discourse.

"Oh, yes, he existed. So much is certain. He proclaimed himself Ashur-uballit the Second and he succeeded in escaping to Harran, where the Belikh joins the Euphrates. There he made a stand, supported by an Egyptian force that had come to the aid of the Assyrians. But they were defeated, and he fled westward across the Euphrates and was never heard of again. It isn't known whether he lived or died. He may have abandoned his new name in order to escape pursuit. In any case, at this point he simply disappears from history.

"It took the invaders several more years to mop up the remnants of the Egyptian and Assyrian forces, but by 605, when they took Carchemish, it was all over, the whole region was in their hands. And that would have spelled the death of these two lying here. I think that they had these few years of grace while the fighting was going on. I think that when he knew the enemy was at the gates he took his own life, probably by poison, and she followed suit."

Not much was said after this. Somerville announced his intention of staying on there for a while. He wanted to look more closely at the contents of the sarcophagus and to arrange for a cover to be made. Palmer was in need of a rest after his vigil, and Patricia wanted to go back to the house with him. The three other men left in a body. Edith waited until everyone else had gone; then she went to her husband and kissed him. "John, you were wonderful," she said. "I was so proud of you."

When she too had gone, Somerville did not approach the sarcophagus but remained where he had been standing to hear the thanks of his departing visitors. He felt the warmth of Edith's kiss on his lips, and it sustained him in the moments of exhausted reaction that followed. Like marionettes, the two of them lying side by side, neat and dutiful and somehow pathetic, their bones perfectly in place. Not waiting to be fleshed again but for some touch on the string that would bring them both upright together . . .

He had been troubled by the thought that some impostor, some false claimant, might be buried here. But he felt certain now, as he stood alone in the silence, that this was not so, could not be so. No man or woman of the time would choose to die under a false identity. Who would wish, as he stood at the threshold of the Underworld, to risk the curse of the god Sin by stealing his name or denying it? Sin-shar-ishkun. Not one of the great Assyrian kings, not like his grandfather Esarhaddon or his father Ashurbanipal. Heir to ruin and destruction. No hero, any more than he was himself—a hero would have died in the flames—but the last of the royal line of Sargon.

His own name would be made now, his own identity confirmed. He would rewrite the final chapter of Assyrian history. In archaeology a discovery as revolutionary as this would generate a vast amount of activity aimed at corroboration or disproof. And the man at the heart of a controversy like that could be sure of fame.

Drawings and notes would have to be made; the attitude and position of the skeletons would have to be carefully recorded, along with the nature of all the objects in the coffin. This before anything was touched. The necklaces would have to be restrung as closely as possible in the original order, which meant much patient work matching the beads. Before the beads could even be handled the loose dust would have to be blown away delicately enough to leave them undisturbed. For the first time now it came fully home to him, the work that would be needed, the labor of preserving this material, much of it no doubt in bad condition. Then there were the skeletons themselves; to get them without damage from the sarcophagus would mean shrouding them separately in thickly waxed linen, wrapping them around so that they could be encased and so lifted clear. Everything—the alabaster and ceramic drinking vessels, the statuette of the god, the jewelry—would have to be packed on the surface and made ready for transport to London. To get the sarcophagus to the surface some system of pulleys would have to be devised, a difficult operation in that narrow space.

With a sudden gesture Somerville raised hands to his temples, stilling the sound, not heard but felt within him, indistinguishable from the pulse of his life in that quiet place, the clash of metal against metal. There were weeks of delicate, painstaking work awaiting them here. Three weeks, four weeks . . . He quitted the chamber with a sensation of escaping the silence there, which had become intolerable now, and began to make his way up the sloping trench on the left side. He had some idea of finding Elias or Halil and arranging for a cover to be made for the sarcophagus. Elias was there, but the first person he really saw on reaching the surface was Jehar, standing in exactly the same position as before.

15.

In the afternoon of that day Major Manning was as usual engaged in watching, from the half-opened window of his room, the comings and goings in the courtyard. Some two hours previously he had seen Spahl come through the gate on foot and cross to his own room, where he had remained—no doubt to keep watch too. He had seen Palmer leave, also on foot, which meant he would be making for the mound. Palmer had been wearing a cartridge belt with a revolver in the holster, the first time Manning had known him to do this. He had also been carrying a small knapsack. He would be going to relieve Somerville, who had not returned with the others. But an hour or so later he had come back alone, this time without the knapsack or the belt or revolver. So Somerville had been unwilling to leave the site. Was it possible they only had one revolver between them? Since Elliott had let fall the fact that he was carrying the report on him, the major had become absorbed to the point of obsession in surmising the motives of everyone as well as observing everyone's movements, as if something missed might give Elliott a crucial advantage. The American was cunning, as criminals often were; he might have made that declaration at breakfast with the idea of acting as a decoy, getting them to track him to some preselected place where he could lie in wait and ambush them; the major included Spahl in these speculations because though not on the same side they were on the same quest. Or then again he might have said it to make them suspect that very thing and slow them down, whereas his real aim was simply to make a run for it at the earliest possible opportunity.

Elliott had kept to his room after luncheon. But now, shortly before, he had suddenly emerged in shirtsleeves, with a towel over his shoulder and made his way across to one of the two bathhouses, which were in the far corner of the courtyard on the side farthest from the gate. Before setting off, Manning noted, he checked his window fastenings and locked his door, slipping the key into his trouser pocket. He was followed almost at once by a house servant carrying two buckets of water from which a thin steam rose and lingered in the windless air.

The bathhouses were in an awkward place; it was only possible for Manning to keep them under surveillance by leaning well out of his window. He saw the houseboy return without the buckets; then he sat back to await the American's return.

But the next person to come to Elliott's door was not Elliott but the Arab who acted as his interpreter. This man knocked repeatedly on the door and called, "Mr. Elliott, sir!" several times, getting no answer.

Manning emerged from his room and walked over to him, "No use knocking," he said, "he's having a shower." But even as he spoke a terrible suspicion came to him. He went quickly across to the bathhouse Elliott had entered and pushed the door open. There was no one there. The two buckets, still faintly steaming, stood on the wooden boards. He ran back to the interpreter, who was still calling, "Mr. Elliott, sir!" He saw Palmer and Mrs. Somerville emerge from their separate rooms to see what the disturbance was.

"Two months' wages!" the interpreter said. "He has gone without paying me." It was clear from his voice and his face that he was close to tears. "He took me from my home and my family," he said. "What shall we do now? How shall I feed my children?" He spoke English well, with an American accent.

"He can't get far," Manning said. "Not on foot and dressed like that."

"He can get far, sir, he can get very far. One of the horses, the one he uses, is missing."

Manning fought down his agitation, summoning his military training to his aid. *Assess the situation; ascertain the direction of enemy fire; issue your orders.* The bathhouse was in that part of the courtyard farthest from the gate, nearest the stockade where the horses were kept. This stockade was not visible from his room. The horse would have been already prepared and saddled, ready to be led quietly away, just in those few minutes, as he had sat back and waited. Elliott would have known he was not being watched; he would have seen I was not leaning out . . . It was quite in keeping with the blackguard's character that he should decamp without paying his dues. To cheat a servant like this! It was late, darkness would fall before very long, but Elliott could not be far ahead, not more than ten minutes.

Spahl, who also kept his window open, had heard this knocking and calling, had seen Manning emerge from his room and question the man at Elliott's door. He knew the man for Elliott's interpreter, knew that he slept in the servants' quarters and accompanied Elliott on his expeditions. He had heard almost everything the man said, as he had spoken in loud and tearful tones. Manning had said little, but Spahl had noted his haste to get out one of the horses.

He would follow, at some distance, keeping Manning in sight. He was a colder-blooded man than the major, less nervy, and he had been on missions of a similar sort before. He knew his duty, but it was more of the bureaucratic than the patriotic sort. The one who lay third always had the advantage. He would let Manning bear the brunt. If the Englishman came off worse, Spahl was confident he could still deal with Elliott at either long range or short; if, on the other hand, Manning succeeded, he could kill him and so obtain the report. If Elliott escaped them both, it would represent a failure and it would go against him. But life was a mixed bag of failures and successes after all. The main thing was to come out with a whole skin.

When, as expected, Spahl had set off after Manning, Alawi waited some minutes, then went to join Elliott, who was comfortably seated in the space between the rear side of the bathhouse and the stockade wall, quite invisible to view. Night was not far off now; the brief Mesopotamian dusk would soon be upon them.

Their horses, already saddled by Alawi and loaded with the things they would need for the journey, were waiting beyond the gate, on the side away from the track to the mound. Alawi had advised the major to take this track. Being alone, he had said, Elliott would risk the open country as little as possible; he would make for the Khabur River and hire a boat to take him down to the Euphrates. When they had discussed the way they would go back to Aleppo when the work was done, this was the route they had planned to take. They had planned it, he said, and now this man he had trusted had treated him thus.

Manning followed this advice and Spahl followed Manning. Meanwhile the man they were hunting, with his friend and associate at his side, the report securely buttoned in the breast pocket of his shirt, was heading in quite the opposite direction.

Somerville had not wanted to leave the site or even to move away from the burial chamber. He had not wanted to return to the house for long enough to put the money together to make the advance payment Jehar had asked for—one-half of the total. He had given him only what he had in his pocket, twelve gold pounds in coin and a handful of gurush. Jehar had been magnanimous; he had found it an occasion to show greatness of soul. He knew the *khwaja* was a man of honor, a man of his word; was he not an English lord? Jehar was content to wait for the money. He had promoted himself on the spot; it was an agreement between gentlemen.

Somerville did not want to think about Jehar and strove to put the man's jubilant face out of his mind, together with all speculation about the time Jehar would choose and the manner of the thing. While he kept his thoughts on the momentous discovery he had made—his, it was his, he had seen the shape of the shaft—he could be convinced that he was justified. He had chosen to believe Jehar's assurances that no one would be hurt.

The boards were over the entrance to the anteroom, and the stone doors that gave admittance to the tomb were drawn together to allow the passage of only one man at a time. He felt secure here; there was nowhere for the moment he would rather be, except perhaps at the Royal Society in London astounding everyone with his revelations. He had the bread and cheese and dried dates that Palmer had brought; he had brandy in a metal hip flask; he had the revolver and the cartridges. He was not much used to firearms but felt, at these close quarters and with the advantage of surprise, more than a match for anyone who came through the narrow aperture into the tomb.

He went to the sarcophagus, looked down at the skulls side by side on their headrest, felt again the curious readiness that skeletons have, the promise of alacrity they show, as if waiting for a call. More suggestion of life in them than there would be in corpses, much more, he thought. Even corpses mummified. The relation between them would almost certainly never be known. Close they must have been, for the king to break with custom and share his death space with her. If she had died on his orders as a forced companion on his journey to the Underworld, or died at the decree of custom, he would not have done this. They had waited together for the approach of the fire, for the end they knew was coming, and when it came, they had died together and the fire had not touched them. The palace apartments, yes—there were the weeping eyes of the lion of empire, the ash and clay compacted in the stone relief of the guardian of the portals, the thick layer of ash that had covered the platform, with the scraps of furniture mixed in it. But the invaders had missed this place; the Babylonians had not encountered the stare of their god.

Not love as we would understand it, not romantic love. But something no less potent. She had been faithful to the death. Suddenly, unexpectedly, he was swept by mingled feelings of envy and grief. She had followed him through defeat and hazardous flight and through the years of obscurity and exile, a failed king . . . Together they had escaped the fire, and together they had lain inviolate here through the centuries. Through me they will be kept alive, he vowed to himself, alive and intact for all the time that is left for people to wonder at such things.

The sound of horses, as first Manning and then Spahl passed along the track, did not come to him down there.

The main problem for Jehar lay in choosing the right time to force the lock and steal the dynamite. The day he would do it was never in question; it was today, the first one, now. But he had to find an hour between the end of work at the sheds and the onset of darkness; he did not dare to show a light, there were people too close.

From a point on the eastern side of the mound he watched and waited. There was already some graining of darkness in the air when the last of the workmen left. By good fortune, the night guard's shack was well behind the sheds, out of the way; he would not begin his rounds—if he began them at all—until night was well advanced.

He had taken the measure of the lock days before, even before making his proposal. He was armed with what he needed, a short spike with one end flattened and an iron bar. One of the few truthful things he had said to Somerville was that he had experience of breaking locks. A certain amount of noise was unavoidable. He hoped the watchman would not hear; if he did, and came to investigate, Jehar knew he would have to kill him, and for this purpose he had a third essential tool: the knife he wore at his belt below the loose-fitting smock.

But no mishap of this sort occurred. He sprang open the lock, entered the shed, and took what he needed without impediment. The dynamite was in boxes lined with thick cloth. He had a canvas bag slung to his body for the blasting caps and the fuses. There was still light enough to see by as he made his way to the preselected place, a shallow declivity immediately below the line of the sheds. He had already, the night before, covered from view by the forward bank of this ditch, worked patiently to make recesses in this bank where the dynamite, bound in bundles of ten sticks, could be inserted and packed around. Three of these holes he had made, at intervals of twenty paces. It was a heavy charge of explosive, but he was resolved to make a thorough job of it and so be sure of his money.

It was now, in a certain way, that Jehar began to pay the price for having turned his life into a story. He had not spoken the truth when he told Somerville that he had great experience in the laying of explosives. In fact he had none at all. It was like the boat building on the Great River that was to be the foundation of his and Ninanna's fortunes; he had never done it, but more than once he had seen it done. He had watched while they inserted the blasting caps and while they placed the fuse into the neck of the cap when it was in place. He knew that the fuse had to be squeezed and crimped when this was done in order to ensure a tight fit. And he knew the dangers of this; he had once seen a man squeeze the explosive instead of the end of the cap and get his hand and forearm blown off. He knew too that the fuse had to be dry and cut level to avoid friction and that great care had to be taken to avoid cracking the outer covering. He did not know what was inside the blasting cap or the fuse or the explosive itself, but he did not need to know these things.

What he needed to know was what Elliott, now some miles away, could have told him: that petroleum is generally less dense than the rock that surrounds it, that it will flow upward to the earth's surface through whatever cracks and pores and fractures it can find, that it sometimes reaches a containing enclosure beneath a layer of impermeable rock and that as this sedimentary layer builds up it presses down on the fluid trap below, creating a condition known as overpressure. Elliott might also have added that such overpressured pockets often contain quantities of gas and might lie close to the surface, in which case they are unpredictable and liable to cause violent eruptions, and that the risk of this is even greater where rivulets of salt water through layers of limestone have dissolved the rock and over long periods of time created a hidden and unsuspected underground landscape of caves and corridors.

It was in happy ignorance of these facts that Jehar now began to position his fuses.

Darkness was falling as Manning rode along the track that ran past the mound toward the German railway sheds. He was beginning to despair now; before long it would be impossible to see anything clearly. The swine had given them the slip; by morning he would be beyond pursuit.

Then, just ahead of him, he saw a figure in movement, head and shoulders only visible, the rest concealed below some dip or hollow in the ground. The figure appeared to be wearing an Arab headdress. Manning, his mind overheated by the violent reversals of the afternoon, remembered the towel Elliott had carried over his shoulder and came to the immediate conclusion that Elliott had used this same towel to disguise himself as an Arab and was now preparing an ambush. At once he dismounted and crept some yards forward, his rifle at the ready. When he came upon a low ridge that offered some cover he went down flat. The movements of the figure were inexplicable. He saw a brief glow of light, then another. "Elliott!" he shouted. "Stand still and come toward me with your hands up." The contradiction in these orders was not immediately apparent to him. "I want that report!" he shouted.

But instead of obeying, Elliott began to run away, like the coward he was.

"Stop or I'll shoot!" Manning shouted.

Jehar understood this; the earlier words had been incomprehensible to him. He understood his danger. But he could not obey because he had lit the fuses and they were less than the span of a man's arm in length. So he went on running, and after a moment more Manning shot him.

Spahl, also lying flat, was close by. Following at a distance he had seen Manning dismount, and he had followed suit. He had been able to get near enough to hear the major's shouted orders and the shot that shortly followed. Evidently Elliott had been hit. This assumption was confirmed a moment or two later when he saw Manning get up and move forward, obviously intending to recover the report. He was training his rifle on the major when a sound louder than any he had heard in his life before stunned and deafened him: A great gout of fire rose high into the air; fire from the base of this fountain streamed toward him like a river in spate, scorching his face and hands, half blinding him. He saw the major stand clear and distinct for one moment, enveloped, like a genie of the fire. Then he was no more. Spahl turned to run, but he could not see where he was going. He knew his clothes were on fire and he knew he was screaming. His rifle writhed and twisted where he had let it fall. The burning stream, traveling now at an appalling speed, caught him, engulfed him, seemed to lift him a little, then let the carbonized remains fall.

Somerville heard the tremendous roar of the gushing oil and gas without knowing what it was. It seemed in these first moments like the feared arrival of the locomotive train, multiplied a thousand times. He went through the aperture in the doorway, moved aside the boards that covered the entrance to the anteroom, and began to mount the steps he had discovered so recently and with such joy. The sound grew louder, deafening. He became aware of intense heat and a terrible stench of decay as if some huge creature were rotting somewhere in the night above him. Looking upward, he saw a flare of light half muffled in black smoke. He had some confused notion of retreating, as if to find safety in the tomb, but even as he turned to descend again the river of fire found the entrance to the shaft and the trenches, swooped down upon him in a threefold stream, consumed him in seconds as he stood there, swallowed up the god Marduk in the anteroom, surged through the opening in the stone doors, flooded into the burial chamber, melted the alabaster vases in the alcoves, swept stinking and shrieking into the sarcophagus, and—in less time than it would take a moth to die in a candle flame—put an end to the long and patient vigil of the bones.

Afterword

It was never discovered who had laid the charge of dynamite and for what purpose. The only two people who could have explained this were both dead. No evidence of theft remained, as the railway sheds were completely destroyed and their contents scattered over a wide area and largely submerged in the tide of oil, which had also killed the night watchman as he dozed in his shack.

Manning and Spahl had been seen setting off for the mound, and it was assumed that they too had died in the inferno, though no trace of them or their horses was ever found. Why they had taken that route, one following behind the other, at that time of day, remained a mystery. Elliott and his interpreter had disappeared at the same time, and there was some speculation between Palmer and Patricia, recalling how close the three men had been, almost inseparable, about a possible plot among them that had somehow gone wrong. But then Hassan, the boy who kept the gate, had come forward to say that he had seen Elliott and Alawi ride off in the opposite direction.

The fame Somerville had failed to find in his lifetime did not come after his death either, though the cataclysmic manner of it, assumed as this had to be—no mortal remains were ever found—together with the expert testimony of Palmer, became elements in the general feeling of apocalypse that pervaded Europe in the months before the war, featured prominently in the press for some days, and provided material for at least one novel. Gaining any general belief in what had been found in the tomb itself was another matter, for the obvious reason that nothing of it was left. Palmer had taken photographs, so much was true, but photographs can be faked, as everyone knows; in terms of what could be recorded, there had been some interesting finds, certainly, but nothing so very remarkable. What chiefly remained was a story, sensational in its nature and so arousing skepticism in the sober world of Mesopotamian archaeology, of the last days of the last Assyrian king. But the story survived the skepticism, as such stories will; in the years that followed an aura of mystery and glamour continued to surround the ultimate fate of Sin-shar-ishkun.

Though cheated of the recognition he had wanted, Somerville achieved a sort of posthumous heroism in Edith's eyes. She married again a few years later—a rising barrister, much resembling her father—but she always remembered how splendid John had been that afternoon, standing beside the skeletons that lay side by side in their coffin amid the scattered jewels, how he had compelled them all, even the odious Elliott. She was glad to think that she had praised him and kissed him on that last day of his life and that she had showed him her admiration for his great enterprise of retelling the history of Assyria. And as the years passed this gladness came to cast a more tender light on their marriage and she grew to believe that she had always supported him, always been staunchly at his side through all the ups and downs of his career.

Palmer and Patricia became Mr. and Mrs. Harold Palmer that summer. They were married in July, just two weeks before the German invasion of Belgium and the British declaration of war. Palmer surprised everyone—himself included—by volunteering for the army. After two years of war as an infantry officer he had his right kneecap shattered by shrapnel from an artillery shell, and the wound left him with a slight limp. He did not return to field archaeology, for which he had never felt much vocation, resuming his career at the British Museum, where he became a senior curator specializing in Akkadian and Babylonian inscriptions. His new translation of the *Gilgamesh Epic* was widely praised, and it was followed by a collection of Sumerian hymns. Patricia spent a good deal of time during the war years on committees of one sort or another, concerned with various projects to raise funds for the war effort. They had several children, who all grew up to exercise the vote, independent of gender. Sometimes, when some reference was made to the ill-fated excavation at Tell Erdek, Palmer would shake his head and say always the same thing: "Poor fellow, he was so afraid of the railway, but if it hadn't been for that terrible accident he would have had all the time in the world to get the stuff out, he would have had the whole season." And this of course was true; by the outbreak of war, which called a halt to it, the line had only got as far as Rais el-Ain, still a dozen miles away.

Ninanna never knew why Jehar failed to return to her. Her life seemed gray without him. The town of Deir ez-Zor soon lost its ravishing colors; only the warmth of his voice had kept them glowing and beautiful. The fat and greedy Pasha, the strangely haunted Englishman, the white minarets and green fields and fountains and birds, soon became like a dream only half remembered. She wept for Jehar, but he had made her a great gift before he went away: He had given her a love of stories. And when a group of Lutheran missionaries, escorted by fervent and heavily armed converts, came to the yards at Jerablus and spoke to people in Arabic, she found the story of Christ, with its drama of betrayal and sacrifice and resurrection, very gripping indeed, and she became a Christian. So devout was she, so eager for repeated tellings of this story, that they engaged her as a native helper and offered to take her back with them to their mission house at Mardin. The uncle opposed this, but since he could produce no evidence of legal right over her, his opposition was easily overcome. At the mission house they taught her to read. She was not a clever girl, but she tried hard and made progress. It was thought for a while that her experience of waiting at table might be put to good use in a very special hotel they were planning to build. But the war came, and the site they had chosen was the scene of great carnage when a regiment of Ottoman troops were taken by surprise and massacred almost to a man by an attack from the air. The site was devastated, pitted with craters made by the bombs. This in itself would not have been reason enough to abandon the plan—the ground might have been leveled out again; the corpses were soon devoured by vultures and crows, and anything of value carried off by looters—but the Society for Biblical Research was riddled with factions, and there was a sizable minority of members who maintained that the Swedes had made a gross blunder, that the site of the Garden of Eden was not in Mesopotamia at all but in Azerbaijan and that God had wished to reveal this error before the hotel could be built by sending a strong message. Passions ran high; there was danger of a schism. Moreover, the markets were uncertain in these postwar years, and the society was experiencing difficulty in raising the capital needed on sufficiently favorable terms. So in the end the idea was dropped.

Elliott and Alawi bade each other farewell when they reached Aleppo. Alawi stayed on there during the war years as an agent for various American business interests, among them the Chester Group. He prospered greatly, as these years saw an enormous expansion in American industry with a consequent need for raw materials from the Near East and for wider export markets—its exports rose tenfold in the course of the war. This vastly increased activity was also of great benefit to Elliott, who continued to work for the Chester Group when he returned to the United States. His report was duly delivered and provided an invaluable basis for preliminary estimates. His loyal service and the greatly increased value of his holding led in 1915 to his being invited to join the board of directors and increase his stock even further. By this time America had become one of the great creditor nations of the world. It was feared by some that this growing interest in the mineral resources of Mesopotamia would lead to political interference in the affairs of sovereign states and so to a policy of what was beginning to be called economic imperialism. But Elliott was too busy getting rich to think much about this.

Rampling learned in due course that Elliott had escaped the consequences of his treachery and had returned to his native land and the warm embrace of Standard Oil and the Chester Group. But Rampling was not a vindictive man, and he believed in the conserving of energy. The harm was done; there was no point in wasting further time on the matter. Disapproval of the American had been necessary during the time he was planning to have him killed. But if they had met now, he would have shaken Elliott by the hand and wished him well.

He was, in any case, extremely busy in these months, working out the financial terms for an agreement on the Baghdad Railway. He was on the brink of success when the Austrian archduke Francis Ferdinand and his morganatic wife, Sophie, duchess of Hohenberg, were shot dead by a Bosnian Serb in Sarajevo.

Shared investment to protect, free competition, Rampling was always to maintain, might have saved the peace even then, had it not been for Austro-Hungarian arrogance and intransigence. But his true success, the accord for which he and his partners had been working in secret for several years, together with members of the government and the high military command, came in May 1916, with the Sykes-Picot Agreement, which defined British and French political and economic interests in the postwar period, when—as was hoped and believed—the

Ottoman Empire would be dismembered. By this agreement Britain was to gain complete control over lower Mesopotamia from Tikrit to the Persian Gulf and from the Arabian boundary to the Persian frontier. This vast territory, which had never been home to a single nation, she was to rename Iraq.

A Note About the Author

Barry Unsworth, who won the Booker Prize for *Sacred Hunger*, was a Booker finalist for *Pascali's Island* and *Morality Play*, and was long-listed for the Booker Prize for *The Ruby in Her Navel*. His other works include *The Songs of the Kings*, *After Hannibal*, and *Losing Nelson*. He lives in Italy.

A Note About the Type

The text of this book is set in New Baskerville, which was designed by George Jones in 1930 for Linotype-Hell. New Baskerville is based on the original font, circa 1752, designed by and named for the British printer John Baskerville. The delicacy and grace of the long, elegant serifs and the subtle transfer of stroke weight from thick to very thin make New Baskerville an ideal text font. ◈